新聞英語

NEWS 必備指南

—— 關鍵句

金利 主編

COVID-19來襲，想要掌握國際間第一手消息？
英語新聞閱讀力必不可少！

松燁文化

目錄

前言

在當今社會，如果你希望憑藉英語技能提高競爭力，過硬的英語能力必不可少。但在英語學習過程中，許多英語學習者都面臨著這樣的困擾：

● 即使認識大量單字，仍然感覺聽懂英語很吃力；

● 學習了許多英語句型，實際溝通時仍然會遇到障礙。

因此，是否只要多聽多看，這些問題就能迎刃而解、輕鬆聽懂讀懂英文內容呢？

勤奮努力可以帶來進步，但有很多英語學習者雖然下了很大的功夫，但學習效果仍不甚理想。

究竟是什麼阻礙了我們進步呢？其實，許多英語學習者都存在這樣一些問題：首先，在選擇英語學習資料方面就會遇到困難。其次，感覺找不到高效的學習方法、抓不住學習重點，無法做到有的放矢地學習。因此，在本書中，我們希望可以幫助讀者解決這些問題。本書具有以下特色：

1. 原汁原味學習內容，有針對性提高聽力程度

英語學習材料成千上萬，如何選擇最合適的內容？

不同的英語學習者程度不同，各自的優勢和薄弱環節也有所不同。因此，選擇適合自己的學習內容才有「對症下藥」的效果。我們選取的材料來自 VOA、BBC 和 CNN 等新聞內容，這些新聞資訊的題材十分廣泛，讀者透過這些原汁原味的新聞內容可以十分有針對性地提高聽力程度。

2. 以句子為單位感受語境，方便活學活用

英語新聞難度大，導致挫敗感強烈。篇幅過長的內容往往傳達著整塊的資訊，而這對理解句意是一個不小的挑戰。為解決這個問題，我們從收集到的新聞材料中選出了包含豐富知識點的句子。相比整個篇章，這些精挑細選的句子更能夠呈現真

實的語言環境，讀者可以領略最具特色的新聞語言，並培養理解能力和表達能力。

3. 詳細講解並拓展知識，事半功倍學英文

面對整個句子找不到重點，不能以點蓋面地學習知識。我們會講解句中最常用的單字、片語的用法，對於那些在新聞中常用的說法更會重點講解。此外，還會根據句子本身擴展實用的相關句子，讓讀者對主句中敘述的事件有一個更全面的了解。我們希望本書能對提高英語聽力程度有所幫助，讓英語學習者不但能聽懂英語新聞，同時還能熟悉新聞中常見的用法，讓英語程度獲得質的飛躍。

編者

Part 1

World Politics & Current Affairs

1   Polls show majorities of Americans favor stricter gun laws and an immigration overhaul. (VOA)

投票結果顯示，大部分美國人支援更加嚴格的槍支管理法案和移民改革。

要點解析

① majorities of 意為大部分，大多數；其單數形式 a majority of 也有相同的意思。

② favor 意為贊成，支持，in favor of 也有相同的意思。此外，favor 還能表示「青睞、喜愛」。

③ overhaul 意為澈底檢修，詳細檢查。

2   A Bangladeshi minister said his government has turned down offers of international help because it was confident it could handle the rescue operation. (BBC)

孟加拉的一位部長表示，政府拒絕了國際社會的援助，因為他們有信心處理好這次救援行動。

要點解析

① turn down 是「拒絕」的意思。此外，它還有「降低、減小」的意思。

② confident 意為自信，常用固定搭配是 be confident of 對……自信。

③ handle 這個動詞很靈活，有「處理、操作、買賣」等意思。

3   Obama asked for Planned Parenthood's help spread in the world, especially, among women. (NPR)

歐巴馬要求美國計劃生育聯合會為全世界提供幫助，尤其是針對女性。

要點解析

① ask for 是「要求，尋找」的意思。常用搭配有 ask for advice「向某人尋求建議」。

② Planned Parenthood 是「計劃生育聯合會」的意思。其中 planned 可以表示「有計畫的，根據計畫的」。

4　　We're learning more as well about one of the two key suspects who were shot and arrested at the crime scene. (CNN)

我們同樣了解到，兩名關鍵嫌疑人中的一人在被警方開槍擊中後在犯罪現場被逮捕。

要點解析

① as well 是「同樣地；也，還」的意思，固定搭配 as well as 是「不但……而且……；和……一樣」的意思。

② key 除了表示「鑰匙」，還可以作形容詞表示「關鍵的」。常用搭配 key factor，即「關鍵因素」。

5　　U.S. President Barack Obama visits a town devastated by a killer tornado and federal investigations continue into the cause of a major bridge collapse in Washington State. (VOA)

美國總統巴拉克·歐巴馬慰問遭龍捲風襲擊的小鎮；另外，聯邦調查局正在繼續調查華盛頓州一座大橋坍塌的原因。

要點解析

① devastate 毀滅；毀壞。此外，它還有「制服，壓倒」的意思。

② killer 除了「殺手」的意思之外，還可以作形容詞，表示「致命的，危險的」。另外，在英語俚語中它還可以表示「極好的，有趣的」等含義。

6　　It would greatly expand financial disclosures and make all of the data searchable so insider trading and conflicts of interest would be easier to detect. (NPR)

這將大幅加強財務披露，並使所有資料都可以被搜尋到，這樣能夠更加容易監測到內幕交易和利益衝突。

要點解析

① financial disclosure 對財務狀況的披露。其中，disclosure 在審計方面有「披露」的意思。此外，它還可以表示「揭發」，如：public disclosure of fact 當眾揭發事實。

② insider trading 內幕交易。insider 來自 inside，表示「內部的人」；對應的 outsider 則是「局外人」。

9

相關句子

In 2001, the FSA was granted the power to prosecute insider trading cases under criminal law. (BBC)

2001 年，英國金融服務管理局得到授權，可以根據刑法檢舉內幕交易案。

---

7   I intend to introduce legislation to increase the resources and direct the Department of Justice to start doing its job. (NPR)

我打算提案，建議增加資源，指導司法部開展工作。

要點解析

① intend 打算。片語 intend to do sth. 表示「打算做某事」。

② introduce 提出。表示「介紹」的意思，但它還可以表示「提出，採用」。

③ 注意：direct 在這句話裡作動詞，表示「指導」。

---

8   A rally demanding a recount in the Venezuelan presidential elections has been called off. (CRI)

一場要求重新計算委內瑞拉總統大選票數的集會被叫停。

要點解析

① recount 重新計算，在投票中經常用到。

② elections election 選舉。

③ call off 取消。在這句話裡表示「制止」的意思。

---

9   President Obama may only have visited one Central American country, but he met with the leaders of all seven Central American nations and the Dominican Republic. (CNN)

歐巴馬總統可能只走訪了一個中美洲國家，但他會晤了七個中美洲國家和多明尼加共和國的領導人。

要點解析

① meet with 表示「和……會晤」。此外，還有「偶然遇見，獲得，符合」等意思。

② Central American Country 指「中美洲國家」。

10   The top leader has said he hopes a deal to secure an international res-
      cue package for the country's banks would be made soon. (BBC)
      最高領導人表示,他希望能儘早達成一項協議,保證挽救該國銀
      行的國際救援計畫能夠馬上實施。

   要點解析
   ① make a deal 表示「成交,達成交易」的意思。類似意思的片語還有 close
      a deal,strike a bargain。
   ② secure 在這句話裡作動詞,表示「爭取到」。
   ③ package 除了我們常用的「包裹,包」的意思之外,還有「一攬子的」的
      意思,常用片語為 package deal,即「一攬子交易」。

11   Secretary of State John Kerry made it clear that American foreign pol-
      icy decisions affect the lives of Americans. (VOA)
      美國國務卿約翰‧凱瑞明確表示,美國的外交政策決策會影響美
      國民眾生活的各方面。

   要點解析
   ① make it clear 中的 it 在這個句子裡是形式賓語,that 後面跟的從句才是真
      正的賓語。
   ② affect 影響。此外,它還有「感動;侵襲」的意思,如:be affected with
      感染……。

12   The U.N. Food and Agriculture Organization, the FAO, hopes to
      change that with a new project called Voices of the Hungry. (VOA)
      聯合國糧食農業組織(FAO)希望透過「飢餓之聲」的新專案
      做出改變。

   要點解析
   ① 在 with a new project 中,with 的用法非常靈活,表示「透過,用」的
      意思。
   ② call 在這個句子裡用來修飾 project,意思為「稱之為,命名為」。

13   The British Prime Minister David Cameron has announced plans to tighten the rules on state welfare to immigrants. (BBC)

英國首相大衛·卡麥隆宣布了一項計畫，該計畫更加嚴格地限制了移民者獲得國家福利的條件。

要點解析

① tighten 是「變緊，緊縮」的意思，在這句話裡引申為「變得更加嚴格」的意思。這個詞的常用搭配有 tighten belt，即節省開銷；而固定搭配 tighten up 表示「加強，變緊」的意思。

② state welfare 國家福利。

14   I think the problems are problems he inherited from the Republicans, frankly, and he's working his best to solve those problems. (CNN)

坦率地說，我認為這些是從共和黨人那裡繼承下來的遺留問題，而他正在竭盡全力解決這些問題。

要點解析

① inherit from 表示「從......繼承、得到、遺傳」等意義。

② frankly 是「坦率地說」的意思，經常用作插入語。類似意思的表達還有 frankly speaking。

③ work one's best 盡某人最大的努力。

15   In the global challenges of diplomacy, development, economic security, and environmental security, you will feel our success or failure just as strongly as those people in those other countries that you'll never meet. (VOA)

在外交、發展、經濟安全和環境安全的全球化挑戰中，你們會強烈地感受到我們的成功與失敗同世界其他地方與你們素不相識的人一樣。

要點解析

① environmental security 是「環境安全」的意思，即由於環境的改變、破壞、退化對人類經濟活動、國家安全和國際和平造成的隱患。

② as strongly as 是「和......一樣強烈」的意思。

相關句子

The future of the United States depends upon three pillars : national security, economic security and environmental security.
美國的未來主要依賴三大支柱：民族安全、經濟安全和環境安全。

---

16   President Obama welcomes South Korean president Park Geun-Hye to the White House.(CNN)
美國總統歐巴馬歡迎南韓總統朴槿惠訪問白宮。

要點解析

① welcome 是「歡迎訪問」的意思，welcome to 是「歡迎到來，歡迎參加」的意思。此外，welcome 還可以作形容詞，表示「受歡迎的」的意思。

---

17   Some government officials toured the area alienated by the twister, telling residents the federal government will do everything in its power to help in the recovery. (NPR)
一些政府官員走訪了龍捲風受災區，並告知當地居民，聯邦政府將盡一切努力來幫助他們重建家園。

要點解析

① tour 在這句話裡作動詞，表示「周遊」。tour 常被用作名詞，表示「迂迴；巡視；遊歷」的意思。「巡迴演唱會」即 concert tour；tour group 即「旅遊團」。
② alienate 疏離；轉移。片語 alienate from 表示「與……疏離；與……隔離」的意思。
③ in power 是「掌權，執掌」的意思。

---

18   That would be paired with heightened efforts to secure U.S. borders and halt the flow of illegal immigrants. (VOA)
我們還將加大力度確保美國邊境的安全，防止大批非法移民入境。

相關句子

① be paired with 與……配對。

② secure 保護，此外還有「爭取；獲得安全；拋錨」等意思，如：secure a ceasefire 爭取停火。

③ flow 作動詞時是指水流「湧動」；作名詞則引申為「大量人或物的流動」，意思非常形象生動。

19　Liberal Democrat Simon Hughes says if the Conservatives are not offering real reform, then his party is not interested. (VOA)

自由民主黨西門‧休斯稱，如果保守黨不能實施真正的改革，那麼他的黨派是不會感興趣的。

要點解析

① reform 作名詞是「改革，改正」的意思；它的同根詞 reformation 則是「革新；改善」的意思。

② party 在這句話裡表示「政黨，黨派」；此外它還有「當事人，一方」的意思，如：third party 協力廠商。

20　The cabinet failed to agree on two important and hotly contested issues: one was the establishment and membership of a commission to oversee general elections; the other was his request that the mandate of the chief of internal security should be extended. (BBC)

內閣無法就這兩項備受爭議的議題達成共識：一項是建立並加入委員會來監督大選；另一項是要求擴大國內治安首領的權利範圍。

要點解析

① fail to 未能，沒能做到。還可以用 fail in doing sth. 表示「未能做到某事」。

② agree on(upon)... 對……取得一致意見。通常指在爭辯思考之後才達到一致。

③ oversee 除了「監督，審查」的意思外，還有「偷看到，無意中看到」的意思。

④ internal security 指「國內治安」。

21　There are committee hearings, filibuster threats and hours of floor debate. (NPR)

這些包括委員聽證會、阻礙議案通過的威脅以及無休止的會場辯論。

要點解析

① hearing 除了表示「聽力，發表意見」的意思外，也常用來表示「聽證會」。常用表達有：committee hearings 委員聽證會；court hearing 庭審。
② filibuster 阻撓議案通過。
③ floor 在政治新聞中不是「地板」，而是「議政廳、與會者、發言」的意思。

22　But a third party, the Liberal Democrats, is turning this election into a three-horse race. (VOA)

但是第三個黨派——自由民主黨的加入將這場競選變成了「三強爭霸賽」。

要點解析

① turn into... 把……變成；此外還有「成為、轉入」的意思。
② three-horse race 是一種比喻的表達方式，將這場政治活動比喻為「三強爭霸賽」。

23　Nevertheless, as concerns rose in India, foreign minister S.M. Krishna called on Indians to assess their options while exploring the possibility of studying in Australia. (VOA)

然而，由於印度國內關注度的不斷提高，印度外交部長克里希納號召印度人民在尋求澳洲求學機會的同時，也要權衡他們的選擇。

要點解析

① nevertheless 通常放在句首表示轉折，意思為「然而，不過」。
② call on 號召，請求。call on sb. to do sth. 表示「號召某人做某事」。此外還有「訪問、拜訪」的意思。
③ assess 評定，對……進行評估。在這句話裡是「權衡」的意思。

24　We got something about Syria that United Nations representative called the first hopeful news in the very long time. (CNN)

我們有了一些關於敘利亞的消息。聯合國代表稱在很長一段時間內終於有了一個好消息。

要點解析

① get something about... 獲知……的消息。其中，something 是泛指的用法，指得到的一些消息。

② in the long time 在長時間內。

---

25 The operator of the Grasberg mine says rescuers have successfully cleared two passengers for heavy equipment that could help crews get to the miner sooner. (NPR)

格拉斯伯格礦場的經營者表示，救援者已經成功救出了兩名乘客，在重型設備的幫助下，營救人員能夠更快地找到礦工。

要點解析

① clear 除了常用的形容詞和副詞用法外，還可以作動詞表示「清空」。在這句話裡是「使……沒有危險」的意思。

② crew 全體工作人員；全體船員。固定搭配為 a crew of 一組工作人員。

③ get to 到達；開始；接觸到。

相關句子

Union leaders said production had been paralyzed at the Grasberg mine, which is run by US firm Freeport-McMoran. (BBC)

工會領導人表示，美國麥克莫蘭銅金公司經營的格拉斯伯格礦場的生產已經癱瘓。

---

26 Allison Keyes reports the questions is whether a conservative republican can win a southern state that twice backed President Obama. (NPR)

據愛麗森·凱斯報導，現在的問題是保守的共和黨人能否得到南部一個州的支援，這個州曾兩次支持歐巴馬總統。

要點解析

① win 除了表示贏得比賽、獎章等之外，還有贏得想要或需要的事物的意思，如：win the support of... 贏得……的支持。

② back 除了表示「後面、倒退」之外，還有「支持」的意思。

27   The judicial elections were introduced by President Evo Morales, who
says they'll make Bolivia's justice system more accountable. (BBC)

司法選舉是由總統埃沃‧莫拉萊斯提出的，他表示這將使玻利維
亞的司法制度承擔更多的責任。

要點解析

① introduce 引進。在這句話裡是「提出，採用」的意思，如：introduce a
system 提出一項制度。

② accountable 有責任的。後面通常接 for，表示「對......負責任」。

---

28   Britain has the second largest NATO contingent in that country after
the United States. (BBC)

自美國之後，英國在那個國家部署了第二大北大西洋公約組
織派遣隊。

要點解析

① the second largest 第二大。這個是序數詞加最高級的用法，表示「第
幾......」的意思。

② contingent 指「員警、士兵、軍車的批次」，此外還可表示「代表團」。

③ NATO 北大西洋公約組織，簡稱北約，是美國與西歐、北美等已開發國
家為實現防衛協作而成立的國際軍事集團組織。

---

29   Judges were chosen directly by politicians before, but now more than
five million people will elect them from a list of candidates who were
put forward by the Bolivian Congress. (BBC)

之前，法官是由政治家直接選舉的，但現在超過五百萬名民眾將
從玻利維亞國會提供的候選人名單中選出法官。

要點解析

① more than 多於，超過。在口語中，還有「非常，極其」的意思，常用搭
配有 more often than not，表示「常常，多半」的意思。

② a list of 一列，一覽表。如：a detailed list of claims 債權清冊。

③ put forward 推薦。此外，還有「把......拿出來給人看，提出，提前」的
意思。

30　Colorado's governor has signed six laws to regulate and tax recreational marijuana use in that state. (VOA)

科羅拉多州州長已經簽署六項法律，對本州用於消遣用途的大麻進行徵稅和控制。

要點解析

① sign 簽署，簽名。常用搭配有 sign up 簽約僱傭；sign for 簽收；sign in 簽到。

② regulate 調節，規定，控制。名詞形式 regulation 就是「規則，校準」的意思。

③ tax 在這句話裡作動詞表示「徵稅」的意思。

31　The United States sees engagement with Burma as a means to encourage further political and economic liberalization. (VOA)

美國把與緬甸的交戰視為一種鼓勵未來政治自由和經濟自由的手段。

要點解析

① see... as 將……視為。look upon as, treat as, regard as 都有相同的意思。

② engagement 在軍事中表示「交戰」。

相關句子

In Burma, the United States continues to press the Burmese junta to allow workers' rights and unions and to discontinue its use of forced labor.

在緬甸，美國持續向緬甸執政團施壓，要求給予勞工權、允許建立工會，並停止強制勞動。

32　This explains that those complications and difficulties are following a pace thought by people who don't know the internal circumstances of the talks. (BBC)

這說明複雜和困難的局勢後有一個階段，人們並不了解談判的內在環境。

要點解析

① complication 這個詞在醫學中用得很多，表示「併發症」；在這句話裡指「複雜的問題」。

② pace 指「每一步」，也有「步速，速度」的意思。

③ internal 是「內部的，內在的，國內的」的意思，與 inner 意思相近。

33　Turkey has increased security forces in the area and its allies have arrived there. (CNN)

土耳其已經在該地區增加了安全部隊，而且其盟軍也已經抵達那裡。

要點解析

① security 安全部隊。

② ally 助手，夥伴。在外交方面常指「同盟國」。

34　I think the biggest mistake that people make is grabbing their social security benefits as soon as they become available at age 62. (CNN)

我認為人們最大的錯誤，就是他們一到 62 歲就想得到社會保障福利。

要點解析

① grab 攫取，霸占。此外還有「將……深深吸引」的意思，如：grab one's attention 吸引某人注意力。

② social security benefits 社保福利。benefit 的複數形式表示福利。

35　The U.S. Supreme Court has a lower court ruling that blocks Indiana from striking Medicaid funding from Planned Parenthood. (VOA)

美國最高法院下屬的一個地方法院不允許印第安那州取消給計劃生育聯合會的醫療補助撥款。

要點解析

① Supreme Court 最高法院。

② block from... 阻止，妨礙……。

③ strike from... 意思為「從……中劃掉」，在這句話裡引申為「取消」。

36　We know that much remains to be done, on democracy, fighting poverty and achieving lasting peace. (BBC)

我們知道，要想實現民主、消除貧困，獲得持久的和平，還有很多要做。

要點解析

① remain 意思為「留下，剩餘」。remain to be done 表示「有待完成」。
② lasting 持久的。同義詞還有 permanent 永恆的。

37　No party is expected to win a majority in the election which will be closely monitored by the organization for security and cooperation in Europe. (BBC)

無法預測哪個黨派能在這場競選中贏得多數選票，該選舉將在歐洲安全與合作組織的密切關注下進行。

要點解析

① be expected to do... 被期待……。在翻譯的時候，可以使用主動語態靈活翻譯。
② closely 密切地，親近地，嚴密地。

38　As a permanent member of United Nations Security Council, Russia has the power to veto resolutions. (BBC)

作為聯合國安全理事會的常任理事國之一，俄羅斯有權否認任何決議。

要點解析

① permanent member 指聯合國的常任理事國。permanent 指「永久的，不變的」。
② veto 反對，否決，禁止。後面通常跟決定或方案等。

39　Court watchers say Anthony Kennedy could side with conservative justices to overturn or limit a major Supreme Court decision from ten years ago that allowed affirmative action. (CNN)

法院觀察家們表示，安東尼·甘迺迪可能會支持保守法官們一起

推翻或限制 10 年前允許平權行動的最高法院的決定。

要點解析

① side with 同意,支持,偏袒。side 作名詞是「方面」的意思,作動詞可以引申為「朝某個方面倒」,即「偏袒,支持」的意思。

② overturn 推翻,顛覆,破壞。這個詞通常用在政治方面,如推翻政府或推翻統治等。

40　A blue-ribbon panel convened by the college board wants the 48-year-old Pell Grant program to focus on students who actually stay in school and graduate, because right now, too many drop out. (NPR)

由學校董事會召集的菁英小組表示,他們希望已有 48 年歷史的佩爾助學金專案能夠關注那些真正想留在學校並想畢業的學生,因為現在有太多的學生選擇輟學。

要點解析

① blue-ribbon 指「一等的,一流的,菁英的」。這裡有一個典故,blue ribbon 原指比賽中第一名獲得的藍綬帶,後來這個詞就用來指代「一流的,菁英的」。

② focus on 集中(精力、注意力)於。還可表示相機「聚焦於」。

③ drop out 輟學,退學。此片語的連寫形式 dropout 作名詞,表示「中途退學,中途退出的人」。

41　Those supporters argued that the president gave his people the sense of national pride. (CNN)

那些擁護者稱其總統賦予了本國人民民族自豪感。

要點解析

① argue 提出理由證明、主張;此外還有爭論、爭辯;說服、勸說的意思。

② sense of national pride 民族自豪感。sense 經常用來表示「……感」,如:sense of humor 幽默感;sense of direction 方向感。

42　The military advice says that extra forces are needed to help maintain progress and dominate the ground more effectively to ensure the safety of the area. (BBC)

軍方建議說，需要額外的部隊幫助維持進展和有效地控制地面主導權，從而確保該地區的安全。

要點解析

① maintain 維持，保持。此外還有「維修，保養」的意思。其名詞形式 maintenance 最常用的意思即「修繕，維修」。

② dominate 支配，控制。此外還有「在......中占首要地位」的意思。其名詞形式 domination 也是「控制、統治」的意思。

③ ensure 確保，使安全。

43　This question reflects just how complicated and at times, how confounding the world can be. But we must be clear-eyed even in our grief. (CNN)

這個問題反映了事情是多麼複雜，而且有時世界是多麼混雜。但即使在悲傷時，我們也必須保持敏銳的洞察力。

要點解析

① reflect 反映，表達。此外它還有「映射，深思，反省」等意思。

② confounding 使人迷惑的，容易搞混的。

44　The supreme leader and his leadership have revived the confidence of people that they can bring the change through the electoral process, through the ballot. (VOA)

這位最高領導人憑藉其領導能力使人民重獲了信心，他們相信可以透過投票選舉過程帶來改變。

要點解析

① revive 表示「再流行，恢復」。在這句話裡是「使......甦醒，復活」的意思。

② bring 最常用的意思是「帶來，拿來」。此外，它還有「促使，使發生」的意思。

③ electoral process 選舉過程。類似說法還有 electoral college，意為「總統選舉團」，是由各州選出的，履行選舉總統與副總統的職責。

45　Any limitation on this fundamental right of self defense makes us more dependent on our government for our own protection. (VOA)

對自我防衛這一基本權利的任何限制，都使我們更加依賴政府對我們自己的保護。

要點解析

① limitation on... 對於……的限制，on 後面接被限制的對象。

② self defense 自我防衛。self 有很多類似的用法，如：self protection 自我保護。

③ dependent on... 依賴於……。這個用法是從動詞片語 depend on 衍生而來的。

46　Senators could decide whether the bill extends equal protections to immigrants whose relationships are not recognized under current federal law. (VOA)

參議員會決定該法案是否延伸至對移民的平等保護，而目前的聯邦法律不認可其關係。

要點解析

① extend to... 延伸至……。其中 extend 意思為「延展，延長」，其名詞 extension 是「伸長，延展」的意思。

② 表示「在……法律下」可以用 under...law 這一說法。

47　But if the coalition sticks to it, it is hard to see that this negotiation framework can ever really get off the ground. (VOA)

但如果該聯盟對此堅持，那麼這一談判框架很難取得進展。

要點解析

① stick to 形容「不放棄，堅持或維持」某事物。此外，它還有「黏住，儘管有困難仍繼續做某事」的意思。

② negotiation framework 談判框架。

③ get off the ground 的字面意是「離開地面」，引申意思為「開始，（使）取得進展」。

48   The unmilitary aircraft has just crashed in the sea after the pilot and
      co-pilot refuse to follow orders. (CNN)
      在機長和副機長拒絕服從命令後，這架違反軍事規程的飛機剛剛
      墜落在海裡了。

要點解析

① unmilitary 字面意思是「非軍事的」，在這句話裡指「違反軍事章程的」。
② crash 墜落，落下。此外，它還有「碰撞，衝；垮台，破產」的意思。
③ follow orders 遵守命令。除了 follow 以外，obey、abide by 也有「遵守」
   的意思。

49   It's been a long and painful process but the country is about to form a
      coalition government. (BBC)
      這是一個漫長而痛苦的過程，但該國還是準備重建一個
      聯盟政府。

要點解析

① be about to... 準備……，這是將來時的形式，通常指準備做經過計畫和思
   考後的事情。
② coalition 結合體，同盟，聯合。co- 這個首碼通常表示「合作」。

50   When President Obama released his budget for the federal govern-
      ment, much of it was spreadsheets and tables. (NPR)
      總統歐巴馬發表了他的聯合政府預算，其中大部分都是「紙
      上談兵」。

要點解析

① release 發表，發布。此外這個詞還有「釋放，解脫，鬆開」的意思，固
   定表達有：press release 新聞稿。
② budget 預算。常用搭配有 make a budget 做預算；此外還可以作動詞，表
   示「編預算，做安排，規劃」等意思。

51   The bill approved by the Republican-controlled House is designed to
      ease deep cuts across the defense department that came into effect.

(BBC)

共和黨控制的眾議院通過此法案，目的是緩和在國防部實施的大幅度消減措施。

要點解析

① ease 緩和，解除，減輕；它作名詞是「悠閒，自在」的意思。at ease 自由自在。

② come into effect 實現，生效。還可以用 put sth. into effect 使......生效。

52　Passengers are already feeling the impact of furloughs that affected the Federal Aviation Administration. (NPR)

乘客已經感覺到停職事件為美國聯邦航空總署帶來的影響。

要點解析

① feel the impact of... 感受到......的影響。

② furlough 停職，暫時解僱。尤指「因無足夠工作可做而停職」。

53　He is one of 100,000 flood victims, nearly half of whom are registering with the government's aid project. (VOA)

他是數十萬洪災受害者中的一人，已有將近一半的人員在政府援建專案中登記。

要點解析

① victim 意為「受害人」，還有被害人，犧牲者的意思。

② register 登記，註冊。此外還有「記下，表達，掛號」的意思，如：registered letter 掛號信。

54　"There weren't too many members of Congress who were aware of this legislation," says one government official. (NPR)

一位政府官員稱，「並沒有太多國會議員知道這項立法。」

要點解析

① be aware of 知道，了解。

② legislation 立法。其動詞形式為 legislate，即「用立法規定」。

55　Obama was welcomed off Air Force One by the country's Foreign Minister Jose Antonio Meade and the US ambassador Anthony Wayne. (BBC)

歐巴馬從空軍一號下來的時候，受到了該國外交部長約瑟‧安東尼奧‧米德和美國大使安東尼‧韋恩的歡迎。

要點解析

① welcome 作名詞和動詞都是「歡迎」的意思。give a warm welcome 意為「給予熱烈歡迎」。

② off 在這句話中作介詞，表示「下（飛機，車等），離開」。

③ Air Force One 空軍一號，是美國總統的專用飛機。這架波音 747 是美國權力的象徵，也叫「空中白宮」。

56　Measuring the scope of world hunger is a long and complicated process. (VOA)

衡量世界飢荒的影響範圍是一個漫長而複雜的過程。

要點解析

① 句首的 measuring the scope of... 是動名詞作主語。

② scope 泛指「（活動，影響等的）範圍」。此外，它還有「餘地，機會」之意。

57　They have been an important part of the Republican base for a long time, and they are extremely dubious of this new approach. (NPR)

在很長一段時間裡，他們曾是共和黨基地的重要部分，並且對這項新方案持極度懷疑的態度。

要點解析

① be an important part of... 是……的一個重要部分。類似意思的表達還有 play an important role in。

② be dubious of... 對……持懷疑態度，猶豫不決的。類似表達還有 be skeptical of。

58　In today's global world, there is no longer anything foreign about foreign policy, more than ever before, the decisions that we made from the safety for our shores don't just ripple outward. (CNN)

在如今這個全球化的世界，外交政策不再是與己無關的事物。比起以往，我們做出的海岸安全決策不僅僅只是對外界產生影響。

要點解析

① no longer 是「不再」的意思，同義表達還有 not any longer。
② make decision 做決定。
③ ripple 起漣漪。這裡是用「激起漣漪」比喻「帶來效果」。這個詞作名詞表示「細浪，漣漪」，我們常說的連鎖反應就是 ripple effect。

59　I think the society must start teaching the children who are adopted, you know sometimes to not concentrate much on the roots. (VOA)

我認為社會必須開始教導那些被領養的孩子，你知道，有時不要那麼在意自己的出身。

要點解析

① adopt 收養。這個詞還有「採用」的含義。值得注意的是：不要和形近詞 adapt「改變，使適合」混淆。
② concentrate on 集中注意力於。
③ root 的原意是「根」，在這句話裡指的是一個人的「出身」。

60　This happened when the Democrats won the last undecided senate seat from November's election. (BBC)

這是在民主黨在 11 月的大選中獲得了最後一個懸而未決的參議院席位的時候發生的。

要點解析

① undecided 是由 decide 衍生的詞，表示「未解決的，猶豫不定的」。
② senate seat 參議院席位。seat 除了「座位」的意思，還可指「席位，職位」。

61　In order to get tax exempt status, which is what it's called, those groups have to fill out an application and submit to other checks from the IRS. (CNN)

為了獲得所謂的免稅資格，那些組織必須填寫一份申請表並提交美國國稅局的一些其他的支票。

要點解析

① fill out 指填寫表格或申請書等；此外還有「變胖，使充實」的意思。
② submit to 提交，呈送。其中 to 是介詞，該片語還有「建議，屈服，遵守」的意思。固定表達 submit oneself to 是「遵守」的意思。

62　It's analysed that President Obama is quite popular in Indonesia because most people believe the president understands Indonesian culture and values. (VOA)

據分析，總統歐巴馬之所以在印尼非常受歡迎，是因為大多數人認為這位總統了解印尼的文化和價值觀。

要點解析

① be popular in... 在……受歡迎。
② value 在這句話裡是「價值觀」的意思。

63　A push to overhaul U.S. immigration laws has been gaining momentum in the Senate. (VOA)

對美國移民法案改革的推動為參議院獲得了勢頭。

要點解析

① push 作動詞的用法比較常見，表示「推，促進」的意思。但是 push 也可以作名詞，有「推」的意思，也可以引申為「決心，進取心」的含義。
② overhaul 作動詞和名詞都是「大修；仔細檢查」的意思。
③ momentum 在物理學中指「動力，動量」，在這句話裡是「勢頭」的意思。固定搭配 gain/gather momentum 意為「增加勢頭」。

64　So Detroit today is announcing a big plan, shutting down more than 40 of its schools. (CNN)

所以，今天底特律宣布了一個即將關閉超過 40 所學校的重大計畫。

要點解析

① announce 意為「宣布」，通常指宣布法案或決策。

② shut down 關閉，臨時性停工。此外，該片語還有「關窗戶，彌漫，籠罩」的意思。

65　One third of the world's population does not have access to a toilet, which has huge social and health implications. (VOA)

世界三分之一的人口沒有廁所可以使用，這一現象隱含著很大的社會和健康問題。

要點解析

① one third of 三分之一的。

② have access to 接近，可以使用；其中 to 作介詞。

③ implication 的本義是「暗示」，在這句話裡引申為「潛在的問題」。

66　Mexico will have an independent body to oversee teaching and the curriculum and teachers and schools will now be assessed. (BBC)

墨西哥將設立一個監督教學的獨立機構，課程、教師和學校都將接受評估。

要點解析

① body 原指身體，但在這句話裡是「機構」的意思。

② oversee 監視，監督；此外還有「俯瞰，眺望」的意思。

③ assess 評定，估價。其名詞形式為 assessment，常用搭配為 make an assessment 進行評估。

67　Greenpeace in Turkey calls the decision to build this new plant a high-risk project. (BBC)

土耳其綠色和平組織稱建造新工廠是一個高風險專案。

要點解析

① plant 除了常見的「植物」這一含義之外，還有「工廠」的意思。

② high-risk 有「高風險的」的意思，對應的 low-risk 則是「低風險的」。

③ Greenpeace 綠色和平組織。這是一個國際性的非政府組織，從事環保工作，總部位於荷蘭的阿姆斯特丹。

68　Mr. Obama arrives with two separate agendas, one public, in which both sides have been keen to strengthen emphasis on the economy and trade; the other is private. (BBC)

歐巴馬此行有兩個獨立議程，一個是公開議程，雙方都熱衷於加強對經濟和貿易的關注；另一個則是私人議程。

要點解析

① agenda 指「議程」，常用搭配為 on the agenda 在議程上。

② be keen to... 熱衷於做……。這個片語可以表達對某項政策或決議的擁護或熱情。

③ emphasis on... 強調……。

69　She has given an emotional final address to her people a day before she abdicates in favour of her eldest son. (BBC)

她在退位前一天對她的人民發表了最後一場充滿感情的演講，並對她的長子繼位表示支持。

要點解析

① address 除了常用的「地址」之意，還有「演講，講話」的意思。

② abdicate 是一個比較正式的表達，表示「放棄權力或高位」。

③ in favour of 支持。

70　President Obama has delivered a national security speech at a time through disruptions from a member of the audience of the National Defense University. (NPR)

當時，總統歐巴馬發表的一場關於國家安全的演講被一名來自國防大學的觀眾數次打斷。

要點解析

① deliver 這個詞有很多意思，可以表示「傳送，發表，釋放」；此外還有「接生」的意思。

② at a time 每次，在某時。注意和 at times「有時」區分。

71   On behalf of President Obama and on behalf of FEMA, we will be here to stay until this recovery is complete. (NPR)

我們代表總統歐巴馬和聯邦緊急事務管理署留在這裡,直到恢復工作澈底完成。

要點解析

① on behalf of 常指「代表某人或某機構」。

② recovery 恢復,痊癒。通常是指病情的痊癒,也可以指「從......中恢復」。

③ complete 在這句話作動詞,表示「完成」。

72   Two senators, for some reason, have come up with a compromise on background checks. (CNN)

不知什麼原因,這兩位參議員在背景調查方面達成了妥協。

要點解析

① come up with 提出,想出。如:come up with an idea 想出主意。

② compromise on... 在......上達成妥協。類似片語還有 open to compromise 尋求和解。

③ check 考核。

73   President Obama has praised his leadership during historic talks at the White House. (BBC)

在白宮的歷史性會談中,總統歐巴馬讚揚了他的領導能力。

要點解析

① leadership 泛指領導,領導層;在這句話裡是「領導能力」的意思。

② historic 歷史性的,有歷史意義的。注意區分它與 historical 的含義,後者表示「歷史上的,有關歷史的」。

74   The top leader himself won't be in the cabinet, but one of his closest political allies will be interior minister. (BBC)

這位最高領導人本人將不會進入內閣,但一位他最親密的政治盟友將擔任內政部長。

要點解析

① cabinet 最基本的意思是「陳列櫃，儲藏廚」，但是最常用的是政治方面的「內閣」。

② interior 內部的，內地的，國內的。其反義詞為 exterior「外部的」。

75　The head of the organization said in a letter of congratulation to the new leader that he hoped for cordiality and sincere friendship. (BBC)

該組織領袖在致新任領導人的祝賀信中表示，他希望得到熱情誠摯的友誼。

要點解析

① hope for... 希望得到......。

② cordiality 親切感，真摯。它的複數形式表示熱情友好的舉動或者言辭。

76　All these challenges can be better addressed in an open democratic so-ciety. (BBC)

所有這些挑戰都能在一個更加開放和民主的社會裡得到更好的解決。

要點解析

① address 除了表示「演說，講話」以外，還有「對付，處理」的意思。

② open 在這句話中是「公開的，坦率的」之意。此外，它還有「無偏見的，空缺的，尚未解決的」等意思。

77　All the delegates are set to vote on who will be next leader. (CNN)

代表們都將投票表決誰將成為下一任領導人。

要點解析

① be set to do... 準備做......，其中 set 在這句話裡是形容詞，表示「處於某種狀態的」。

② vote on... 在......方面投票。

78　All the people are looking to the new government with hope that it will be able to solve the country's deep economic and security problems. (VOA)

人民都期望新政府能解決該國嚴重的經濟和安全問題。

要點解析

① look to 指望，依靠。此外，還有「照管」的意思。

② be able to... 能夠......。這個片語所描述的能力通常是透過努力獲得的。

79　In a Baltimore company called "Ellicott Dredges" he announced steps to speed up major infrastructure projects. (NPR)

在巴爾的摩一家名為「埃里克特挖掘機」的公司裡，他宣布採取措施加快實施重大基礎設施專案。

要點解析

① speed up 加快速度。在這句話裡 speed 作動詞。

② infrastructure 基礎結構，基礎設施。這是一個集合名詞，指為社會生產和居民生活提供公共服務的物質工程設施，如：公路、機場、通訊等，也包括教育、科技、醫療衛生及文化等社會方面的基礎設施。

80　I hope the court rules that a student's race and ethnicity should not be considered when applying to the University of Texas. (CNN)

我希望，法庭規定，在學生申請德州大學時不應該考慮其種族和民族問題。

要點解析

① rule 通常作名詞，表示「規則，習慣」；此外它還可以用作動詞，表示「統治，控制」。

② apply to... 向......提起申請。類似的片語 apply to sb. 表示「適合某人」；apply sth. to 表示「把某物應用在......上」。

81　Visiting another countries and working with their leaders is one of biggest parts of his new job. (CNN)

訪問其他國家並與這些國家的領導人會面是他新工作最主要的一個部分。

① work with... 與......一起工作。可引申為「與......合作」的意思，即：cooperate with。

② biggest part 比重最大的部分。big 原指「大的」，在這個語境中，指「比重大的」。

82　At the White House, Press Secretary Jay Carney urged the public to withhold judgment until all the facts were clear. (NPR)

在白宮，新聞發言人傑伊·卡尼呼籲公眾在事實水落石出之前不要妄加評斷。

要點解析

① withhold 抑制，制止。此外，這個詞還有「拒絕，忍住」的意思，如：withhold laughing 忍住不笑。

② clear 在這句話裡指「清楚明白的」，還有「無疑的，確信的」等含義。常見固定搭配有 clear away 把......清除掉；clear off 離開。

83　President Barack Obama has arrived in Costa Rica to attend the summit of Central American leaders. (BBC)

總統巴拉克·歐巴馬已經抵達哥斯大黎加，準備出席中美洲領導人峰會。

要點解析

① arrive in 意為「抵達，到達」，通常後面接城市、國家等較大的地點；而 arrive at 則是接小地點。

② 表示「出席會議」常用 attend 這個動詞，這個詞還有「上課」的意思，如：attend class。

③ summit 的原意是「山的最高點，峰頂」，在這句話裡是指「峰會」。

84　Countries like Britain want their EU contributions to fall in line with national austerity cuts. (BBC)

英國等國家希望他們為歐盟所做的貢獻符合國家的緊縮削減政策。

要點解析

① in line with... 與......一致，符合。fall in line with 和 keep in line with 都可以表示「與......保持一致」。
② austerity 樸素，緊縮。它的形容詞為 austere，意為「樸素的，嚴峻的」。

85　He made no public statement, but the outgoing minister said parliament's secretaries would take charge of the ministries until a cabinet is appointed. (BBC)

雖然他沒有發表公開聲明，但即將離任的部長表示，在內閣被任命之前，議會大臣將負責掌管各部門。

要點解析

① outgoing 特指「即將離職的，離任的」，還有一個常用意思是「外向的，開朗的」。
② take charge of 負責。相當於 be responsible for 和 take responsibility of。
③ appoint 任命，委派。此外，這個詞還有「約定，指定時間地點」的意思。

86　We all believe in the constitution, we all know what all these amendments are about and what they're supposed to do and we're going to make sure that during this debate we keep the constitution in mind. (BBC)

我們都相信憲法，知道所有這些修正法案的內容和作用，我們確保在辯論的過程中將憲法銘記於心。

要點解析

① be supposed to do 理所應當做某事。這個片語的含義類似於 should do。
② make sure 確保，確信。該片語後面通常接從句或者介詞 about，of，表示確信的對象。
③ keep...in mind 將......銘記於心，也可以將 keep 換成 bear。

87　Mr. Kerry told business leaders in Cairo that in order to get the economy back on its feet, it was vital to establish a sense of security. (BBC)

凱瑞先生告訴開羅的商界領袖，為了使經濟復甦，建立安全感至關重要。

要點解析

① in order to do... 為了⋯⋯。這個片語常用來表示目的。

② get back on one's feet 讓⋯⋯重新站穩腳跟，表示「恢復到穩定的位子」。

③ a sense of security 安全感，類似的表達還有 a sense of humor 幽默感。

88　The initial count favored him but the recount gave the majority to his rival. (BBC)

他在首輪計票中略勝一籌，但在重新計票後，他的對手贏得了多數選票。

要點解析

① favor 有利於，有助於，在這句話裡指「占優勢」。此外它還有「喜愛，偏愛」的意思。favor 還可以作名詞，有「喜愛，恩惠」的含義，如：win sb.'s favor 獲得某人好感。

② rival 競爭者，匹敵者，此外，還可作為形容詞表示「競爭的」。

89　The government said it respected the judges but they'd failed to take into accounts steps taken by the government to make its austerity measures fair to all citizens. (BBC)

政府表示尊重法官的判決，但法官們並沒有考慮到政府為了讓緊縮措施對所有公民都公平而採取的行動。

要點解析

① fail to 未能。相當於 fail in doing sth.，後者也表示「未能做⋯⋯」。

② take sth. into account 考慮。

③ take steps 採取步驟，與 take measures 含義類似。

90　He is urging church leaders to go out into their communities and help the poor around rather than focus on the internal politics. (NPR)

他呼籲教派領袖要走進社區去幫助周圍窮困的人，而不要只關心內部政治。

要點解析

① go out 出去，參加社交活動。此外它還有很多其他的意思，如「燈熄滅，過時，花掉，退去」等。

② rather than 而不是，寧可……也不願。這個用法是否定 rather 前面的事物，肯定 than 後面事物。

③ focus on 這個片語的基本意思是指「將光線聚焦於」，常表示「集中於，以……為重點」。

---

91 He travels the area for talks on lasting economic and trade co-opera-tion. (VOA)

他前往該地區就長期經濟貿易方面的合作進行會談。

要點解析

① travel to... 去……，經常用來指「去……旅行」。

② talk on... 在……方面的會談，on 後面接談論的對象或話題。

---

92 The founding fathers gave senate that power in constitution that's called vice consent. (CNN)

開國元勳賦予參議院憲法上的權利被稱作「代為同意」。

要點解析

① constitution 憲法，是法律中常用的專有名詞。

② vice 作為形容詞有「代替的」的含義。consent 同意，意見一致，如：mutual consent 雙方同意；by common consent 一致同意。

---

93 The two leaders had a meeting in a bid to revive the peace process. (BBC)

為恢復和平進程，這兩位領導人進行了會面。

要點解析

① in a bid to 為了，試圖，力求，和 in order to 一樣表示目的。

② revive 復興，恢復，重演，re- 這個首碼表示「又」的意思。

---

94 As Prime Minister, I renew my commitment here today, to do all of my powers to attack the additional difficulties and put an end to this crisis once and for all. (BBC)

身為總理，我今天在這裡重申我的承諾，我將盡最大努力解決其

他的困難，並一勞永逸地解決這場危機。

要點解析

① renew 更新，重新開始；commitment 是「承諾」的意思。

② put an end to... 結束......，相當於 end。這個片語比較正式，後面可以直接跟名詞。

③ once and for all 一勞永逸地，最後地。

95　The acting president fired him and replaced him with one retired military official. (VOA)

代理總統解僱了他，由一位退役的軍官接替他的職位。

要點解析

① acting 代理的，裝腔作勢的；這裡的 acting president 指「代理總統」。

② fire 除了「火」之外，作動詞還可以表示「解雇，開除」。

③ replace with... 以......替換，可以用 by 代替 with。

96　He announced plans to cut another 30,000 public-sector jobs and added that civil servants would be required to work an extra hour a day. (BBC)

他宣布，計劃裁減 30,000 個公共部門職位，並表示公務員每天將額外工作一小時。

要點解析

① public-sector 是「公關部門」，其中 section 在這句話裡指「部門」；civil servant 就是「公務員」的意思。

② add 原指「增加」，在這句話裡是「補充說」的意思。

③ work extra hour 就是常說的「加班」的意思，也可以用 work overtime 表示。

97　A new coach was especially meaningful for that small community. (VOA)

一個新的主帥對那個小團體來說具有特別的意義。

要點解析

① meaningful 有意義的，常用搭配是 be meaningful for。

② community 的常用意義是社區，此外，還可表示「生態群落，團體」。

98　The Italian President Giorgio Napolitano has used his inaugural address to demand a new government and urgent reforms to break the political deadlock in the country. (BBC)

義大利總統喬治‧納波利塔諾利用就職演說要求組建新政府，並督促進行改革，打破國家政治僵局。

要點解析

① inaugural address 是「就職演說」，其中 inaugural 表示「開始的，就職的」。

② urgent reform 緊急的改革。

③ break the deadlock 打破僵局，類似的表達還有 break the ice 打破沉默。deadlock 意為「僵局，停頓」。

99　President Obama's stimulus and health care programs ballooned the size of government. (NPR)

歐巴馬總統的刺激政策和醫保專案擴大了政府規模。

要點解析

① stimulus 刺激，激勵；如：fiscal stimulus 財政刺激。這個詞的動詞形式為 stimulate。

② balloon 在這句話裡作動詞，表示「像氣球般鼓起來」，這個用法非常形象，具有比喻意義。

100　One government official said he would take charge of administrative tasks until elections are held. (VOA)

一位政府官員稱他會負責管理行政事務，直到舉行大選。

要點解析

① take charge of... 意思是「負責 ......」。

② hold election 舉行大選。在英語中，general election 即「大選」的意思，表示選舉總統的活動。

101 The attorney general accuses the union leader of having used the money to fund her lavish lifestyle including on plastic surgery, a private jet and two homes in Santiago. (BBC)

首席檢察官指控工會領導人濫用工會資金滿足她自己奢華的生活方式，包括整型、購買私人飛機以及在聖地牙哥購買兩處房產。

要點解析

① attorney general 是「首席檢察官」。
② accuse sb. of... 指控某人……，of 後面通常接表示罪行的動名詞或者名詞。
③ lavish 浪費的，奢華的；此外，還可作動詞，表示「揮霍」。
④ plastic surgery 整型外科手術，簡稱「整型」。

102 A key goal is to prevent multi-national firms exploiting legal loopholes to minimize their tax payments. (BBC)

一個關鍵性的目標是防止跨國公司利用法律漏洞將納稅額減到最小。

要點解析

① prevent (from)... 阻止……做，在這個句子中後面接的 exploit 要用動名詞形式，類似意思的片語還有 stop from，prohibit from。
② multi-national firm 跨國公司，multi- 意為「多」，經常用來作為首碼。
③ loophole 漏洞，多指法律方面的漏洞，還可表示牆上的窺孔。

103 The national transportation says the board is investigating along with Connecticut officials. (NPR)

國家運輸局表示董事會正在和康乃狄克州的官員一同進行調查。

要點解析

① board 董事會，還可以用 executive board 表示董事會。
② along with... 與……一起，連同……一起；此外還有「加之，除……之外還有」的意思。

104 NPR's Ari Shapiro reports Obama travelled to Baltimore to talk about economic growth and infrastructure. (NPR)

據美國國家公共電台的阿里・夏皮羅報導，歐巴馬走訪了巴爾的摩，探討關於經濟成長和基礎設施的情況。

要點解析

① talk about 談論，討論；此外還有「說起……，提到……」的意思。

② infrastructure 基礎設施，公共建設；如：economic infrastructure 經濟基礎設施。

---

105 Many older Americans worry that their care will be affected by cuts in federal payments to hospitals and other providers. (VOA)

許多年長的美國民眾擔心聯邦政府針對醫院和其他服務提供者的財政削減會影響他們的醫保。

要點解析

① be affected by 受……影響，類似的片語還有 be influenced by。

② cut 作名詞表示「削減，減少」。

③ provider 供應者，如：service provider 服務提供者，technology provider 技術供應商。在這句話裡是指一些公共服務的提供者。

---

106 President Obama has spent most of the week in reactive mode, dealing with three separated controversies about the IRS, the justice department and Benghazi. (NPR)

總統歐巴馬本週大部分時間都在應答關於美國國稅局、司法部門以及班加西的三個獨立的爭議。

要點解析

① reactive 反應的，反應性的；是動詞 react 的形容詞形式。in...mode 是「處於……模式」的說法，如：「處於震動模式」就是 in vibrate mode，在這句話裡是用來表示「處於某種狀態」。

② deal with 處理。此外還有「應付，涉及，對待」的意思。

③ controversy 爭論，競爭，爭辯。

107   The White House says the president's council, Catherine Rommel
       alerted some senior staff members after she learned inspector general
       of the internal revenue service was looking into special scrutiny if con-
       servative groups were plying for tax exempt status. (NPR)

       白宮方面表示，總統顧問凱薩琳‧隆美爾意識到美國國稅局檢查
       長在對申請免稅的保守團體進行特殊審查，隨後她對一些高級官
       員做出了警告。

要點解析

① alert 作為動詞、名詞、形容詞表示「警惕，警告」，如：smart alert 智慧
   提示；be alert to 對……警覺；be on the alert for 準備應對。
② look into 調查；此外還有「觀察，窺視，瀏覽」的意思。
③ ply 是「使用，辛勤工作，定期來往」的意思，比如：ply for hire 指車輛
   往來「攬客」。

108   People can begin signing up for insurance exchanges to get health cov-
       erage. (NPR)

       人們可去保險交易所註冊以獲得醫療保險。

要點解析

① sign up for 報名參加，選課，註冊；類似意思的片語還有 log in，register
   for。
② insurance exchanges 保險交易所，exchange 在這句話裡作名詞，表示「交
   易所」；作動詞時最常用的意思是「交換，調換」。
③ coverage 覆蓋，覆蓋範圍，在這句話裡指「保險範圍」，新聞中還常用
   到「報導」之意，如固定搭配：news coverage 新聞報導。

109   The Somali president, regarded as the country's most legitimate leader
       since the state Politicians in Washington will be monitoring the effects
       of those cuts and the public's reaction as federal services are reduced.
       (VOA)

       華盛頓的政客將時刻監控這些削減政策的效果，以及大眾對於聯
       邦服務減少做出的反應。

要點解析

① monitor 監控，監聽；它還可以作名詞，表示「監控器，監督員」；固定搭配有 monitor system 監控系統；remote monitor 遙控器。

② cut 在新聞中，多數是表達「削減」的意思，既可作名詞也可以作動詞。

③ reaction 反應，感應；固定搭配：reaction to 對……做出反應。

110　The organization runs... runs schools, medical clinics and a job creation program, but financial support for these programs hasn't kept up with the overwhelming need and deepening poverty of refugees. (BBC)

這個組織開辦學校、發放食物，此外，該組織還開辦學校、醫療診所和創造就業專案，但是對這些專案的財政支援並不能滿足難民龐大的需求，也無法緩解他們日漸加深的貧困狀況。

要點解析

① financial support 意為「財政支援」。

② keep up with... 緊跟，與 ...... 同步。

相關句子

To help restore conditions following a fire, the UN supplies Palestinian refugees with emergency supplies and assistance.

為協助開展火災後的恢復工作，聯合國為巴勒斯坦難民提供了緊急賑災物資和協助。

111　We look forward to working closely with the government and all other stakeholders. (BBC)

我們期待與政府和所有其他利益相關者緊密合作。

要點解析

① look forward to 期待，希望；to 為介詞，後面跟名詞和動名詞形式。

② work with 與……合作，與……共事；此外還有「對……起作用」的意思，相當於 take effects on。

③ stakeholder 利益相關者，股東。

112　You just find in a particular atmosphere that you have to end up com-
promising some basic values. (NPR)
你會發現在那樣一個特殊的氛圍中，你最終不得不放棄一些基本
的價值觀。

要點解析

① end up 完整型式為 end up with，後面接動名詞和名詞，表示「以......結
束」。

② compromise 作名詞和作動詞都有「妥協，和解」的意思，常見搭配：
reach a compromise 達成妥協；make a compromise 做出讓步。

③ remind 提醒，常用搭配為 remind sb. of sth. 提醒某人某事。

113　Obama's trip comes hours after he nominated longtime fundraiser,
philanthropist Penny Pritzker to run the Commerce Department and
economic advisor Michael Froman to be the next trade representative.
(NPR)
在提名長期籌款人慈善家潘妮・普利茨克執掌商務部，經濟顧
問邁克爾・弗曼擔任下任貿易代表幾小時後，歐巴馬才開始
他的行程。

要點解析

① come hours after...直譯為「在......發生幾小時以後」，引申為「在......之
後」的意思。

② nominate 提名，任命為......；be nominated for 被任命為......。

③ run 經營，管理。

114　I'm directing agencies across the government to do what it takes, to
cut timelines for breaking ground on major infrastructure programs in
half. (NPR)
我正在指導各政府機構採取措施，將開辦大型基礎專案的期限減
少一半的時間。

要點解析

① timeline 時間軸，要事年表，在這句話裡指「限期」。

② break ground 字面意思是「動土」，可以引申為「創辦，開辦」。

③ in half 分成兩半；divide/tear/cut/split sth. in half 把……分／撕／切／劈為兩半。

---

115 Other advocates say there are many other steps that need to be taken, including a strengthening of police and court systems. (VOA)

其他支持者表示還需採取其他許多步驟，包括加強警力和法院體系。

> **要點解析**

① advocate 作名詞意為「提倡者，支持者」；後面常跟介詞「of」，表示「是……的宣導者」。

② take steps 採取步驟（行動），take measures 也表示這一含義。

---

116 These two countries have traditionally enjoyed close economic and diplomatic ties. (BBC)

這兩個國家一向有著緊密的經濟和外交關係。

> **要點解析**

① diplomatic 外交的，老練的；如：diplomatic relations 外交關係；diplomatic mission 外交使團。

② tie 關係，紐帶；economic tie 經濟關係。

---

117 Mr. Obama is expected to discuss immigration and trade with leaders attending the summit. (BBC)

預計歐巴馬將與參加峰會的領導人討論移民和貿易問題。

> **要點解析**

① immigration 移民，常用搭配有：illegal imagination 非法移民；immigration policy 移民政策。

② attend the summit 出席峰會，attend 常用的搭配還有 attend a concert 聽音樂會；attend church 做禮拜；attend school 上學；attend a meeting 參加會議。

> **相關句子**

At this APEC CEO Summit, you will discuss the important matter of world economic development and you will also discuss how to strengthen mutual cooperation. (VOA)

在此次亞太經合組織工商領導人峰會上，各位可以討論世界經濟發展的大事，也可以討論加強相互合作的問題。

118　Her policies, especially some economic ones, urged her support and criticism from the British people. (CNN)

英國民眾對她的政策，尤其是一些經濟政策褒貶不一。

要點解析

① policy 政策，方針；常用搭配：monetary policy 貨幣政策；economic policy 經濟政策；foreign policy 外交政策。

② economic 容易和 economical 弄混淆，economic 表示「經濟上的」；economical 則表示「節約的，合算的」。

③ criticism 批評，苛求。常用搭配：literary criticism 文藝評論；criticism and praise 批評和讚揚。

119　The Senate and then the House passed the bill in largely empty chambers using a fast-track procedure known as unanimous consent. (NPR)

眾議院跟著參議院走了捷徑——在大多數議員未出席的情況下以全體同意的方式通過了這個議案。

要點解析

① chamber 原指「室，房間」，在這句話裡指「（立法或司法機關的）會議室，議院」。

② fast-track 快捷通道，有「捷徑」的意思；如：fast-track claim 簡易賠案；fast-track entrance 快速通道入口。

③ unanimous consent 一致同意。

120　Obama says Turkey is important ally in global effort to end crisis. (NPR)

歐巴馬表示，土耳其在終止危機的全球努力過程中是一個重要盟友。

要點解析

① ally 同盟國。這個詞也可以作動詞，經常跟 to、with 連用，表示「使國家聯盟」。

② global effort 全球努力，global 意為「全球的」，常見搭配：global economy 全球經濟；global warming 全球變暖。

相關句子

Then Barack Obama heads to Turkey for the last stop on his first trip to Europe as president. (VOA)

巴拉克‧歐巴馬前往土耳其，這是他以總統身分進行首次歐洲之行的最後一站。

121　Like people everywhere, they also deserve a future of hope, and their rights will be respected. (CNN)

與世界各地的人民一樣，他們也應該擁有一個充滿希望的未來，他們的權利將會得到尊重。

要點解析

① deserve 應受，應得；如：deserve consideration 應受考慮；deserve charity 應受施捨。

② respect 在這句話裡作動詞。表示「尊敬，欽佩」；作名詞時還有「方面」的意思，常用搭配：in respect of 關於，涉及；in this respect 在這方面；in all respects 在各方面。

122　The president's plan has already drawn criticism from both the left and the right for it's offered to trim spending on Medicare and social security and it's called for hundreds of billions of dollars in new taxes. (NPR)

總統的計畫遭到了左翼和右翼的批評，因為該計畫需要削減醫療和社保經費，以及增加數千億美元的新稅收。

要點解析

① trim 修剪，削減；如：trim off 修剪掉；trim down 裁剪。在這句話裡與 cut 的含義用法相同。

② call for 需求，相當於 demand。

123　We think that it is still too early to decide whether to attend because it is not clear what this conference is about. (VOA)

由於還不清楚會議的內容，我們認為現在就決定是否參會還為時過早。

要點解析

① too...to... 太......而不能。但是注意，當這個片語與 can't 一起用的時候，表示「太......都不為過」，比如：can't be too careful 就表示「越仔細越好」。

② be about 關於......，此外還有「正忙於......」，「大約」等意思。

124　President Obama has urged Congress to pass a bill to avert billions of dollars of automatic spending cuts. (BBC)

歐巴馬總統督促國會透過一項議案來避免上百億美元的自動開銷削減。

要點解析

① pass a bill 透過議案，bill 指「政府法案，議案」。

② avert 避免，防止......發生。

③ automatic 自動的，無意識的；如：automatic operation 自動操作；automatic system 自動系統；automatic equipment 自動設備。

125　He told the BBC that he was determined to meet the huge challenges facing his country and to bring about change. (BBC)

他告訴英國廣播公司，他已經下定決心迎接本國所面臨的巨大挑戰，並帶來改變。

要點解析

① be determined to do... 決定做......，這個片語可以用來表示決心。

② bring about 引起，造成，帶來。

126　The senate judiciary committee has unanimously approved the justice department lawyer to fill the post. (NPR)

參議院司法委員會一致同意由司法部律師擔任這一職位。

要點解析

① senate 國會，議會，參議院。常用搭配有：senate finance committee 參議院財政委員會；senate banking committee 參議院銀行業委員會；senate budget committee 美國參議院預算委員會。

② fill the post 任職，其中 fill 是「擔任（職務等），任職」的意思，post 是「職位」的意思。

127　Additionally, changes in health care laws give millions more Americans access to health insurance and care. (VOA)

此外，醫保法案的改革讓超過數百萬名美國民眾有機會享受醫療保險和保健。

要點解析

① additionally 此外，加之；類似意思的表達還有：moreover，besides。

② give access to 中 to 是介詞，後面接名詞或動名詞，片語的意思是「接近，准許出入，得以進入」。

128　This was an important final stop-off for Mr. Obama recognizing what he called an invaluable ally. (BBC)

歐巴馬認可了他最重要的盟友，這也是他旅程中重要的一段停留。

要點解析

① stop-off 中途分道，中途停留；類似意思的表達還有 stopover。

② recognize 察覺，賞識，認可，recognize as 公認。

129　Margaret Thatcher was one of the best the Britain has had and White House Secretary Jay Carney praises Thatcher as a champion of liberty and a true friend of the U.S. (NPR)

瑪格麗特·柴契爾是英國歷史上最傑出的領導人之一；白宮祕書卡尼稱讚柴契爾是一位自由的捍衛者，是美國真正的朋友。

要點解析

① praise as 讚美……為……。

② champion 除了「冠軍」之外，還有「擁護者」的意思。

相關句子

More recently, Margaret Thatcher's 1981 budget cuts heralded real reforms in Britain and, eventually, a period of growth and prosperity.

更近一些，瑪格麗特‧柴契爾 1981 年的預算削減為英國帶來了真正的改革，以及一個時期的成長和繁榮。

130　We continue to work very closely with our neighbouring countries in order to promote economic cooperation. (CNN)

我們繼續與鄰國展開非常密切的合作以促進經濟合作。

要點解析

① work closely with 密切合作，緊密配合。

② in order to... 為了……，以便……；一般在句中作目的狀語。

③ economic 經濟的，經濟上的，其名詞形式是 economy。

131　President Medvedev says there is a need to eliminate Interior Ministry functions that are redundant or not relevant to police work. (VOA)

總統梅德維傑夫表示，有必要撤銷冗餘或與員警工作不相關的內務部職能。

要點解析

① eliminate 消除，擺脫；如：eliminate poverty 消除貧困；eliminate noise 消除雜訊；eliminate illiteracy 掃盲。

② redundant 多餘的，累贅的；相關的片語有：redundant information 資訊冗餘；redundant system 系統冗餘。

132　The Dutch government has announced plans to give police much greater powers to fight cyber crime. (BBC)

荷蘭政府已經宣布計畫，給予警方更多的權力來抗衡網路犯罪。

要點解析

① power 職權，許可權，權利範圍；相關片語：in power 執政的，當權的。

② fight 企圖戰勝，如：為……進行戰鬥；fight for 為……而戰；fight against

對抗；fight with 與......並肩戰鬥。

③ cyber 網路的；cyber terrorism 網路恐怖主義；cyber attack 網路攻擊。

133　The European Union has suspended most of the sanctions it imposed on some auxiliary persons after the country approved a new constitution curbing the president's powers. (BBC)

在該國通過一項新憲法削弱總統的權利之後，歐盟取消了針對一些相關人士的處罰。

要點解析

① suspend 延緩，推遲，暫時取消；如：suspend payment 停止支付；suspend operation 暫停運行；suspend one's business license 暫停營業執照。

② sanction 處罰，制裁；新聞中常見的搭配有：economic sanction 經濟制裁；general sanction 全面制裁。

③ impose on 施加影響於，強加；常用搭配有：impose restriction on 施加限制；impose punishment on 施加處罰；impose sanctions on 實施制裁。

134　Let it be our task, every single one of us to honor the strength and the resolve and the love these brave Americans felt for each other and for our country. (VOA)

讓這成為我們的任務，讓我們每個人向這些勇敢的美國人的堅強、決心以及他們對彼此和對我們國家的愛致敬。

要點解析

① let it be... 讓它成為......。此外，單獨使用時它還有「順其自然」的意思。

② every single... 經常用在口語中，用來加強語氣，表示「每一個」的意思。

135　It's expected that they will give their backing to results which awarded a narrow victory to make him the chosen successor. (BBC)

他被選為繼承人，預計他們會對這個險勝的結果予以支持。

要點解析

① give one's backing to... 支持......，其中 backing 在這句話裡是 back 的動名詞，表示「支持」的意思。

② award 授予，贈與。

③ narrow victory 險勝，通常用在選舉或比賽之中。

④ chosen successor 選定接班人；chosen 已選定的；successor 繼承人。

---

136   Two of America's thorniest issues—immigration reform and gun control—will be the focus of deliberations in the U.S. Senate. (VOA)
      美國的兩大棘手問題——移民改革和槍支管制將成為美國參議院商議的核心。

要點解析

① thorniest 是 thorny 的最高級形式，表示「最棘手的，最痛苦的」。

② deliberation 表示在做出決定前的「商議，協議」；如：democratic deliberation 民主審議；under deliberation 在考慮中。

---

137   United States will take all necessary steps to protect its people and to meet our obligations under our alliances in the region. (BBC)
      美國將採取一切必要措施保護其人民，履行該地區聯盟的義務。

要點解析

① take steps 採取措施，相當於 take measures。

② meet one's obligation 履行某人的義務，meet 有「滿足，達到（目標），應付」的意思，比如：meet requirement 符合要求；meet challenge 迎接挑戰。

---

138   With the proper use of technology, we will be able to say we have a degree of border security that will enable people to move toward a path to citizenship. (VOA)
      在技術的正確利用下，我們可以說在一定程度上實現了邊境安全，並且促使人們朝合法公民的方向前進。

要點解析

① a degree of 一定程度上的，如：a high degree of 高度的，a certain degree of 一定程度的。

② border security 邊境安全，border 是「邊境」的意思，相關片語還有：border guard 邊防人員；border trade 邊境貿易等。

③ move toward 走向，前往。

139　Two sides have different views on what might happen for peace talks to begin. (NPR)

雙方就開始和談的條件持不同觀點。

要點解析

① side（衝突中的）一邊，一方；常用搭配：both sides 雙方。

② view on... 對……的看法。口語中表示「觀點，看法」的詞還有 perspective，opinion，attitude。

140　Standing outside the plaza tower elementary school which has been demolished by the tornado, Obama pledged the federal government will help the community throughout the rebuilding process. (NPR)

站在遭到龍捲風破壞的廣場高塔小學外，歐巴馬承諾，聯邦政府將幫助社區進行重建工作。

要點解析

① demolish 摧毀，成為廢墟；在口語中還能表示「吃光」。

② tornado 龍捲風，此外還能表示「極具破壞力的人（或物）」。

③ pledge 許諾，保證；pledge oneself 宣誓，保證。

相關句子

Preside nt Obama has been visiting the area worst affected by a violent tornado, which killed more than 130 people in the American state of Missouri. (BBC)

歐巴馬總統走訪了受龍捲風影響最嚴重的美國密蘇里州，在這裡已有超過 130 人遇難。

141　The spokesman said that improving the country's economy would go long way towards solving its other problems. (BBC)

發言人表示，改善其經濟對於解決國家的其他問題有著非常深遠的意義。

要點解析

① improve 改善，提高；常用搭配有：improve relationship 改善關係；improve health 改善健康狀況。

② go a long way 除了字面意思「走很長的路」之外，還有「對......有很大幫助」的意思，後面通常接介詞 to / towards。

142　The Chinese government is working on imposing a ban on all forms of tobacco advertising, sponsorship and promotion of tobacco products. (VOA)

中國政府擬禁止一切形式的菸草廣告、贊助以及菸草產品的促銷。

要點解析

① be working on... 致力於 ......，從事於 ......

② impose 利用，施加影響，常與介詞 on 連用。

③ all forms of 各種各樣的。

143　There is more lifting ahead; the estimated gap between what is being spent on surface transportation and what is needed adds up to more than $800 billion. (NPR)

未來還將有更多提升；據估計，地面交通的資金投入與實際需要的總共相差 8,000 多億美元。

要點解析

① lifting 提高；上升，這個詞還能作形容詞表示「舉起的」，相關搭配有：lifting jack 千斤頂；lifting beam 起重橫梁。

② gap 差距；分歧，常用搭配有：income gap 收入差距，generation gap 代溝。

③ surface transportation 地面交通。

144　But some Republican lawmakers say those same qualities give them pause about voting to confirm Perez as a Cabinet member. (NPR)

但是一些共和黨議員表示，那些相同的品質讓他們對是否投票選舉佩雷斯成為內閣成員感到猶豫。

要點解析

① give sb. pause 字面意思為「讓某人停頓一下」，其實際意思為「讓某人仔細考慮；躊躇一下」。

② vote to do 投票做某事。此外，vote 還有名詞用法，比如：casting vote 決定票；popular vote 普選；individual vote 個人投票。

145　The interior minister said about 750 people were transferred to holding centers in the southern cities of Crotone and Bari. (VOA)

內政部長稱大約有 750 人被轉移到南部城市克羅托內和巴里的收容中心。

要點解析

① interior minister 內政部長，相關表達有 former interior minister 前內閣部長；current interior minister 現任內閣部長。

② transfer to 轉移到，調往，移至；其中 to 是介詞，後面接名詞或動名詞形式。

146　Since moving to the Boston area, they have been embraced by the community. (VOA)

自從搬到波士頓地區之後，他們在社區中受到了擁護。

要點解析

① move to 搬到；移居到。關於 move 的片語有：on the move 在活動中；move on 往前走；make a move 搬家；move out 搬出。

② be embraced by 受到擁護。其中 embrace 有「樂意採取，利用」之意，如：embrace an opportunity 抓住機會。

③ community 社區；團體，如：international community 國際社會；community health 社區健康；community development 社區發展。

147　He'd built up an unassailable lead, and it's now been decided he'll be the Socialist Party candidate for the upcoming presidential election. (BBC)

他建立了不可動搖的領導地位，現在這使他在即將舉行的總統選舉中成為了社會黨候選人。

要點解析

① build up 增進；逐步建立，關於它的搭配有：build up confidence 增進信心；build up health 增進健康；build up one's body 增強體質。

② unassailable 不容置疑的；無懈可擊的，相當於 indubitable，invulnerable。

③ upcoming 即將來臨的，還可以用 around the corner 來表示。

148　They are trying to establish that dictatorship or democracy is a frame of mind. (BBC)

他們試圖表示獨裁或民主是一種心態。

要點解析

① dictatorship 專政；獨裁權。比如：military dictatorship 軍事獨裁國家；dictatorship of proletariat 無產階級專政。

② democracy 民主，與 dictatorship「專政」相對。

③ frame 有「框架」的意思，而 frame of mind 則表示「心態」。

149　He has defended a 10 bn euro bailout deal to save the country's banks from collapse. (BBC)

他為 100 億歐元的救助計畫進行辯護，目的是讓國家銀行免遭破產。

要點解析

① defend 保衛，守護；defend against 防衛；defend with... 用......防衛；defend oneself 自衛。

② bailout 緊急救助，新聞中常見的搭配有：bailout period 緊急救助階段；government bailout 政府救助。

③ collapse 倒塌，瓦解；這裡指「銀行破產」。

150　If the resolution doesn't pass, and that's not unusual, then the government can use a continuing resolution—basically the budget numbers from the past year continue into the new year. (CNN)

如果決議沒有通過也是正常的，這樣政府就可以採用持續決議──基本上就是將去年的預算數目持續到新的一年。

要點解析

① resolution 在這句話裡是「決議」的意思，新聞中常見的搭配有：major resolutions 重大決議；draft resolution 提案。此外，在口語中還能表示「決心」的意思，比如：make a resolution 下決心。

② continuing 持續的，繼續的。常用搭配有：continuing education 繼續教育；continuing operation 持續經營；continuing breach 持續違約。

③ basically 主要地，基本上。類似的詞還有 mainly，mostly，primarily 等。

---

151 Russia will take measures to help India meet a shortage of electricity for its booming economy. (VOA)

俄羅斯將採取措施幫助印度解決其繁榮的經濟帶來的電力短缺問題。

要點解析

① a shortage of 缺乏，還可以在 shortage 前加上 desperate，sever 等定語來表示缺乏的嚴重性；此外這個片語後面常接的名詞有 capital 現金，fund 資金，grain 糧食，labor 勞動力等。

② booming economy 繁榮的經濟。

③ nuclear power plant 核電站，plant 在這句話裡不是「植物」的意思，而是「工廠，電廠」的意思，如：treatment plant 汙水淨化廠；thermal power plant 火力發電廠。

---

152 Venezuela has the largest oil reserves in the world, along with Saudi Arabia, that oil wealth enabled Chavez to offer up free education and health care in his own country. (CNN)

和沙烏地阿拉伯一樣，委內瑞拉是世界上石油存儲量最大的國家，石油財富使查維茲能為自己的國家提供免費的教育和醫療保險。

要點解析

① take measures 採取措施，採取手段，take effective measures 表示「採取有效措施」。

② oil reserve 儲油量，此外，新聞中常見的搭配還有：cash reserve 現金儲備；foreign exchange reserve 外匯儲備。

③ along with... 與……一起；加之，關於它的片語還有 get along with 相處；

go along with 贊同。

---

153 He opened his Asia tour to restore normal ties and take a leading role in stabilizing the region. (NPR)

他開啟了他的亞洲之旅,希望以此來恢復正常關係,並對該地區的穩定發揮主導作用。

要點解析

① restore 恢復,修復。

② leading 主要的,常見搭配有:play the leading role in 起到主要作用;leading position 首要位置;leading technology 領先技術;leading edge 前端。

③ stabilize 穩定,安定,如:stabilize the market 穩定市場;stabilize prices 穩定物價。

---

154 Even as they agreed to start indirect talks, both sides disagreed whether the negotiations had officially begun. (VOA)

即使他們同意啟動間接和談,雙方就是否開始正式談判仍然存在分歧。

要點解析

① agree to... 同意做……,相關的片語還有 agree with sb. 同意某人;agree on... 一致同意做……

② indirect talks 間接會談;indirect 間接的,direct 直接的。

③ officially 官方地;正式地。

---

155 While yesterday, there was another major quake, this one had magnitude of 8.6. (CNN)

然而就在昨天,發生了另一場 8.6 級的大地震。

要點解析

① major quake 大地震,此外還可用 mega seism 來表示「大型地震」。

② magnitude 震級,相當於 earthquake magnitude。

156   He greeted him at his new retirement home, a converted monastery on the edge of the country's gardens. (NPR)

他在剛入住的養老院接待了他，該養老院位於該國花園邊上一所改建的修道院裡。

要點解析

① greet 歡迎，迎接，口語中「迎賓」可以說成 greet guest，此外，greet 還有「對……做出反應」的意思，通常後面接介詞 with。

② convert 轉變；改建，常見搭配：convert into 轉變成。

③ on the edge of... 在……的邊緣；瀕臨。

157   Investigators with a national transportation safety board are being dispatched to the site of collapsed bridge in Washington State. (NPR)

美國國家運輸安全委員會的調查人員已被派往華盛頓州坍塌大橋的事故現場。

要點解析

① board 可以表示「委員會；局」。比如：tourist board 旅遊局。

② dispatch to 將……派遣到，網上購物裡的「發貨」即 dispatch an order。

③ site 現場；site investigation 現場調查；on the site 在現場。

158   The top leader has passed into law sweeping reforms of the country's education system. (BBC)

最高領導人批准了對全國教育體系進行大規模改革的法律。

要點解析

① pass into law 通過法案。

② sweeping reforms 全面改革，其中 sweeping 表示「澈底的，廣泛的」。

159   Our position on settlements and outpost and on the legalization is that we are opposed to it. (NPR)

我們對定居點、警戒部隊及合法化均持反對態度。

要點解析

① settlement 定居點，其動詞形式是 settle，表示「定居」的意思。

② outpost 警戒部隊。

③ be opposed to... 反對……；與……相對，比如：be firmly opposed to... 堅決反對……；be bitterly opposed to 立場反對。

160　The findings suggest that for large segments of the military, repeal of don't ask, don't tell, though potentially disruptive in the short term, would not be the wrenching, dramatic change that many have feared and predicted. (CNN)

調查結果顯示，軍隊中大部分人希望取消「不問，不說」的政策，儘管可能造成短期混亂，但是不會讓多數人感到擔憂，並出現能預測出的令人痛苦的巨大變化。

要點解析

① segment 部分；分割，如：large segments of... 大部分的……

② repeal 撤銷；廢止，這是一個新聞常用詞，一般指法令等的廢除或撤銷，後面常接介詞 of，也可以直接接名詞，比如：repeal the law 廢除法令。

③ in the short term 短期內；就眼前來說。

161　He said the 49 countries who attended had come to a four-point plan. (BBC)

他表示 49 個出席國已經達成了一個四點計畫。

要點解析

① attend 出席，參加，到會。

② come to 歸結為，此外它還有「涉及」的意思，形式是 it comes to 表示「一提到……」，它還有「復甦；參加活動；總計」的意思。

162　The United States regulators have approved modifications made by the aircraft giant Boeing to the battery system for its 787 Dreamliner, a key step if the plane is to return to the sky after being grounded. (BBC)

美國監管機構批准航空龍頭波音公司對其 787 夢幻客機電池系統制訂的條款修訂，如果該客機在停飛後重新飛行，這將是關

鍵的一步。

要點解析

① modification 修改；緩和，常用搭配有：equipment modification 設備修改；data modification 資料修改。

② be grounded 可以表示「使停飛」，ground 作動詞有「使擱淺」的意思。

163　The Senate passed the food-safety bill, it will give the FDA (Food and Drug Administration) more power to order product recalls. The government wouldn't have to wait for companies to issue volunteer ones and House passed the similar bill last year. (CNN)

參議院透過了食品安全法案，這將給予美國食品及藥物管理局更多下令召回產品的權力。這樣政府不必等待公司自願召回，而去年眾議院也透過了類似法案。

要點解析

① give power 給予力量；給予權利。

② product recall 產品召回，其中 recall 意為「召回；撤銷」，通常在產品出現問題時，生產商有義務將這些產品召回。常用搭配有：beyond recall 不可挽回；recall from... 從……處召回。

③ issue 發布；分配，關於它的搭配有：issue in 導致；issue from... 從……流出。

④ pass 通過，比如：pass the bill 通過議案。

164　He offered potential partner a minority role in a government. (VOA)

他為其潛在合作夥伴在政府中提供了一個少數黨派的角色。

要點解析

① potential 表示「潛在的；可能的」。

② partner 合作夥伴。

③ minority 作名詞可以指「少數民族，少數派」；作動詞可以表示「少數的」。

165　Rare bipartisanship has emerged on both issues, boosting prospects for legislative action. (VOA)

在兩黨在這兩個議題上進行了罕見的合作，為立法行動增加

了可能性。

要點解析

① bipartisanship 兩黨合作；兩黨制。

② emerge 浮現；擺脫，如：emerge as 成為；emerge from 冒出。

③ boost 促進；支援。常用搭配：boost up 向上推。

166　To me, that is the essential core principle behind our founding documents—the idea that we are all created equal. (VOA)

對我而言，人們生而平等的理念是建國的基本核心原則。

要點解析

① core principle 核心原則，其他與 principle 相關的片語還有：working principle 工作原理；basic principle 基本原理；on the principle of... 根據……的原則。

② founding 創辦的；發起的；founding member 創辦會員；founding father 創建人。

167　Some lawmakers want to know exactly what took place at the IRS, and whether those activities were known or even sanctioned by the Obama administration. (VOA)

一些立法者想知道國稅局到底發生了什麼事，歐巴馬政府對這些行為是否知情或甚至已經做出制裁。

要點解析

① take place 發生；舉行。類似意思的片語還有 happen, occur。

② sanction 制裁；處罰；批准。sanction a proposal 批准一項議案。

168　She had only very general information about the then incomplete orbit which she passed onto some senior staffers. (NPR)

她對當時不完整的勢力範圍只有大概的了解，然後她把資訊傳給了一些高級官員。

要點解析

① orbit 在這句話裡表示「勢力範圍；生活常規」。

② senior 高級的；年老的；資深的。如：senior management 高級管理。

③ staffer 職員。與 staff 比較，這個詞更多用來指政治組織或者新聞機構的工作人員或職員。

169　As part of a latest drive by the Saudis to cut the expatriate workforce that brought in some new laws which would penalize companies if they don't employ at least one Saudi. (BBC)

沙烏地阿拉伯政府為減少外來工作人員頒布了新的法律，規定每家公司至少僱用一名沙烏地阿拉伯人，否則將受到處罰。

要點解析

① expatriate 移居國外的；被流放的。如：expatriate officer 外籍雇員；expatriate staff 離國服務的工作人員。

② workforce 勞動力；雇員總數。

③ bring in 引進；生產；帶入。

170　Under French law, that status means Lagarde could still be charged later on in the case, but can have legal representation and access to court file as the probe continues, a process that could take months or even years. (NPR)

根據法國法律，這種情況意味著拉加德之後可能仍會被起訴，但在調查進行期間，她可以有法律代表，查閱法院檔，這一過程可能會花費幾個月甚至幾年的時間。

要點解析

① charge 控訴;指責。如:charge... to... 歸咎於;charge for... 為......收取費用。

② have access to 使用；接近；可以利用。其中 to 為介詞，後面接名詞或動名詞形式。

③ probe 調查；查究。它還可做動詞，常見搭配：probe into 探究。

Part 2

Business & Finance

1   Microfinance is a movement within international development to pro-
    vide financial services to the poor. (VOA)
    小額信貸是在國際化發展過程中為貧困人群提供經濟服務的
    一種活動。

要點解析

① microfinance 小額信貸。
② 英語中常用 the 加上形容詞表示一類人，如：the poor 貧困人群，the
   young 年輕人。

相關句子

Under the World Trade Organization's financial services deal, banking markets
in many countries are opening up. (CNN)
在世界貿易組織的金融服務協定激勵下，許多國家都將開放本國的
銀行市場。

2   Sir Alan announced that some episodes have been 「specifically made
    to wards recognition of what difficult times we are in」. (BBC)
    艾倫爵士宣稱，一些事件已經「讓我們明確地意識現在所處的困
    難時期」。

要點解析

① 在人名前面大寫的 Sir 不是「先生」的意思，而表示「爵士」這一頭銜。
   如果是「先生」，應該用 Mr。
② episode 是名詞，意思是「事件；經歷；插曲」，如：The episode was a
   huge embarrassment for all concerned. 這個事件令所有有關人員都感到非
   常尷尬。
③ recognition 的意思是「識別；承認」。如：Their recognition of the new
   law is unlikely. 這項新法律不大可能獲得他們的承認。

相關句子

This weekend, Project Green Search will announce its selection of a new
model for the environmental "Green Revolution". (VOA)
本週末，綠色搜尋專案將宣布「綠色革命」新任環保小姐的人選。

3　The restrictions on foreign monetary exchange do not just hurt big business. (VOA)
限制外幣兌換交易不會只對大公司造成傷害。

要點解析

monetary 貨幣的；金融的，財政的。如：monetary policy 貨幣政策。

相關句子

The central bank's easy monetary policy has also been heavily criticized by some Republican presidential candidates. (BBC)
中央銀行寬鬆的貨幣政策也遭到了一些共和黨總統候選人的嚴厲指責。

4　With India's economic growth at its lowest point in a decade, some are questioning whether the South Asian nation should still be counted among the world's most influential, emerging economies. (VOA)
由於印度的經濟成長處於十年以來的最低點，這個南亞國家作為世界上最具影響力的新興經濟體之一的地位受到了很多人的質疑。

要點解析

① count 除了「計算」的意思以外，在這句話裡還可以表示「認為」的意思。
② emerge 是動詞，意思是「浮現，暴露」。emerging 則是其現在分詞作形容詞，表示「新興的，出現的」，如 emerging market 新興市場；emerging economy 新興經濟；emerging technology 新興技術。

相關句子

India's economy grew at an annual rate of 8.6% in the three months to March, largely thanks to growth in manufacturing, official data has shown. (BBC)
官方資料顯示，由於製造業的成長，印度經濟在一至三月期間的年度經濟增速高達 8.6%。

5　The EU, the world's biggest importer of bananas, is to cut the duty it imposes on Latin American producers of the fruit, while bananas grows in former European colonies will gradually lose the preferential terms they've enjoyed. (BBC)

作為世界上最大的香蕉進口方,歐盟將削減拉丁美洲香蕉生產商的關稅,而前歐洲殖民地將逐漸失去他們在香蕉種植方面享受的優惠條件。

要點解析

① EU 是 European Union 的縮寫,即「歐盟」。

② duty 作名詞既有「責任,義務」的意思,也可以表示「稅收」,如:duty free 免稅。

③ impose 強加;徵稅;以……欺騙。常用片語為 impose on,如 impose punishment on 施加處罰;impose fines on 罰款。

相關句子

The UK government has applied to the European Commission for the power to cut the duty by 5p a litre. (BBC)

英國政府已賦予歐盟委員會將汽油稅每升降價 5 便士的權力。

6　Shareholders have spoken Jamie Dimon can keep both his titles, chairman and CEO, only 32% of shareholders voted today at the bank's annual meeting in favor of a measure that have split Dimon's roles. (NPR)

股東們表示傑米‧戴蒙可以繼續同時擔任董事長和執行長兩個職位,在今天的銀行年度會議上,只有 32% 的股東投票贊成分離戴蒙職務的提議。

要點解析

split 的意思是「分裂,分開」,作動詞。常見搭配是:split up,表示「分開,分離」。

相關句子

Later this month shareholders of BSkyB will vote on whether Mr Murdoch should stay as chairman. (BBC)

本月晚些時候,英國天空廣播公司的股東們將投票決定是否繼續由梅鐸擔任董事長。

7　　Cyprus found itself at the brink of economic disaster. (BBC)

賽普勒斯處在經濟危機的邊緣。

要點解析

① 片語 at the brink 的意思是「瀕於......的邊緣」。如：at the brink of collapse 瀕臨崩潰的邊緣；at the brink of meltdown 瀕臨崩盤之際。

② disaster 災難，economic disaster 表示「經濟浩劫，經濟危機」。

8　　The computer first went on sale for 666 dollars but at today's auction it fetched a price 1,000 times higher. (BBC)

這台電腦的上市價格為 666 美元，但今天的拍賣價格卻比上市價格高了一千倍以上。

要點解析

① on sale 上市；出售；for sale 則表示「打折出售，降價出售」。

② auction 拍賣，auction house 可以表示「拍賣行」。

③ fetch a price 賣個......的價錢，如：fetch a high price 賣個好價錢。

相關句子

The auction house is suing the company that provided it with the phony items. (BBC)

拍賣行將起訴向他們提供假貨的那家公司。

9　　The president said they are working together to rebuild the economy, after a series of emergency measures to end the recession and help key industries survive. (VOA)

總統表示，在採取一系列結束經濟衰退的緊急措施，幫助重點行業得以生存之後，他們正在共同努力重建經濟。

要點解析

① rebuild 重建，這個單字的詞根是 re-，表示「一再，重新」，如：rearrange 重新安排，reclaim 取回，reappear 再次出現。

② recession 經濟衰退，不景氣。

③ key 在這句話裡作為形容詞，表示「關鍵的」的意思。

相關句子

Economists fear a similar wave of protectionism today could plunge the world back into recession. (NPR)
經濟學家擔心當下類似的保護主義風潮會使世界經濟重新陷入衰退。

10　Federal Reserve chairman Ben Bernanke usually speaks about what the nation's central bank is doing to boost the economy. (NPR)
美聯儲主席本・柏南奇經常談論美國央行為刺激經濟發展所做的努力。

要點解析

① speak about... 提到……，談論。其仲介詞 about 後面加談論的內容。
② boost 促進；增加；宣揚。

相關句子

Devolving the power to cut corporation tax is the Northern Ireland Executive's key idea to boost the economy. (BBC)
透過移交權力來削減公司稅費是北愛爾蘭政府刺激經濟發展的主要理念。

11　People are angry at events since some of Switzerland bestknown companies, multibillion pound losses at banking giant UBS, thousands of redundancies at a pharmaceutical company Novartis while big pay awards for bosses continued. (VOA)
瑞士的一些嚴重虧損的知名企業，比如虧損數十億英鎊的龍頭瑞士聯合銀行，裁員數千人的諾華製藥公司，仍然在向管理層支付高額獎勵，這令人們非常憤怒。

要點解析

① multibillion 數十億的。
② redundancy 過多，冗長，在商務英語中則有「裁員」的意思。
③ pharmaceutical 製藥的，配藥的。

12   As Syria's economy continues to suffer, primitive refineries are spring-
      ing up in backyards across the country. (VOA)
      敘利亞的經濟仍在走下坡路，但是原油冶煉廠卻如雨後春筍般在
      全國各地興建起來。

   要點解析
      ① refinery 精煉廠，冶煉廠。
      ② spring 最常見的意思是「春天」，在這句話裡作為動詞使用，表示「生長；
        湧出；跳躍」。而 spring up 表示「出現；湧現」。
      ③ backyard 後院，這裡可理解為「地方」。

   相關句子
      Supplies shrank mostly on the Gulf Coast, as refineries cut back on crude
      imports. (NPR)
      由於煉油廠減少了原油的進口量，墨西哥灣沿岸地區的石油供應
      大幅減少。

13   U.S. nurses are caught between a sour economy, a demographic bump
      and a flood of unemployed new graduates. (VOA)
      美國護士處在經濟衰退、人口激增以及一大批未就業應屆畢業生
      的環境中，步履維艱。

   要點解析
      ① be caught 在這句話裡表示「陷於」，引申為「步履維艱」的意思。
      ② sour 酸的，酸味。這裡引申為「不景氣的，衰退的」。
      ③ demographic 人口學的，人口統計學的。
      ④ flood 原意為「洪水」，片語 a flood of 表示「如洪水般襲來」，即「大量
        的，一大批的」。

14   The International Monetary Fund has told governments across the
      world that further action is needed to help return the global financial
      system to stability. (BBC)
      國際貨幣基金組織要求全球各國政府採取進一步行動以恢復全球
      金融體系的穩定。

要點解析

① the International Monetary Fund 國際貨幣基金組織。該組織與世界銀行同時成立，並列為世界兩大金融機構之一，總部設在華盛頓。

② stability 穩定性。

相關句子

The global economy is sluggish and the current, relatively high oil prices are not helping. (BBC)

全球經濟呈現疲軟之勢，而如今相對較高的油價也絲毫不能起到拉動作用。

15　The Chairman of the US Federal Reserve Ben Bernanke has described the America's economic situation as far from satisfactory. (BBC)

美聯儲主席本·柏南奇認為美國的經濟形勢實在不容樂觀。

要點解析

① US Federal Reserve 美國聯邦儲備委員會，簡稱美聯儲，美國最高貨幣政策主管機關。

② far from... 是「離……很遠」的意思，這裡的 far from satisfactory 表示「遠遠不能令人滿意」，即「不容樂觀」的意思。

16　There is a container terminal and we have started exporting livestock. (VOA)

這裡有一個集裝箱碼頭，我們已經開始從這裡出口家畜。

要點解析

① container 容器；集裝箱，相關片語有：container transport 集裝箱運輸；container ship 貨櫃船；container port 貨櫃港口。

② terminal 作形容詞用，表示「末期的，末端的」，如：terminal cancer 晚期癌症；作名詞使用表示「終端；終點站；航空站」。我們乘坐飛機時常說的 T1、T2 的 T 指的就是 terminal 航站樓。

③ livestock 家畜。

17   The Mexican telecommunications magnet Carlos Slim has topped the
      Forbes magazine's list of the world's richest people. (BBC)
      墨西哥電信大亨卡洛斯‧史林榮登《富比士》雜誌世界富
      豪榜首位。

   要點解析
   ① telecommunication 電信，通訊。
   ② magnet 磁鐵，有吸引力的人／物，此處引申為「巨擘，大亨」。

18   The long-term strength of the Indian economy is supposed to be its
      young population. (VOA)
      印度經濟的長期優勢在於其人口的年輕化。

   要點解析
   ① strength 力量；優點。與其相對應的詞語是 weakness 缺點，弱點。
   ② be supposed to be... 應該，被期望……。

19   The networks have really started to depend on the dual revenue stream
      to enable them to pay for programming, including sports programming
      and scripted dramas. (NPR)
      廣播電視網已經真正開始取決於其雙重的收入來源，使其有能力
      為節目付費，包括體育類節目和改編劇碼。

   要點解析
   ① dual 作為形容詞有「雙重的」意思。其常用搭配有 dual system 雙重系統。
   ② revenue 稅收，另外還有「收益」的意思。其常用片語有 sales revenue 銷
     售收入；revenue stream 收入來源。
   ③ scripted 作形容詞的時候有「照稿子念的；改編的」的意思。

20   The video sharing site YouTube is launching its first pay channels
      which will allow content providers to sell its subscriptions through
      their videos. (BBC)
      影片分享網站 YouTube 推出首個支付平台，這將允許發布者透過
      他們的影片提供付費訂閱。

要點解析

① launch 作動詞有「發射；下水」的意思；作為名詞還有「汽艇，投放市場」的意思。

② channel 作名詞時有「通道，頻道以及海峽的」意思。常用片語有 channel capacity 通道容量，通道傳輸能力。

③ subscription 捐獻；訂閱；簽署的意思。常用片語有 public subscription 公開發售。

相關句子

Bonnier, the magazine publisher, plans to sell annual subscriptions to the digital version of Popular Science for Android users but will not charge for articles on its Web site. (BBC)

雜誌發行商邦尼集團計劃出售可供安卓用戶訂閱的《通俗科學》電子版，但其網站上的文章則會全部免費開放。

21　Spain recently requested a multi-billion-dollar bailout from its European partners to help its struggling banking sector. (BBC)

西班牙最近請求其歐洲夥伴國提供數十億美元的救援資金來幫助該國舉步維艱的銀行業。

要點解析

① bailout 是「緊急救助；跳傘」的意思。常用搭配有 government bailout 政府緊急援助。

② struggling 作形容詞有「努力的，奮鬥的」的意思，但這裡是「苦苦掙扎」的意思。

③ banking sector 是「銀行業」的意思。類似的片語還有：business sector 商界。

22　He said it highlights the microfinance industry's success in the face of the global financial crisis. (VOA)

他說這也強調了即使面臨全球金融危機，小額信貸產業依舊能成功。

要點解析

① highlight 作動詞有「強調，突出以及使顯著」的意思；在作名詞的時候，

表示「有最精彩的部分」的意思。

② microfinance 小額信貸，微型金融。

相關句子

Called "the Banker to the Poor," Yunus is seen as one of the pioneers of microcredit and the microfinance industry. (VOA)

尤努斯被譽為「窮人的銀行家」，他被視為小額信貸和小額貸款行業的先驅。

---

23 The internet company Yahoo has bought an application created by a British teenager in a deal reported to be worth tens of millions of dollars. (BBC)

網路企業雅虎在一場交易中買下了一位英國少年創作的應用程式，報導稱這筆交易價值上千萬美元。

要點解析

① application 是「應用，申請」的意思，常用片語有 application letter 求職信。

② deal 作名詞有「交易，政策，待遇」的意思；作動詞時，常用片語有 deal with 處理。

---

24 A US jury has awarded damages of $240 m to a group of disabled former workers for the years of physical and mental abuse at a turkey processing company which employed and housed them. (BBC)

美國一陪審團支付給一群在火雞加工廠工作和居住期間遭受多年身心虐待而殘疾的老工人 2.4 億美元的賠償。

相關句子

① award 作動詞有「授予，判定」的意思；作名詞有「獎品，判決」的意思。

② damages 是 damage 的複數形式，在表示「損害賠償」的時候要用複數形式。

---

25 Greece has agreed its first major privatisation in a programme of "selling state assets" in order to cut the country's debts. (BBC)

希臘已同意首次私有化，實施名為「出售國有資產」的專案，以

削減本國債務。

要點解析

① major 作形容詞有「主要的，主修的，較多的」等意思。常用片語有 major in 主修，專攻。

② debt 債務；借款。其常用片語有：national debt 國債。

相關句子

Greece will benefit far more from a well-designed privatisation scheme than a fire-sale to raise cash. (BBC)

比起拋售資產籌集現金的方式，希臘將從精心策劃的私有化計畫中獲得更多好處。

26　Obama says his budget will curb spending and cut corporate tax breaks—while boosting funding for infrastructure and education. (VOA)

歐巴馬表示，他的預算將控制支出、減少企業稅收減免，同時還會增加公共設施和教育的資金投入。

要點解析

① budget 作動詞有「安排，做預算」的意思；作名詞時有「預算費用」的含義。

② curb 作動詞有「控制」的意思。

③ infrastructure 基礎設施；公共設施。

27　Domestic manufacturers of auto parts are looking outside India for business, and steel companies are also feeling the pinch. (VOA)

本土汽車零件廠商正向印度以外的地方尋找商機，鋼鐵公司也覺得處境困難。

要點解析

① domestic 作形容詞表示「國內的；馴養的」意思，常用片語有 domestic flight 國內航班。

② auto 汽車，是 automobile 的縮寫。此外還有「自動」的意思。

③ feel the pinch 這個片語經常用於口語，表示「感到經濟拮据；手頭拮据」

的意思。

28　An investigation of the United States has found that the country's top financial regulator, the Securities and the Exchange Commissioner SEC, fail to uncover the 65 billion dollar fraud carried out by the convicted financier Bernard Madoff. (BBC)

美國一項調查發現，國家最高金融監管機構——美國證券交易委員會沒有發現已獲罪的金融家伯納‧馬多夫透過詐騙行為獲得650億美元。

要點解析

① regulator 調節器；校準者；監管機構。
② un 這個詞根通常用於表示否定，因此 uncover 就表示「揭開……的蓋子」或者「揭露；發現」。同樣表示否定的詞根還有 im，in，dis。如：impossible 不可能；indirect 不直接的；disable 有殘疾的。
③ fraud 欺詐；騙子；冒牌貨。

相關句子

Bernard Madoff's properties in Florida, Long Island, and the South of France have been confiscated along with his luxury yacht. (BBC)

伯納‧馬多夫在佛羅里達、長島以及法國南部的資產連同他的豪華遊艇已經全部被沒收。

29　The ruling struck down more than a billion Euros in spending cuts as unfair to public sector workers and pensioners. (BBC)

此裁定認為 10 億歐元的開銷削減對公共部門的員工和退休員工不公平。

要點解析

① strike down 是「打垮，取消；殺死」的意思，其相關用法有 strike sb. down 將某人打倒。
② pensioner 領養老金者，領取撫恤金者。這個詞來自 pension 養老金。

30　Understanding the financing models, understanding how to ask for money, having the courage, the familiarity and the experience going in and teeing up funding, that's something training can provide. (VOA)

透過培訓，我們可以了解融資模式、融資方法，有勇氣、熟悉並掌握資金運作的經驗。

要點解析

① familiarity 是形容詞 familiar 的名詞形式，意為「熟悉，通曉」。

② tee 作名詞時，表示「球座；(套圈等遊戲的) 目標」，作動詞的意思是「置球於球座上；準備發球」。片語 tee up 的意思是「安排」，此處引申為「運作」。

相關句子

Nicaragua relies on international economic assistance to meet internal- and external-debt financing obligations. (BBC)

尼加拉瓜需要依賴國際經濟援助才能擔負起國內外債務融資的責任。

31　Researchers have found that uniform pricing actually accentuates the differences between products, which makes it harder to choose. (Scientific American)

研究者發現統一標價實際上突出了商品之間的差異，從而使選擇更難進行。

要點解析

① uniform pricing 單一定價，統一標價。

② accentuate 為動詞，有「強調，重讀」的意思。

32　The steep fall in sales reflects the frustration and despondency of those most affected by India's slumping economy. (VOA)

銷售量的暴跌反映了印度的經濟不景氣所導致的挫折和沮喪。

要點解析

① frustration 表示「挫折，失望」。

② despondency 是「洩氣，意氣消沉」的意思。如：diligence dismisses despondency 勤奮能驅除沮喪。

③ slumping 作名詞有「滑塌，坍塌」的意思。常用片語有 slumping market 蕭條的市場。

33 Parliament in Greece has approved a bill allowing the government to cut 15,000 jobs in the country's civil service. (BBC)

希臘議會透過了一項議案,允許政府減少 15,000 個行政部門職位。

要點解析

① bill 作名詞有「法案;帳單;清單」的意思。
② civil service 公務員,也可以指「行政部門」。

---

34 The Commerce Department says sales rose to a seasonally adjusted annual rate of 454,000, reaching the secondhighest level since the summer of 2008. (NPR)

美國商務部表示,經過季度性調整後的銷售量已增加到 454,000,達到了自 2008 年夏天以來第二高的程度。

要點解析

① seasonally 季節性地,週期性地。
② adjusted 是「調整過的,調節了的」的意思。

---

35 The corporation's head of strategy, James Purnell, said it had reached the point where good money was being thrown after bad. (BBC)

公司的策略負責人詹姆斯 · 珀內爾表示,在經歷了一段艱難時期之後,公司的大筆投資都已付諸東流。

要點解析

good money 不能從字面上理解為「好錢」,而應該翻譯為「大筆投資,許多錢」;throw good money after bad 想挽回損失反而白白送掉錢,相當於中文裡的「賠了夫人又折兵」。

相關句子

Who say that turning around a failing school means just throwing good money after bad. (BBC)

有人曾經說過,要把一個虧損的學校扭虧為盈可以說是填無底洞。

36　The U.S. Supreme Court is citing with Monsanto in a fight over genetically engineered soybeans. (NPR)

美國最高法院在一場關於基因改造大豆的爭論中引用了孟山都公司的例子。

要點解析

① cite 是「引用」的意思。

② genetically engineered 基因改造工程。

37　The nation isolates itself from most of the rest of the world, so it doesn't have many trading partners. (CNN)

由於這個國家從世界大多數國家中孤立自己，因此並沒有很多的交易夥伴。

要點解析

① isolate... from 使與……隔離。常見用法有 isolate oneself from others 自絕於人。

② trading partner 交易夥伴。

38　The U.S. government has begun a crash diet of automatic spending cuts in pursuit of better fiscal health. (VOA)

美國政府已經開始自動削減日常開銷以追求更好的財政狀況。

要點解析

① crash 作名詞表示「猛撞，撞毀；墜落」的意思。

② fiscal 與 financial 都表示「財政的，財務的」，但是在使用的時候 fiscal 更多強調國家財政策略，如：fiscal year 財政年度；fiscal policy 財政政策；而 financial 則強調金融事務，如：financial investment 金融投資；financial assistance 財政援助。

39　The ministers said conditions had improved, but economic and financial recovery was uneven and unemployment a worry. (BBC)

部長們發表聲明表示，雖然目前情況已有改善，但經濟和金融的復甦仍不穩定，失業情況也靈熱令人擔憂。

要點解析

① recovery 恢復，復原，economic recovery 經濟復甦
② uneven 不平坦的；不均勻的。

40　The head of Mexico's teachers union Elba Esther Gordillo has been formally charged with the use of illicit funds. (BBC)

墨西哥教師工會負責人戈迪略被正式控告非法挪用資金。

要點解析

① charge with 是「控告」的意思。其常用用法有 charge sb. with 指控某人做某事。
② illicit 非法的，不正當的。常見片語有 illicit trading 非法貿易。

41　President Barack Obama says foreign-born workers have always con-tributed to America's economic prowess. (VOA)

歐巴馬總統稱外籍工人一直在為美國的經濟實力做出貢獻。

要點解析

① foreign-born 在國外出生的。常用片語有 foreign-born spouse 外籍配偶；the foreign-born 移民，僑民。
② contribute to 有助於，捐獻。常見用法有 contribute significantly to... 大大有助於……

42　For years, an argument in Washington has raged between reducing our deficits at all costs, and making the investments we need to grow the economy. (VOA)

多年來，在不惜一切減少赤字和為經濟成長進行投資這兩方面，華盛頓進行了激烈的爭論。

要點解析

① rage 作動詞時有「發怒；流行」的意思。
② deficit 赤字，不足額。常用片語有 budget deficit 預算赤字。
③ at all costs 是「無論如何，不惜一切代價」的意思。

43   The U.S. deficit is projected at $900 billion this year, down slightly
      from previous years. (VOA)
      預計美國今年的赤字為 9,000 億美元，與去年相比有稍有下降。

要點解析

① project 作名詞表示「專案」，作動詞表示「投影」。在這句話裡是「預估」
的意思。
② slightly 輕微地，纖細地。

44   If we have trouble moving grains down the river, if that slows down, it
      affects prices that we can get, mostly because the price of transporta-
      tion gets higher because they can't haul as much. (VOA)
      運輸速度降低使我們在向河流下游運送穀物時遇到麻煩，無法運
      送太多穀物而使交通費用增加，影響了穀物的價格。

要點解析

① transportation 是「運輸系統；運輸工具」的意思。常用片語有 transportation engineering 運輸工程。
② haul 作動詞時有「拖；改變主意；改變方向」的意思。常用片語有：
haul off 退卻；駛離。

45   For those in the market for a new car, this could not be a better time,
      as dealers are offering discounts to get people in the door. (VOA)
      對那些想要買新車的人來說，現在是最好的時機了，經銷商們為
      了吸引顧客都在提供折扣。

要點解析

① dealer 經銷商，商人。常用片語有：securities dealer 證券交易商。
② offer 作動詞時有「提供；出價；出現」的意思。
③ discount 作名詞時有「折扣，貼現率」的意思。

46　A Board's spokesperson says that consumers were worried about higher taxes in federal spending cuts are showing more optimism. (NPR)

一位委員會發言人稱，此前擔心聯邦政府為削減開銷而增稅的消費者現在顯得更為樂觀。

要點解析

① spokesperson 發言人，代言人。

② consumer 消費者。常用片語有 consumer demand 消費者需求。

③ be worried about... 為……而擔心，憂慮。常用片語有 be very worried about 牽腸掛肚。

47　But domestic concerns are also a challenge for his push to join the trade pact. (VOA)

但是國內對他推動加入貿易協定的擔憂也是一種挑戰。

要點解析

① concern 在這句話裡表示「擔憂」的意思。這個詞還可以表示「關注」。

② pact 協定；公約。常用搭配有 trade pact 貿易協定。

48　The U.S. subsidiary of an Indian pharmaceutical company has pleaded guilty to multiple felony charges, including making false statements. (NPR)

印度一家製藥公司的美國分公司已經承認了包括發布處假言論等在內的多項重罪。

要點解析

① subsidiary 作名詞有「子公司，輔助者」的意思。常用片語有 subsidiary company 附屬公司。

② pharmaceutical 製藥的。常用片語有 pharmaceutical chemistry 藥物化學。

③ plead 有「藉口，懇求以及辯護」的意思。常用片語有 plead with... 向……懇求。

49　The labor department released its producer price index fell 0.70, the

steepest dropping more than three years. (NPR)
勞工部公布生產價格指數下降了 0.70，這是三年多以來下降幅度
最大的一次。

要點解析

① release 在文中是發的意思，此外還有「發射；釋放」之意。

② index 作名詞時有「指標，指數，索引」的意思。常用片語有 performance index 性能指標。

50　Federal Reserve Chairman Ben Bernanke signaling the Fed will maintain its stimulus efforts testifying before the joint economic committee.
(NPR)
美聯儲主席本·柏南奇在國會聯合經濟委員會作證時暗示，美聯
儲將繼續實行刺激措施。

要點解析

① signal 通常作名詞使用，表示「訊號，暗號；徵兆」。在這句話裡作動詞
表示「暗示」，相當於 indicate。

② stimulus 刺激因素。

相關句子

The Republican candidates, however, have labeled President Barack Obama's
2009 stimulus efforts a failure. (NPR)
不過，共和黨候選人認為歐巴馬總統在 2009 年實行的刺激政策是
失敗之舉。

51　They are still struggling over how to improve the agency for bailing
out governments with less the resources to help Italy or Spain should
they be needed. (BBC)
他們仍在爭論應該如何幫助該機構利用盡量少的資源，在義大利
和西班牙政府需要幫助的時候伸出援手。

要點解析

① 片語 struggle over 有「為……而努力」的意思。

② 單字 bail 作動詞使用,有「保釋;幫助脫離困境」的意思;片語 bail out 則表示「緊急援助」。

52　But as countries buy and sell fruits, vegetables, timber and other products, they also may be putting domestic plants at risk. (VOA)

國家間買賣水果、蔬菜、木材和其他產品時,他們也許會將本地工廠置於危機之中。

要點解析

① timber 木材,木料。相關表達有 timber tree 成材木。

② put...at risk 是「使……處於危險境地」的意思。

53　The European Central Bank has said it will cut off emergency support to Cypruss financial institutions if no satisfactory deal is reached. (BBC)

歐洲中央銀行曾表示,如果沒有達成令人滿意的協議,他們會中斷對賽普勒斯財政機構的緊急援助。

要點解析

① cut off 是「切斷;剝奪繼承權」的意思,這個片語加上連字號變成 cut-off,意思是「截止,界點」。常用片語有 cut-off date 截止日期。

② institution 制度;公共機構,常用片語有 academic institution 學術機構。

54　The clothing retailer Primark has said it'll compensate some of the victims of a Bangladesh textile factory which collapsed. (BBC)

服裝零售商普里馬克曾表示他將對孟加拉一個倒閉紡織廠的一些受害者進行賠償。

要點解析

① retailer 零售商,如:retailer price 表示「零售價格」。

② compensate 補償;付報酬。常用片語有 compensate sb. for sth. 因……賠償某人。

③ textile 作名詞時有「紡織品,織物」的意思。常用片語有 textile industry

紡織工業。

---

55 The cuts are a key requirement for Greece to receive another bailout from the European Union. (BBC)
這個削減開銷的措施是希臘從歐盟獲得另一筆救助金的主要條件。

要點解析

① requirement 是「要求，必要條件以及必需品」的意思。
② 「獲得」救助金的動詞可以用 receive 表示。

---

56 We hear a lot from our retirement planners that you need pretty much a million bucks to retire. (CNN)
我們聽到很多退休規劃者表示，你需要幾乎一百萬美元才能退休。

要點解析

① retirement 退休；退役。常用片語有 retirement benefit 退休金。
② buck 在美國俚語中可以表示「一美元」；此外還有「雄鹿；紈絝子弟」的意思。

---

57 To help finance social programs, he nationalized, or seized control of, major businesses, including oil companies. (VOA)
為了扶持金融社會專案，他實行了國有化，控制了包括石油公司在內的主要企業。

要點解析

① nationalize 是「使國有化，使民族化，使成國家」的意思。
② seize 是「抓住；理解；逮捕」的意思。常見搭配有 seize power 奪取政權。

---

58 One government official delivered the commerce address today to US military academy of West Point. (NPR)
一位官員今天在美國軍事學院西點軍校發表了商業演講。

要點解析

① deliver 作動詞有「交付；發表；履行」的意思。

② commerce 貿易；商業。常見片語有 electronic commerce 電子商務。

③ academy 學院；學會；專科院校。常見片語有 academy of sciences 科學院。

59　Other treaty standards are being looked at for possible revision, in-cluding guidelines for sea containers. (VOA)

其他條約標準正在審查並可能受到修改，包括海運集裝箱的指導條例。

要點解析

① treaty 條約；談判。常見片語有 unequal treaty 不平等條約。

② revision 修正；複習。

③ guideline 指導方針。常見片語有 course guideline 課程綱要。

60　The German finance minister said it was wrong to expect a definitive solution from the summit. (BBC)

德國財政部長認為，期待這次峰會能達成最終方案的想法是錯誤的。

要點解析

① definitive 作形容詞有「決定性的；最後的；限定」的意思，常見片語有 definitive edition 最終版；權威版。

② solution 解決方案，常見片語有 optimal solution 最優解。

③ summit 作名詞有「頂點，最高級會議」的意思，常用片語有 summit con-ference 峰會。

61　The new service was a pilot one which would allow program makers to set their own distribution services through the site. (BBC)

這項新服務是個試點，旨在幫助節目製作者透過該網站建立自己的分銷服務。

要點解析

① pilot 在句中是形容詞，表示「試點」的意思。作動詞可以表示「試駕；

試用」；作名詞有「飛行員；領航員」的意思。

② distribution 分布，分配，常用片語有 uniform distribution 均勻分布。

62　It's incredibly important that companies and individuals pay the tax that is due. (NPR)

企業和個人需要繳納應交稅款，這一點至關重要。

要點解析

① individual 個人，個體；此外，它作形容詞還有「個人的，個別的以及獨特」的意思。

② incredibly 難以置信地；非常地。經常用來表達不可思議的程度。

③ due 作形容詞有「到期的；應付的」的意思。常用搭配有 due to 由於。

63　He talked about the need to create jobs and called for a freeze on some government spending. (CNN)

他談到了創造就業的需求，並呼籲凍結一些政府支出。

要點解析

freeze 有「凍結，凝固」的意思。如：freeze over 凍結，全面結冰；credit freeze 信用凍結。

64　In the statement the European commissioner says there are only hard choices left but help from the EU he said can help minimize the economic damage. (BBC)

歐盟委員會專員稱目前只有艱難的選擇，但他表示歐盟的援助能幫助將經濟損失降到最低。

要點解析

① commissioner 是「理事；委員；行政長官」的意思。常見搭配有 deputy commissioner 副局長。

② minimize 最小化。在這句話裡是「降到最低」的意思。

65 College graduates hoping to enter the job market still face a daunting economy. (NPR)

期待進入職場的大學畢業生們仍然面臨著嚴峻的經濟形勢。

要點解析

① graduate 除了常作動詞表示「畢業」以外，還可以用作名詞，表示「畢業生」。

② face 作動詞表示「面臨」，相關的片語還有 face up to 正視；face the music 面對現實。

③ daunting 使人畏縮的；令人望而生畏的。比如：daunting challenge 嚴峻挑戰。

---

66 He hopes this season brings greater crop yields fueled by just the right amount of rain. (VOA)

他希望這場及時雨能為這一季度帶來更大的糧食產量。

要點解析

① crop yield 糧食產量。其中 yield 作名詞表示「產量」，作動詞表示「產出，屈服」。

② fuel 在這句話裡作動詞，表示「供以燃料；加燃料」，引申為「加劇」的意思。此外它還可作名詞，意為「燃料」，固定搭配有 fuel oil 燃油。

---

67 He said he'd heard encouraging things about a new plan, though he had reservations about a lack of detail. (BBC)

他稱這項新計畫振奮人心，雖然他對細節的不確定持保留意見。

要點解析

① encouraging 令人鼓舞的，如：encouraging news 振奮人心的消息。

② reservation 的常用含義是「預約」，但在這句話裡是「保留」的意思。

---

68 Bank earnings in the US are on the rise as the industry rebounds from the financial crisis. (BBC)

隨著工業從金融危機中復甦，美國銀行業的盈利也正在增加。

要點解析

① earnings 收入。如：expected earnings 預期收益；earning capacity 盈利能力；earnings ratio 市場盈利率。

② on the rise 正在成長，與其相對的是 on the fall 正在下降。

③ rebound from... 從……中恢復；彈回來。類似搭配還有：rebound effect 回彈效應；on the rebound 在失望之際，rebound in prices 價格回升。

相關句子

Commercial banks will be buried in consumer loan and mortgag e write downs. (BBC)

商業銀行或將專注於消費者貸款和抵押貸款資產減值。

69　The oil price now seems to be leveling out, and you would expect it to go down a bit rather soon. (VOA)

油價現已逐漸平穩，並且你會期待盡快出現小幅下調。

要點解析

① level out 把……弄平；達到平衡，還可以用 level off 來替換。

② rather soon 很快，rather 是程度副詞，表示「相當地」意思。

70　His start-up company was backed by investors including the Chinese entrepreneur Li Ka-shing and the artist Yoko Ono. (BBC)

他的創業公司得到了投資人的贊助支援，包括中國企業家李嘉誠和藝術家小野洋子。

要點解析

① start-up 作形容詞表示「起動階段的；開始階段的」。如：star-up time 啟動時間；star-up cost 開辦費用，在這句話裡是指「創業型的」。另外，這個詞作名詞也可以表示「創業公司」。

② back 這裡當做動詞，表示「支持，資助」，常與 up 連用。常用的片語有：back down 放棄；back off 後退；back into 倒車撞上。

③ entrepreneur 企業家；雇主。相關搭配有 private entrepreneur 私營企業主；entrepreneur spirit 企業家精神。

71 　Investors concerned about global energy demand took profits ahead
　　of big economic data this week from China and US which will release
　　May's unemployment report tomorrow. (NPR)
　　中國和美國本週會公布重要經濟資料，投資者擔心全球能源需求
　　會在此之前獲利，明天，兩國將公布五月份的失業報告。

要點解析

① concern about 關注；擔憂。關於 concern 的搭配還有：of concern 重要的；
concern oneself in 干預。
② take profit 獲得利潤。與 profit 相關的搭配還有：small profits 薄利，而
huge profits 則表示「暴利」。
③ ahead of... 在……前面；領先於；提前。

72 　People who trade in their animals will receive money, a new vehicle or
　　help with a business plan. (BBC)
　　從事動物交易的人會得到錢、一輛新車，或者一份對他們有幫助
　　的商業計畫。

要點解析

① trade in 買賣；從事於。比如：trade in furs and skins 做皮貨生意。此外，
它還有「低價購物」的意思，如：trade in old refrigerator 低價購買舊冰箱。
② vehicle 車輛；交通工具。
③ help with 在某方面幫助；幫助做某事。如：help sb. with sth. 幫助某人做
某事。

73 　Youssef said it is normal for lenders or aid donors to have conditions
　　that allow them to exploit the country they are helping, either through
　　political concessions or the economy. (VOA)
　　約瑟夫表示，放款人或者捐助人要求他們幫助的國家透過政治或
　　經濟特許權允許他們利用該國資源的現象很正常。

要點解析

① aid donor 捐助者；援助國。
② exploit 開發；（尤指為利益而）利用。如：exploit business opportunity 利

用商業機會。

③ concession 讓步；授予；在政治方面，表示「特許權」，如：political concession 政治特許權。

74　The state has even resorted to issuing IOUs to companies it does business with and to individuals who are owed tax refunds. (BBC)

該國甚至發欠條給合作公司和應該得到退稅的個人。

要點解析

① resort to 依靠；求助於；訴諸。其中 to 是介詞，後面需要跟名詞或者動名詞形式。

② issue 在這句話裡是動詞，表示「發行」。IOU 則是 I owe you. 的諧音，表示「欠條」。

③ do business with... 與......做生意。

④ tax refund 退稅；稅費返還。其中 refund 還可以作動詞，表示「償還」。

75　This economic downturn has created this tension in terms of people staying in the workforce right at the same time we have been working hard to increase the number of graduates to meet that growing health care need. (VOA)

對於那些身處勞動力市場的人來說，這次的經濟低迷使他們陷入緊張狀態，而與此同時，我們也在努力增加畢業生人數以滿足日益成長的醫療保健需求。

要點解析

① in terms of... 就......而言。類似意思的表達還有 as far as... is concerned。

② workforce 勞動力，此外它還有「雇員總數」的意思。

76　Investors hope more confident consumers will continue to push their spending higher. (NPR)

投資者希望更多有信心的消費者能夠加大消費力度。

要點解析

① push 常用的意思是「增加；促成；推」。常用搭配有：push forward 推進；

push for 奮力爭取；push on 推進；push up 增加。
② spending 花銷；花費。常見表達有：consumer spending 消費性開銷；public spending 政府開銷；spending power 消費力。

77　The country's government voted against the idea, so onto the next plan, that also involves a bank deposit tax, but not on as many people. (CNN)
該國政府投票反對這個想法，所以接下來的計畫將涉及到銀行存款稅，但只針對少數人實行。

要點解析

① vote 投票，voted against 表示「投票反對」，還可以用 ballot against 表示類似的意思。vote for 則表示「投票支持」。
② involve 包括；使陷於，如：be involved in... 陷於，捲入......。
③ deposit 存款，常見搭配有：deposit insurance 存款保險；deposit account 存款帳戶；bank deposit 銀行存款；deposit money 銀行活期存款；deposit slip 存款單。

78　Oil and gas exports account for almost 70 percent of Russia's export earnings and cover half of the federal budget. (VOA)
石油和天然氣出口大約占俄羅斯出口總收益的 70%，是聯邦政府預算的一半。

要點解析

① account for... 共計達到......；（在數量、比例上）占......。此外，這個片語常見的意思還有「對......負責；導致；對......做出解釋」。
② cover 包括；涉及，常用搭配有：cover up 掩蓋；cover for 代替。
③ federal budget 聯邦預算，其中 federal 是「聯邦制的」，如：federal reserve 美國聯邦準備委員會；federal government 聯邦政府；federal funds 聯邦資金。

79　Rising stock prices and home values along with steady job growth are contributing to that optimism. (NPR)
日益成長的股價和房價以及穩定的就業成長令人樂觀。

要點解析

① along with... 連同……一起；順沿。此外，go along with... 表示「與……一起」，這個片語也有「贊同」的意思。

② contribute to 有助於；捐贈；促成。其名詞形式的 make contribution to... 表示「對……做出貢獻」。

③ optimism 樂觀，如：blind optimism 可以表示「盲目樂觀」。

80　Africa's economic growth rate for this year would improve to 4.3 percent from 1.6 percent, although he noted this rate is still too low to meet the Millennium Goal of halving poverty. (VOA)

非洲今年的經濟成長率將從 1.6% 提高到 4.3%。但他指出這個比率仍然太低，無法滿足將貧困人口減半的千年目標。

要點解析

① note 在這句話裡作動詞，表示「注意到；提到」；作名詞時，這個詞可以表示「便條；筆記」，常用表達有：take note 注意到，記筆記；note down 記下某事；make a note of 把……記下來。

② millennium 千年期；一千年。

③ halve 使減半；把……分開來，如：halve the risk 使風險減半。

81　A top executive at News Corp. dropped a bombshell this week when he said the company is considering taking Fox's over-the-air network to cable. (NPR)

一位新聞集團的高管本週發布爆炸性新聞，稱公司正在考慮將福斯集團的無線網路改為有線電視網路。

要點解析

① bombshell 突發事件；引起震驚的人或物，本意則是「炸彈」。固定搭配 drop a bombshell 原指「投下炸彈」，引申為「說出爆炸性消息」，十分形象。

② over-the-air 無線的，相當於 on air。

③ cable 電纜，常指「有線」，常見搭配有：optic cable 光纜；by cable 用電報發出；cable network 有線電視網路。

82　The sanctions actually did stop production because foreign operators pulled out. (VOA)

由於國外營運商的撤離，國際制裁確實造成了生產暫停。

要點解析

① sanction 制裁；處罰，這裡的意思是「國際制裁」。常見搭配還有：legal sanction 法律制裁；economic sanction 經濟制裁。

② pull out 離開；從……退出。

83　When a country's economy grows too much too quickly, there's a chance it can start supplying things that aren't in demand. (CNN)

當一個國家的經濟成長過快時，就有可能出現供大於求的現象。

要點解析

① chance 在句中表示「可能性」，相關搭配有：stand a chance of 有可能，take a chance 碰運氣，冒險。

② in demand 受歡迎；銷路好；有需求。

84　The report only counts people as unemployed if they are actively out there looking for work. (CNN)

這份報告直接將那些正在積極找工作的人視為失業者。

要點解析

① count as 視為；當做，相當於 treat as，perceive as。

② look for 尋找，句中 look for work 指「找工作」，相當於 hunt for job。

85　As Egypt's economy falters, its government is trying to find relief anywhere it can. (VOA)

由於埃及經濟不景氣，政府正全力尋求救濟。

要點解析

① falter 原指「蹣跚；遲疑」，還可以指「變弱」。在這句話裡可以理解為「（經濟）不景氣」，相關搭配 falter out 可表示「支支吾吾說出口」。

② relief 救濟；減輕，常用搭配有：in relief 顯著地；relief work 救濟工作；relief fund 救濟金；relief material 救濟物資等。

③ anywhere 隨時隨地，相關的片語有：get anywhere 有點成就。

86　He not only has to find all his online purchases; he has to figure out
which online sellers already charged him sales tax, and which didn't.
(NPR)

他不僅要找到所有的線上購買者，還需要找到哪些賣家徵收過銷
售稅，哪些沒有。

要點解析

① figure out 估計出；弄清。
② charge 索價；收費，常用搭配還有：charge for 索價；charge with 控告等。

87　Our investigations showed that the ring has placed bets of more than
60 million Euros, giving a profit of 8.5 million Euros. (CNN)

我們的調查顯示這個圈子的賭注已超過 6,000 萬歐元，牟取了
850 萬歐元的利益。

要點解析

① ring 戒指，除了這個意思，作名詞時還有「環狀物；圓形場地」的意思，
常用搭配有：ring road 環形公路。另外這個詞也能作動詞，表示「按鈴；
回想」，如：ring a bell 使人回憶起。
② bet 打賭，相關搭配有：bet on... 對……下注；a good bet 極有可能。短句
I bet. 表示「我確信」。

88　The financial hit to the government from bailouts during the financial
crisis is shrinking. (NPR)

經濟危機期間，緊急救助使政府的財政損失有所減少。

要點解析

① hit 可以表示「打擊；（唱片、電影或戲劇的）成功，（網站的）點擊」，
固定搭配有：hit the ball 成功；hit it off 合得來；hit the road 開始流浪，
上路。
② bailout 緊急救濟，通常指政府對陷於財政困難的企業，特別是大公司的
救濟。常用表達有：bailout loan 緊急援助貸款；bailout package 緊急援
助計畫。

③ shrink 畏縮，縮小，shrink from 在……面前畏縮；shrink wrap 收縮包裝。

89　He says that while unemployment remains at about 7.5%, the economy continues to add about 180,000 jobs a month. (NPR)

他說，在目前的經濟形勢下，即使失業率保持在 7.5% 左右，每月仍有大約 18 萬的新增職位。

要點解析

① unemployment 失業；失業率。unemployment benefit 則表示「失業救濟」；unemployment pension 則是「失業津貼」的意思。

② add 增加；附帶說明。片語 add up 表示「合計；加起來」。

90　Intelligence officials are telling CNN that at least 20 people were killed today in the accident. (CNN)

情報官員向 CNN 透露，今天至少有 20 人死於此次事故。

要點解析

① at least 至少，與其相對的是 at most，意為「最多」。

② suicide 作動詞可以表示「自殺」；作名詞時，commit suicide 也可以表示「自殺」。相關搭配有：suicide bombing 自殺性爆炸；attempted suicide 自殺未遂。

91　The report is seen as more evidence the job market is slowly returning to health. (NPR)

這份報告更能證明就業市場正在緩慢復甦。

要點解析

① job market 就業市場，工作市場；enter the job market 進入就業市場；flood the job market 湧入就業市場。

② return to 恢復到，回到某種狀態，其中 to 是介詞。return to health 本是「恢復健康」的意思，但在這句話裡指代「經濟復甦」。

92   Health economists say if the economy improves, many older work-
      ers will be willing to leave their jobs and make room for newcomers.
      (VOA)
      健康經濟學家稱，如果經濟得到改善，很多大齡員工會願意把他
      們的工作職位讓給職場新人。

要點解析

① be willing to... 願意做......，相當於 would like to。
② make room for... 讓出地方給......。在這句話裡指「為......騰出空位」。

93   He and members of his team have been warning for days about the
      damage they say the cuts will cause to the U.S. economy. (VOA)
      這幾日，他和他的團隊成員收到了削減預算會對美國經濟造成損
      害的警告。

要點解析

① warn about... 就......提出警告。如：warn sb. about doing 警告某人不要做
   某事。
② cut 切口；（分攤到的）份額。注意此時 cut 指的是「對財政預算的削減」。
③ cause damage to... 對......造成損壞，如：cause damage to property 造成財
   物損失。

94   U.S. business and union leaders are reporting a deal on a guest worker
      program for low-skilled laborers, potentially removing a key obstacle
      to an overhaul of federal immigration laws. (VOA)
      美國商界和工會領袖正在申報一個聘請低技能外來員工的專案，
      這有可能消除全面改革聯邦移民法律這一重要障礙。

要點解析

① deal 交易。這個詞還「待遇，分量」的意思。相關搭配為：big deal 重要
   的事，good deal 划算。
② obstacle 障礙，干擾，妨礙物。
③ overhaul 澈底檢修，詳細檢查，在這句話裡有「澈底改革」的意思。常
   用搭配為：major overhaul 大修；light overhaul 小修。

95   The company president testified before congress, in support of the Keystone XL pipeline, saying it will create jobs. (NPR)

公司總裁在國會作證支持「拱心石」輸油管專案,稱這將會創造就業職位。

要點解析

① testify 證明,作證,如:testify against 做出......不利的證明;testify to 證明。

② in support of 支持;擁護。

③ pipeline 管道,補給線,運輸車隊,如:gas pipeline 天然氣管道;pipe-line construction 管道施工。

96   The Dutch government has advised retailers to clearly label those products. (BBC)

荷蘭政府建議零售商要明確標記那些商品。

要點解析

① retailers 零售商,independent retailer 獨立經營的零售商。

② label 標注,貼標籤於;be labeled as... 被歸類為......。這個詞也可以作名詞,比如:bar code label 條碼標記,brand label 品牌標籤。

97   Senior African finance officials say per capita income in Africa fell for the first time in a decade because of the global economic recession. (VOA)

非洲高級財政官員表示,由於全球經濟衰退,非洲人均收入在十年內首次下降。

要點解析

① per capita 人均,每人。capita 原指「頭數」,在這句話裡指「人頭」。相關搭配有:per capita income 人均收入;per capita housing 人均住房。

② economic recession 經濟衰退,economic slump/decline 也可以表示「經濟衰退」。

98　Employment consultant says she has seen a change in the job market since starting her training and recruiting company. (VOA)

應徵顧問表示自從創辦培訓和招募公司以來，她就注意到了人才市場的變化。

要點解析

① consultant 顧問；諮詢員；會診醫生。

② recruit 應徵，吸收新成員。相關搭配有：recruiting manager 應徵經理；recruiting talents 應徵英才。

99　A United Nations report says the money migrants send does more to reduce Asian poverty than the total amount of international development aid. (VOA)

聯合國一份報告指出，移民消費降低了亞洲的貧困度，其成效比全部的國際發展援助還要大。

要點解析

① migrant 移民者，如：migrant worker 外來工；migrant labor 流動勞動力。

② aid 援助，接濟，常見搭配有：with the aid of... 在......的幫助下；give aid to... 在......予以幫助；first aid 急救；aid in 幫助......等。

③ poverty 貧困，常見的搭配有：in poverty 處於貧困中；poverty alleviation 扶貧；eliminate poverty 消除貧困。

100　The spokesman says his country is not seeking to activate a Euro Zone and International Monetary Fund (IMF) rescue plan designed to prevent a default. (VOA)

發言人表示，他們國家並非為了刺激歐元區，也不是為了國際貨幣基金組織防止違約的援救計畫。

要點解析

① seek to do... 試圖做......，相當於 try to do。

② activate 刺激；使活躍。

③ default 可以表示「缺席」，但在這句話裡的意思是「違約」。相關搭配有：default on/in 不履行......；by default 由於棄權而輸掉；in default 違約。

④ Euro Zone 指「歐元區」，是由採用歐元作為單一的官方貨幣的國家組成的區域。歐元區由歐洲中央銀行負責制定貨幣政策。目前歐元區共有 17 個成員，另有 9 個國家和地區採用歐元作為單一貨幣。

101　Over $40 billion worth of the new shares will go to the government to pay for the right to exploit Brazil's offshor e reserves. (BBC)
價值超過 400 億美元的新股將支付給政府以獲得巴西近海石油開採的權利。

要點解析

① worth of... 價值……，比如：50,000 pounds worth of antique 價值五萬英鎊的古物。
② share 在這句話裡表示「股份」，如：state share 國家股；market share 市場占有率；listed share 上市股份。
③ offshore 常表示「離岸的」，但在這個句子中意為「近海的」。reserve 在這句話裡作名詞，意為「儲備」。

要點解析

The deals come a year after China Development Bank loaned state-owned oil giant Petroleo Brasileiro, or Petrobras, $10 billion to help develop Brazils massive offshore reserves. (BBC)
在中國國家開發銀行向石油龍頭巴西國家石油公司（Petrobras）貸款 100 億美元幫助開發巴西龐大的近海石油儲備一年之後，這筆交易才發生。

102　The technology giant Apple has been defending itself against accusations that it's avoided paying billions of dollars in tax. (BBC)
科技龍頭蘋果公司對逃稅百億的控訴進行了辯護。

要點解析

① giant 除了「巨人」的意思之外，還有「大企業，大國」的意思。
② defend against oneself 是「為自己辯護」；而 accusation 是動詞 accuse 的名詞形式，意為「控訴」。

103　The flight cancellations are expected to have additional reperc ussions for smaller Southeast Asia countries, where travel and tourism is a major share of the economy. (VOA)

航班取消預計會對一些東南亞一些小國造成額外影響，因為旅遊業占據著那些國家經濟的主要占有率。

要點解析

① cancellation 是動詞 cancel 的名詞形式，意為「取消，撤銷」。

② be expected to 有望做某事；被期待做某事。

③ repercussion 反響，後果。如：painful repercussion 沉痛後果。

④ share 在這句話裡作為名詞，表示「占有率；股份」。

104　It tells us the nationa l unemployment rate, how many jobs were added or lost in the previous months, and it's one thing experts look at to get an idea of how the overall economy is doing. (CNN)

這告訴我們全國的失業率以及前幾個月增加或減少的工作職位，專家會由此得出經濟的整體趨勢。

要點解析

① add 表示「增加」，相關搭配有：add up 合計；add in 把......包括在內；add weight to 進一步證明。其反義詞 lost「失去；減少」。

② overall 總體的。

相關句子

The national unemployment rate sits at 9.6 percent, and economists expect little change between now and Election Day in November. (VOA)

全國的失業率仍然維持在 9.6%，經濟學家認為這個數字在 11 月份的選舉日來臨之前不會有太大的變化。

105　The Brazilian oil company Petrobras has unveiled plans to sell more than $64 billion of new stock in what some analysts are describing as the world's biggest ever share offering. (BBC)

巴西石油公司 Petrobras 披露了其將出售超過 640 億美元新股票的計畫，一些分析家稱，這是全世界有史以來最大的一次股票發行。

要點解析

① unveil 公開，揭露；如：unveil the mask 揭開那層面紗。另外這個詞也可以表示「揭露事實」，即：reveal the fact。

② stock 在這句話裡指「股票」，也可以用 share 表達同一個的意思。

③ offering 作為名詞，表示「祭品，提供」；這裡可理解「發行」，如：share offering 股票發行；rights offering 附權發行；offering price 報出價格。

相關句子

And on Feb. 19, China Development Bank struck a similar deal with Petrobras, the Brazilian oil company, agreeing to a loan of $10 billion in exchange for oil. (BBC)

而在 2 月 19 日，中國國家開發銀行與 Petrobras 公司達成了類似協議，巴西石油公司同意中國以 100 億美元的貸款換取石油。

---

106   It's a reform of the public sector that the government says is long over-due and should now pave the way for almost 9 billion Euros of bailout money from Greece's international creditors. (BBC)

政府表示這是一項長期未兌現的公共部門改革，這將為希臘獲得國際債權人的近 90 億歐元的救援款做好準備。

要點解析

① sector 部門。相關片語有：public sector 國營經濟部門；financial sector 財政部門；private sector 私營部門。

② overdue 過期的，未兌的；相關片語：overdue fine 過期罰金；overdue note 逾期票據

③ pave the way for... 的意思是「為……鋪平道路」，也可以指「為……做好準備」。

---

107   We keep saying when the oil flew then the nation glow, so yeah, I think South Sudan's economy is going to revive. (BBC)

我們仍然表示，只要石油價格高漲，國家就會繁榮發展。所以我認為南蘇丹的經濟即將復甦。

要點解析

① flow 是「飛翔」的意思，在這句話裡是指價格「飛漲」。glow 的意思是「容

光煥發；熱情洋溢」，這句話是將 nation 擬人化了。

② revive 恢復；復甦。

108　Ever since broadca sting started, no antenna manufacturer, no tele-vision manufacturer has been required any kind of transmission fee. (NPR)

自從廣播節目開播以來，所有天線製造商和電視機製造商被要求過支付任何形式的轉播費用。

要點解析

① broadcasting（電台或電視台的）播放。廣播節目如：broadcasting station 廣播電台；radio broadcasting 無線電廣播。

② antenna 天線，這個詞也可以表示「觸角」。常見搭配有：receiving antenna 接收天線；satellite antenna 衛星天線。

③ transmission 傳遞，播送。

109　Nearly 5,000 farmers in those areas are exporting organically-grown produce to Europe, after gaining organic and fair-trade certification with help from the U.N. (VOA)

來自那些地區的大約 5,000 名農民在聯合國的幫助下獲得了有機食品和公平貿易認證之後，將有機產品出口到歐洲。

要點解析

① organically-grown 有機培植的，如：organically-grown vegetables 有機蔬菜。

② fair- trade 公平貿易。公平貿易是一項有組織的社會運動，提倡一種關於全球勞工、環保及社會政策的公平性標準，該運動特別關注那些從開發中國家銷售到已開發國家的外銷產品。

③ certi fication 證明，保證。quality certification 品質認證；professional certification 專業資政。

相關句子

Since organic farming is time-consuming, organically grown produce tends to be expensive. (VOA)

由於有機耕作十分耗時，因此有機農作物的價錢通常比較昂貴。

110   Kids nowadays are too materialistic, with their inflated sense of entitlement, and now flat screens and cell phones. (NPR)

現在的孩子權利感膨脹，用著平板電腦和手機，太過物質欲。

要點解析

① mate rialistic 物質主義的，如：materialistic society 物質社會。

② inflated 誇大的；脹氣的；成長的。inflated price 表示「飛漲的物價」；entitlement 則表示「權利；津貼」。

③ flat screen 和 cell phone 分別指「平板電腦」和「手機」。

相關句子

Money could mess them up—give them a sense of entitlement, prevent them from developing a strong sense of empathy and compassion. (NPR)

金錢會讓孩子們暈頭轉向，錢給予他們權利，卻讓他們變得缺乏同情心。

---

111   According to the state's budget, the state receives at least $45 million in federal funding, including administrative costs and federal grants under a program called Temporary Assistance for Needy Families. (NPR)

根據預算，該州獲得了至少 45 億美元的聯邦資助，其中包括「貧困家庭臨時援助專案」的行政費用和聯邦補助金。

要點解析

① funding 資金，通常指「政府或組織為某目的而提供的資金」。如：initial funding 啟動基金；public funding 公共基金。

② grant 補助金，如：government grant 政府補助金；land grant 政府贈地。

---

112   He gave his last public address to tens of thousands of people in the church's administrative center. (VOA)

他在教堂管理中心對成千上萬的人民發表了最後一次公開演說。

要點解析

① tens of thousands of 數以萬計。新聞用語裡常用數詞的複數表達「約數」，例如 hundreds of 數以百計，thousands of 數以千計，millions of 數千萬等。

② admin istrative center 管理中心，其中 adminis trative 是「管理的；行政的」
的意思。相關搭配還有：administrative region 行政區域。

113　Post-Soviet Russia is widely seen as an industrial rust belt. (VOA)
人們普遍認為後蘇聯時期俄羅斯的繁榮工業已一去不復返。

要點解析

① post 經常當做詞綴，表示「後……的」。如：post war 表示「戰後」，
post-Soviet Russia 表示「後蘇聯時期」。
② rust belt 鐵銹地帶，指代從前工業繁盛至今衰落的已開發國家的地區。

相關句子

As the US was pulling out of a mild recession in the early' 90s, post-Soviet
Russia was plunging into a decade-long depression that saw the country's
gross domestic product slump by over half. (VOA)
1990 年代早期，美國已走出了一段略有衰退的時期，而後蘇聯時期的俄
羅斯卻陷入長達十年之久的蕭條，國民生產總值下降一半以上。

114　The Cyprus deal protects small savers, but depositors with more than
100,000 euro face big losses. (BBC)
賽普勒斯協定保護了小額儲戶，但是儲蓄金額超過 10 萬歐元的
儲戶面臨重大損失。

要點解析

① depositor 存款人。常用搭配有：small depositor 小額存戶；bank depositor
銀行儲戶；overdrawn depositor 超支戶。
② loss 虧損；損失。常用組合有：at a loss 不知所措；water loss 失水量；
weight loss 失重。

115　Evidence of India's slowing economy can be seen from local car deal-
erships to job training workshops where unemployed young people get
interview advice. (VOA)
從本土汽車經銷商，到就業培訓班中接受就業培訓的失業青年，
印度經濟緩慢成長可見一斑。

要點解析

① dealership 代理權，經銷權。

② workshop 可以表示「作坊，研討會」。如：processing workshop 加工作坊；workshop section 工段。但在這個句子中，workshop 表示「研習班，培訓班」。

相關句子

With India's economy slowing—growth could dip below 8% this year, from a peak of 9-10%—and interest rates rising, borrowers will be under more strain. (VOA)

隨著印度經濟發展放緩，今年的經濟成長從最高的 9-10% 跌至 8% 以下，利率在上升，借款人的壓力也隨之增大。

116　The Euro Zone is offering a ten-billion euro loan while insisting on extra cash from Cyprus itself. (BBC)

歐元區提供 100 億歐元的貸款，同時堅持要求賽普勒斯額外籌措資金。

要點解析

① loan 貸款；借出。常用搭配有：on loan 借貸；bank loan 銀行貸款；mortgage loan 借貸貸款；student loan 助學貸款。

② insist on 堅持；強調。on 可以省略。

117　It's difficult to estimate how much damage agricul tural pests do every year, but it's believed to be in the billions. (VOA)

蟲害每年對農業造成的損失難以估計，但相信已達到百億。

要點解析

① estimate 預估。常見搭配有：estimate for... 對……估價；cost estimate 成本估算；rough estimate 粗略的估計。

② pest 害蟲，瘟疫。如：insect pest 害蟲；pest management 病蟲害治理。

118　This place, for whatever reasons, is still growing, and it is likely to continue to grow and at a pace to pick another big emerging economy where people seem to think that everything is wonderful. (VOA)

不管出於什麼原因,這個地方仍在發展,並且極有可能繼續成長,繼而發展出一種新興經濟,讓人們覺得一切都是那麼美好。

要點解析

① pace 速度,步調。固定搭配有:keep pace 起步並進;at a snail's pace 慢條斯理地;set the pace 領先;at a good pace 相當快地。

② emerging 新興的。如:emerging economy 新興經濟;emerging market 新興市場;emerging industry 新興產業。

119　The first lady's husband, President Obama, was speaking yesterday too, talking about his proposal for the U.S. government's budget. (CNN)

第一夫人的丈夫——總統歐巴馬昨天也進行了發言,談到了他關於美國政府預算的提案。

要點解析

① talk about 談及;談到。

② proposal 表示「提案,議案」;也可以指「提議」。如:design proposal 設計方案;the proposal for... 針對……的提議;technical proposal 技術建議。

120　Almost 68% of voters backed plans given shareholders a veto on compensation and banning big payouts for managers leaving or joining companies. (BBC)

接近 68% 的選民支援給予股東補償否決權,並禁止向管理者提供高額的離職或到職補貼。

要點解析

① veto on... 反對……。相關搭配有:put a veto on 否決;禁止。

② compe nsation 賠償;補償。如:compensation system 補償制度。

③ pay out 支出;花費。如:payout ratio 股息支付率。

相關句子

The people of Switzerland have voted overwhelmingly to adopt measures restricting the salaries of top managers. (BBC)

瑞士公民以壓倒性的票數支持採取措施，對高層管理者的薪資進行嚴格的限制。

121　The Claims Administrator overseen the compensation of what to businesses damaged by the BP oil spill in Gulf of Mexico. (BBC)

索賠管理人就英國石油公司對墨西哥灣石油洩漏事件造成商業損失的賠償進行了審查。

要點解析

① oversee 監督；審查；偷看到。

② compensation 賠償。

③ damage 表示「傷害」。在這個句子中，可以表示「造成損失」。

④ spill 溢出。常見搭配有：oil spill 漏油；spill over 溢出；chemical spill 化學品溢漏；gulf 有「海灣」的意思。

122　Chinese tourists have overtaken Germans and Americans as the world's biggest spending travelers. (BBC)

中國遊客已經趕超德國和美國遊客，成為世界上最大的消費旅遊族群。

要點解析

① over take 趕上，相當於 catch up with。

② spending 花費；開銷。如：Your spending should not go over your income. 你的支出不應該超過你的收入。

相關句子

All the attention to Chinese tourists, is due to their increased purchasing power. (BBC)

所有對中國遊客的關注都是因為他們不斷成長的購買力。

123　The U.S. patent system, authorized in the Constitution, gives temporary economic incentives to inventors to advance science. (NPR)
由《憲法》授權的美國專利制度為發明家們提供臨時經濟激勵以
鼓勵他們發展科學。

要點解析

① patent 專利的。常見片語有：national patent 國家專利；patent law 專利法；
patent application 專利申請。
② authorize 批准；認可，授權。
③ incentive 是名詞，表示「動機；激勵」。常見搭配有：incentive compensation 獎金；incentive mechanism 激勵機制。

124　Part of why Web content became shorter and less substantive was that
publishers believed in order to have a successful digital business model, they had to produce things as quickly and as cheaply as possible.
(NPR)
網路內容變得越來越簡短，越來越沒有實質內容的部分原因是出
版商認為他們需要盡可能迅速地以低成本發行內容，從而建立成
功的數位化商業模式。

要點解析

① substantive 有實質的；實質性的。常見搭配有：substantive law 實體法；
substantive characteristic 本質特徵；substantive right 實體權利。
② digital 在這句話裡是形容詞，表示「數字的；數位的」。此外，還可以
作名詞，表示「數位」。
③ model 模型；模範。常用搭配有：business model 商業模式；system model 系統模式；optimiz ation model 最佳模型。

125　President Obama challenged his Republican opponents to support
plans for tax cuts and loans for small businesses which they have so
far blocked. (BBC)
歐巴馬總統向共和黨對手發起挑戰，支持為那些目前被限制的小
型企業減稅，並提供貸款方案。

要點解析

① opponent 對手，常見搭配有：political opponent 政敵；opponent party 對方當事人。

② block 阻止，在這句話裡可以理解為「限制」。如：block up 妨礙；block out 封閉。

126　India's slowing economy is hurting an auto industry that was once a top choice for global companies looking to expand. (VOA)

印度經濟的發展緩慢對其汽車行業產生了影響，該國的汽車行業曾一度是全球汽車企業最希望拓展業務的地方。

要點解析

① auto 汽車，是 automobile 的簡寫形式。相關搭配有：auto industry 汽車工業；auto insurance 汽車保險。這個詞也有「自動」的意思，如：auto switch 自動開關。

② expand 擴張，使膨脹；這裡指「擴展業務」。如：They hope to expand their company. 他們想擴大公司的規模。

127　The meeting's resolution reaffirmed their commitment not to... (NPR)

會議決議重申他們不會加入 ......

要點解析

① commitment 承諾；信奉。常見搭配有：make a commitment 承諾；financial commitment 財務承諾；public commitment 公開投入。

② domestic 國內的，如：domestic price 國內價格；domestic flight 國內航班。

③ growth 成長，發展。

128　As Egyptians face a crumbling economy, a rise in decline in basic services, many count on one sector of society to keep the nation from the potential of failed statehood. (VOA)

埃及人民面臨著經濟破碎和基礎服務水準下降的問題，因此許多人都指望某個社會部門能避免國家垮台。

要點解析

① crumbling 破碎的，這個詞來自動詞 crumble「破粹；崩潰」。

② decline 下降；衰退。常見片語搭配有：production decline 產量遞減；on the decline 在衰退；economic decline 經濟衰退。

③ count on 指望；依靠。相當於 depend on。

④ fail 意為失敗，statehood 指「國家地位」，因此 failed statehood 的意思就是「國家的衰敗，垮台」。

129　Media in Cyprus say an investigation into what went wrong at the island's banks has found that important data has been deleted from computers of the largest lender—the Bank of Cyprus. (BBC)

賽普勒斯媒體表示，在調查該島國銀行時發現，最大貸方──賽普勒斯銀行的電腦裡有一些重要資料已被刪除。

要點解析

① go wrong 弄錯；出毛病。

② delete from... 從……中刪除。

要點解析

Cyprus central bank governor Athanasios Orphanides said one of the ECB's options would be to offer banks liquidity for 12 months, double the current maximum period for the ECB's loans to banks. (BBC)

賽普勒斯央行總裁阿沙納斯歐斯‧歐菲尼德斯表示，歐洲央行可以選擇為銀行提供 12 個月的流動資金，而這比當前歐洲央行給其他銀行提供貸款的最長期限長一倍。

130　US automakers continue taking steps towards increasing fuel economy. (NPR)

美國汽車製造商繼續採取措施提高燃料節約率。

要點解析

① take step 採取措施；take measures 也可以表示「採取措施」。

② fuel 燃料，如：fuel consumption 耗油量。句中出現的 fuel economy 意為「燃料經濟性」，即「節約燃料」。

131　A lot of the entry level jobs the young people used to count on, like those at clothing stores or restaurants for example are going to more experienced or more educated workers. (CNN)

大量年輕人指望的入門級職業，像服飾店或餐廳的工作，現在都需要更有經驗或受過更好教育的人。

要點解析

① entry level 入門級，入學程度。

② used to 過去常常，常與 be、get、become 連用；後面接名詞或動名詞。

③ experienced 和 educated 分別表示「有經驗的」和「受過教育的」，在描述職業資歷時常會用到。

132　One creative approach was taken by Virginia, which actually eliminated its gas tax while raising sales taxes and imposing a tax on wholesale fuel. (NPR)

維吉尼亞州採取了一個有創意的手段，在增加銷售稅並且徵收燃料批發稅的同時，實際上是取消了天然氣稅。

要點解析

① eliminate 消除；淘汰。如：eliminate illiteracy 掃盲；eliminate ignorance 掃除愚昧。在這個句子中，climinate 表示「取消」。

② impose 利用；欺騙；徵稅。常用搭配 impose on... 表示「利用......；欺騙......；施加影響於......」。

③ wholesale 批發的；大規模的。如：wholesale trade 批發貿易；wholesale business 批發業務。

133　After years of corporate mergers in the financial industry, the president is calling for legislation to prevent the further consolidation. (VOA)

金融行業經歷了數年的企業併購之後，總統呼籲立法以防止進一步的合併。

要點解析

① merger 合併；併購。如：merger and acquisition 收購兼併；merger agreement 合併協議；consolidation 則也有「合併」的意思。

② call for 要求；提倡；為......叫喊。

③ legislation 立法；法律。常見搭配有：labor legislation 勞工法；delegated legislation 經授權的立法。

相關句子

There is evidence that corporate mergers have continued to proliferate throughout the century (often failing to produce the efficiencies promised by consolidation). (VOA)

有證據顯示企業併購情況在本世紀一直有增無減（但往往沒有產生合併預期的成效）。

134　The extremes of unrestricted wealth and greed are driving poverty. (BBC)

無限制的財富和貪婪加劇了貧窮。

要點解析

① unrestricted 自由的；不受限制的。如：unrestricted transfer 無限制轉讓。
② greed 貪婪，如：greed for money 貪財。
③ drive 在這句話裡是「推動，驅使」的意思，相當於 boost。

135　Over the course of two academic years, each of the eight schools gets on average between \$70,000 and \$80,000, either in monetary or in-kind support. (NPR)

為期兩年的課程中，這八所學校中的每一所平均都得到了七至八萬美元貨幣和非貨幣的收入。

要點解析

① on average 平均地；通常地，相當於 in general。
② monetary 財政的；貨幣的。如：monetary system 貨幣制度；monetary assets 金融資產。
③ in-kind 表示「以貨貸款；非現金的」。常見搭配有：in-kind lease 實物租賃；in-kind benefits 實物福利；in-kind sponsor 實物贊助。

136　When the Federal Aviation Administration said it would have to close about 150 towers to cut costs, the airports protested. (NPR)

當聯邦航空管理局表示，必須關閉 150 座發射塔以減少開銷時，機場表示了抗議。

要點解析

① tower 在這句話裡指「（無線電或電視訊號的）發射塔」，常用搭配有：radio tower 發射塔。

② protest 抗議；斷言，如：protest against... 對……抗議；without protest 心甘情願地；under protest 抗議中；極不樂意地。

137　Facebook has released a new piece of software that it hopes will put the social network the center of Smartph ones that run Google's Android operating system. (BBC)

臉書發表了一款新軟體，希望使社群網路成為裝有 Google 安卓系統的智慧手機的核心。

要點解析

① software 軟體。「一款軟體」可以說 a piece of software；而 a suite of software 則表示「一套軟體」。

② social 社交的，social network 表示「社群網路」。常見搭配還有：social life 社群生活；social behavior 社交行為。

③ smartphone 智慧型手機。

④ operating 操作的。相關片語有：operating system 作業系統；operating procedure 作業程序。

相關句子

And Facebook users, by tagging friends in the pictures they upload, allow the service to recognise these people on other pictures. (BBC)

臉書使用者透過在上傳的圖片中圈出好友，可以允許此服務在其他照片上認出這些人。

138　Also the Syrian government didn't really have anywhere to put the oil. It had limited capacity to put the oil through their refineries. (VOA)

敘利亞政府也沒有任何地方可以儲存汽油，煉油廠中儲存汽油的空間也很有限。

要點解析

① capacity 能力，容量；在這句話裡是「容量」的意思。例如：That is roughly half of its capacity. 這大約是其容量的一半。

② refinery 精煉廠。如：oil refinery 煉油廠；refinery gas 煉廠氣。

---

139   They'd concluded that the man who'd handled the investment should now reimburse them. (BBC)

他們得出結論，那個負責投資的人現在應該賠償他們。

要點解析

① conclude 推斷；結束；下結論。常見搭配有：conclude with... 以......結束；conclude a contract 訂立合約；conclude an agreement 達成協議。

② handle 在這句話裡當做動詞，表示「處理」。此外，handle 還可以作名詞，表示「把手，手柄」。

③ reimburse 償還，賠償。

---

140   Nearly 500,000 people stopped looking, and some experts say that's why the unemployment rate went down. (CNN)

將近 50 萬的人不再繼續求職，專家說這就是失業率降低的原因。

要點解析

go down 在這句話裡是「下降」的意思。此外還有：「趴下；(電腦) 出故障；引起......反響」的意思。

相關句子

The ten percent unemployment rate has meant that many people are struggling with their house payments. (VOA)

10% 的失業率意味著許多人在還房貸的時候會感到捉襟見肘。

---

141   But Economist Mark Vitner with Wells Fargo says much of the rise was fueled by investors snapping up houses rather than by families buying homes to live in. (NPR)

但是美國富國銀行的經濟學家馬克‧維特納認為，上漲的大部分原因是由於投資者搶購房屋，而不是家庭自住購房。

要點解析

① fuel 作動詞時，表示「供以燃料」。在這句話裡可以理解為「推動」。

② snap up 搶購，爭購；其中 snap 是「採取突然的舉動」的意思。這個詞

也可以作名詞，表示「突然的行動」；常見片語搭配有：in a snap 馬上。

---

142 Many job applicants are optimistic that the economy will bounce back.
(VOA)

很多求職者都非常樂觀，認為經濟會迅速恢復。

要點解析

① applicant 申請人，請求者；job applicant 表示「求職者」。
② bounce 跳，彈起；bounce back 表示「反彈；迅速恢復活力」，在這句話裡是指經濟的「迅速恢復」。與 bounce 相關的搭配還有：bounce off 反射。

---

143 New fuel economy standard require automakers fleet to an average of
45 miles a gallon by 2025. (NPR)

新的燃料經濟性標準要求汽車製造商在 2025 年使平均油耗接近每加侖 45 公里。

要點解析

① fleet 在這句話裡作動詞，表示「迅速移動，飛躍」的意思。此外，fleet 還可以作形容詞，表示「快速的，敏捷的」。
② gallon 加侖，是容量單位。

---

144 For the last decade, Russia has been the world's largest energy exporter. (VOA)

近十年來，俄羅斯已經成為世界上最大的能源出口國。

要點解析

① decade 十年，over the past decade 表示「在過去的十年裡」。
② exporter 出口商，與其意思相反的是 importer「進口商」。

相關句子

Many economists say that oil and gas revenues are dropping and that Russia is starting to re-industrialize. (VOA)

許多經濟學家表示石油和天然氣收入正在下降，而俄羅斯開始再次進入工業化時代。

145 One side of that is that young people aren't getting the early working experience that would help them later on. (CNN)
其中一個方面是年輕人無法獲得對他們日後有幫助的早期工作經驗。

要點解析

① side 在這句話裡作名詞，表示「方面」。此外它還可作動詞，表示「支持；同意；贊助」，也可以用 aspect 表達這個意思。
② later on 隨後，以後。

146 These i nclude steps to impose new oversight and controls on hedge funds and complex financial instruments known as derivatives, and protections for consumers of financial products. (VOA)
這些步驟包括對避險基金和複雜的金融衍生品實施新的監管，以及對金融產品消費者的保護。

要點解析

① oversight 監督，照管。類似意思的表達還有 supervision, surveillance。
② hedge fund 避險基金，對沖基金。其中，hedge 表示「避險」。
③ financial instrument 是「金融票具」的意思，其中 instrument 的意思是「工具」。
④ derivative 衍生物，派生物。相關片語有：financial derivative 金融衍生產品。

147 He says more money could be freed up for direct investment if costs were reduced. (NPR)
他表示如果成本降低，可以釋放出更多的錢直接用於投資。

要點解析

① free up 空出來；開放（市場、經濟或體制）。常見表達有：free up a market 開放市場；free up economy 開放經濟；free up system 開放體制。
② investment 投資，投入。如：foreign investment 國外投資；direct investment 直接投資；investment bank 投資銀行。

148　The Federal Reserve came under fire again as some lawmakers re-
newed calls to reduce the Central Bank's authority. (VOA)

隨著一些立法者再次呼籲削弱中央銀行的權利，美國聯邦準備委
員會再次受到了猛烈的抨擊。

要點解析

① comeunder fire 字面意思是「受到炮火的攻擊，遭到射擊」，也可以指「受
到批評」。
② lawmaker 立法者；立法議員。
③ authority 權威；權利；當局。如：authority on... 有關......的權威；tax authority 稅務機關。

149　Although economic and financial conditions have improved, they
decided they still need to keep up the initiatives intended to restore
growth. (BBC)

儘管經濟和金融形勢有所改善，他們仍然決定要繼續維持經濟成
長的主動性。

要點解析

① keep up 保持，常用搭配有：keep up with... 和......保持聯絡；趕得上。
② initiative 主動權；首創精神。
③ restore 恢復；還原。

150　They fear that the uncertainty will damage the fragile Euro zone. (BBC)

他們擔心這種不確定性會對脆弱的歐元區造成損害。

要點解析

① uncertainty 不確定，不可靠；相關片語有：uncertainty analysis 定性分析。
② fragile 脆的；易碎的。如：fragile goods 易碎商品。這個詞也可以用來比
喻，如：fragile dream 易碎的夢。

151　Worries about the Greek economy's potential meltdown have sent jit-
ters through world markets. (VOA)

對希臘經濟潛在危機的擔憂讓整個世界市場都充滿不安。

要點解析

① meltdown 由片語 meltdown「融化」衍生而來，意思是「災難，澈底垮台」；如：financial meltdown 金融危機。

② jitter 在這句話裡作名詞，表示「振動，緊張不安」；作動詞表示「抖動；戰戰兢兢」。

152　It seems that when the Fed is responsible for monetary policy and bank supervision, its performance in both suffers. (VOA)

當聯邦調查局負責貨幣政策和銀行監督的時候，似乎這兩面的表現都會受到影響。

要點解析

① be responsible for... 對……負責任；是……的原因。

② supervision 監督，管理；如：technical supervision 技術監督；financial supervision 財政監督；supervision and control 監督控制。

153　In fact, he says, figuring out what you owe and paying your debt is the foundation of the US tax system. (NPR)

他說，事實上算清你所欠債務並償還是美國稅務體系的基礎。

要點解析

① figure out 算出；理解；斷定。figure sb. out 表示「了解某人」；而 figure sth. out 表示「弄懂某件事情」。

② owe 欠，應給予。常用搭配有 owe to，意為「把……歸功於」。

③ foundation 根據，基礎。常見搭配有：economic foundation 經濟基礎；foundation stone 基石。

154　The BBC World Service director Peter Horrocks said Sri Lanka's state broadcast was warned last week about interference in breach of its broadcasting agreement with the BBC. (BBC)

英國廣播公司全球服務主管彼得·赫魯克斯表示，斯里蘭卡國家廣播因違反與英國廣播公司的廣播協議，上週遭到了警告。

要點解析

① broadcast 廣播；傳播。相關的表達有：live broadcast 現場直播；broadcast media 廣播媒體；broadcast station 廣播電台。

② interference 干擾，衝突。如：inference in 干擾；inference with 妨礙。

③ in breach of 違反，破壞。

155　The agreement creates one of Asia's biggest trading areas and integrates India's fast growing economy with 10 of its neighbors. (VOA)

這份協定創建了亞洲最大的貿易地區之一，使印度快速成長的經濟和它的十個鄰國聯合起來。

要點解析

integrate 使……完整；表示……的總和。相關搭配有：integrate with 結合。如：We should integrate all our services. 我們應該整合我們所有的服務。

156　A family friend worried about his own autistic son's future, help to shape Penchback's legacy. (CNN)

一位家族朋友擔心他自己患有自閉症的兒子的未來，於是幫助皮巴克整理遺產。

要點解析

① autistic 孤僻的；自閉症的。

② shape 是「成型，塑造」的意思。但在這個句子中，可以表示「進行合理安排」的意思。

③ legacy 遺產；傳統。

157　Bank of America took over Merrill Lynch to save it from collapse in a deal ba cked by American taxpayers' money. (BBC)

在一項有美國納稅人資金支援的交易中，美國銀行接管了美林證券公司，讓其免於倒閉的危機。

要點解析

① take over 接管；接收；採用。

② collapse 倒塌；瓦解。

③ deal 在這句話裡作名詞，表示「協議」。

---

158   So if the produce gets a couple of days old, maybe we can't sell it to
       our customers, but we certainly don't want it to go to waste. (VOA)
       如果產品已經上市幾天，也許我們不能把它賣給顧客，但當然我
       們也不想浪費。

要點解析

① 這裡的 get a couple of days old 是擬人的用法，直譯為「已經有幾天那麼
  老」，引申為「已經上市幾天」的意思。
② go to waste 表示「被浪費掉」。

Part 3

Science & Technology

1   The researchers also found that, in the process of being selected for color, size and taste, domestic watermelon lost many of the genes that helped their wild ancestors resist disease. (Scientific American)
     調查者還發現，在選擇顏色、大小和味道的過程中，本土西瓜失去了許多能幫助野生原種預防疾病的基因。

要點解析

     ① in the process of... 在……的過程中，process 除了「過程、步驟」之外，作動詞時還有「處理加工」的意思。
     ② wild ancestor 野生原種。

2   Professor Shahabi says his program uses historical data to predict traffic conditions even before the driver leaves the house. (VOA)
     謝哈畢教授稱他設計的程式甚至可以在駕駛者離開家之前就利用歷史資料預測交通狀況。

要點解析

     predict 預測；預言。形容詞為 predictable，意為「可預言的；可預報的」。

相關句子

     They also wrote a program that counted traffic. The traffic counting program was so successful that they started a company to sell it to city governments. (BBC)
     他們還編寫了一個計算交通流量的程式，該程式非常成功，於是他們成立了一家公司，將這款程式銷售給各個城市的政府。

3   Scientists say they've come closer to finding the enigmatic invisible substance known as dark matter which is thought to make up a considerable part of the universe. (BBC)
     科學家們表示已經進一步探究了暗物質這種神祕的隱形物質，暗物質被認為是宇宙的重要組成部分。

要點解析

     ① enigmatic 神祕的；高深莫測的。

② substance 物質，實質。常見搭配有：in substance 實質上；organic substance 有機物；active substance 活性物質。這裡的 dark matter 是專有名詞「暗物質」。

③ make up 組成。此外還有「彌補；整理；化妝」的意思。

4　Stanford professor Clifford Nass says this kind of synthetic conversation is possible because of advances in voice and language recognition. (NPR)

史丹佛大學教授柯利弗德‧納斯表示，對於嗓音處理和語言辨識的改進讓這種類型的人工合成會話成為可能。

要點解析

① synthetic 綜合的，合成的，人工的。相關片語有：synthetic method 綜合法；synthetic rubber 合成橡膠。

② advance in... 在……的改進；進步，相當於 develop。

5　Noel Sharkey, a Professor of Artificial Intelligence and Robotics, and Chairman of the International Committee for Robot Arms Control, says it marks the final step in the industrial revolution of war. (VOA)

諾埃爾‧沙基，人工智慧機器人專家及國際機器人武器控制委員會主席，他表示這標誌著工業革命戰爭的最後一步。

要點解析

① chairman 主席；副主席可以用 vice chairman 來表示。

② mark 標誌，記號。相關片語有：trade mark 商標；mark on... 在……上做記號；mark with 在……上面標上……。

③ industrial revolution 工業革命，產業革命。

6　The X-47B drone, currently undergoing flight testing, is one of the world's most advanced, able to take off from an aircraft carrier. (VOA)

X-47B 目前正在進行飛行測試，這是世界上最先進的無人駕駛機之一，能夠從航空母艦上起飛。

① undergo 經歷，忍受。如：undergo surgery 進行手術；undergo examination 經歷審查。

② take off 起飛；脫下；離開。

③ carrier 載體；運輸工具。如：aircraft carrier 航空母艦。

7　Among Maimon's more controversial findings is the correlation between the number of foreign students logged into the college network and the frequency and origin of the cyber attacks. (VOA)

麥農還有一個更具爭議的發現，大量外國學生登入大學校園網路與網路攻擊的頻率及來源之間存在關聯性。

要點解析

① controversial 有爭議的；引起爭議的。

② log 把……記入航海日誌；航行（……距離）；飛行（……小時）。在網路用語中 log 還有「登陸」的意思，常用片語為 log on 登入，log off 登出。

③ cyber 電腦的，網路的。在網路時代，cyber 這一詞綴就構成了許多新詞，如 cyberspace 網路空間；cyber romance 網戀；cyber nut 網蟲。

8　They will fire darts from small air rifles to collect blubber and skin for genetic testing, and to attach satellite-tracking tags to monitor the whales. (VOA)

他們會用氣槍發射飛鏢來收集鯨脂和皮膚進行基因測試。此外，他們還在鯨魚身上附上衛星追蹤標籤來監視牠們。

要點解析

① dart 作名詞表示「飛鏢」，但在這句話裡是動詞，表示「投射；投擲」的意思。

② satellite-tracking 是一個合成詞，表示「衛星追蹤的」。其中 satellite 是「衛星」，tracking 是 track 的現在分詞作形容詞。

9　Past research has found increased stress and more intra-species and inter-species aggression among animals that have been fed by humans.

(Scientific American)

過去的研究發現，被人類餵養的動物承受的壓力更大，物種內和物種外的攻擊行為也更嚴重。

要點解析

① intra 和 inter 是兩個常見的詞根，其中 intra 表示「內部的」，如 intraparty 黨內的；intranational 國內的；而 inter 則表示「在......之間；相互」，如 interaction 相互作用；interfere 干涉；intersect 交叉。

② aggression 是形容詞 aggressive 的名詞形式，意思是「侵略；進攻」。

10　The American billionaire and world's first space tourist Dennis Tito has announced he will fund a manned mission to Mars in 2018. (BBC)

美國億萬富翁，世界首位太空旅行者丹尼斯‧蒂托宣布，他將投資 2018 年的載人火星任務。

要點解析

① fund 在這句話裡是動詞，表示「投資；資金」的意思；這個詞也可以作名詞，常用片語有 relief fund 救濟金。

② mission 是「派遣；代表團」的意思，常見片語有 strategic mission 策略任務。

11　Professor Jerry Seigel from the University of California, Los Angeles, conducted a study of the sleep times of a broad range of animals and found that they vary widely. (BBC)

來自加州大學洛杉磯分校的教授傑里‧西格爾進行了一項針對眾多不同動物睡眠時間的研究，發現差距很大。

要點解析

① conduct 是「管理；行為；實施」的意思，在這句話裡是「主導實驗」的意思。常用片語有 conduct pass 安全通行證。

② vary 變化；違反；使多樣化，常用片語有 vary from... 不同於......。

12　In the age of hundreds of cable channels, millions of 140-character bulletins and an untold number of cat videos, a fear has been growing among journalists and readers that long-form storytelling may be getting lost. (NPR)

在一個擁有上百個有限頻道、上百萬條 140 字的新聞快報，以及數不清的搞笑影片的時代，記者和讀者開始擔心長篇幅的敘事方式將失去市場。

要點解析

① untold 既有「未說過的，未透露的」意思，也可以表示「數不清的」意思。
② cat video 搞笑影片，喜劇影片。

13　Scientists realized that what we see in the night sky is not the whole story, that the stars are not alone, that something must be filling the gaps in the galaxies. (BBC)

科學家意識到我們在夜空中看見到的並非全部，星星並不是孤立存在的，星系間的空隙是一定存在著某些物質。

要點解析

① the whole story 的字面意思是「全部的故事」，有「原委；詳情」的含義。
② gap 間隙；缺口；空白。
③ galaxy 銀河；銀河系。

14　As many San Franciscans have noticed, sourdough bread stays fresher longer than the regular stuff. (Scientific American)

正如許多舊金山人已經注意到的一樣，酵母麵包比其他普通麵包的保存期限更長。

要點解析

① notice 作名詞表示「通知；警告」；在這句話裡 notice 作動詞，意思是「注意到；留心」。
② sourdough 直譯的意思是「發酸的麵糰」，也可以表示「酵母」。

15　The thing is, not everyone bouncing around on bad roads has a smart phone—or the app, for that matter—to help gather the data. (NPR)

最重要的是，並非每個在糟糕的道路上奔走的人都有智慧手機，

或是應用程式，可以幫助收集資料。

要點解析

① bounce 彈跳；彈力；活力。bounce around 則引申為「四處奔走」的意思。
② gather 收集；收割；聚集。常用片語有 gather ceremoniously 隆重集會。

16　They synthesized completely artificial voices, and recorded sentences before varying the pitches and resonance. (NPR)
他們合成了完整的模擬語音，並且在改變句子的語調和回音之前將它錄了下來。

要點解析

① artificial 人造的;非原產地的。常用片語有 artificial intelligence 人工智慧。
② pitch 在句子中是「音高，音調」的意思。此外，作動詞表示「為……定調」。
③ resonance 共振；反響。其常用片語有 resonance frequency 共振頻率。

17　So your listening history helps determine whether you'll like a new song— or tell it to hit the road. (Scientific American)
所以你的聽歌歷史紀錄會決定你是否喜歡這首新歌，或讓直接播放。

要點解析

① listening history 的字面意思是「聽過的歷史記錄」，在這句話裡指代「聽過的歌」。
② hit 的含義有很多，本意是「打擊；碰撞」，也有「偶然發現；傷……的感情」的意思。hit the road 在口語中可以表示「上路」，而「命中率」可以用 hit ratio 來表示。

18　The commercial spaceship is 60 feet long, made of lightweight, fuel-efficient material and can carry eight people out of this world and back. (BBC)
商用太空船有 60 英尺長，由超輕的節能材料構成，能承載八個人往返地球。

① commercial 商業的，營利的。commercial use 即意為「商業用途」。

② lightweight 重量輕的，無足輕重的人。其常用片語有 lightweight construction 輕型結構。

19　Meteorologist said these houses are on the seismic fault that can shift on rare occasions. (CNN)

氣象學家表示，這些位於地震斷層上的房屋幾乎不可能發生移動。

要點解析

① meteorologist 氣象學家；氣象工作者。

② seismic 地震的，因地震引起的。

③ fault 故障；錯誤；缺點。在地質專業中，fault 還有「斷層」的意思。

相關句子

The dam was completed less than two years ago despite concerns raised at the time about building it so close to a seismic fault line. (CNN)

這個大壩完工還不到兩年，而當時就已經有人因其距離地震斷裂帶太近表示擔憂。

20　Some opponents of these GMOs want them banned. Others say foods whose DNA has been changed need at least to be labeled. (CNN)

一些基因改造生物的反對者們希望對此加以禁止。其他人則表示已經改變 DNA 的食物至少需要標注出來。

要點解析

① opponent 對手；反對者。其常用片語有 political opponent 政敵。

② label 作名詞可以表示「標籤」；在這句話裡作動詞，表示「貼標籤」的意思。

21　The thing about an autonomous robot is you couldn't hold it accountable. (VOA)

關於自主式機器人有一點是：你無法追究其責任。

要點解析

① autonomous 是「自治的；自主的；自發的」意思；其常用片語有 autonomous navigation 自動導航。

② accountable 有責任的；有解釋義務的；可解釋的。

相關句子

"Higher climbing efficiencies will extend the battery life of a self-contained, autonomous robot and expand the variety of tasks the robot can perform," he says. (VOA)

他說：「更高效的攀爬能延長這種自主協調機器人的電池壽命，讓它們有更多的用武之地。」

---

22   We all experience circadian rhythms, due to molecular clocks in our cells. (Scientific American)

由於我們身體中的細胞分子生理時鐘的存在，我們都會經歷晝夜生物節律。

要點解析

① circadian 生理節奏。常用搭配有 circadian rhythm 晝夜節律。

② due to 由於，應歸於。其常用搭配有 give due consideration to 適當考慮。

---

23   Now scientists have discovered these so-called fairy circles are indeed created by wee little creatures—termites. (Scientific American)

如今，科學家已經發現這些所謂的仙女環實際上是由白蟻這種極小的生物構成的。

要點解析

① wee 極小的，很早的。如 wee hours 凌晨。

② termite 白蟻。

要點解析

Wood debris is even proving to be difficult to dispose of in parts of Louisiana because of concerns about the termite. (CNN)

在路易斯安那州的部分地區，由於乳白蟻的侵襲，甚至連木頭碎片都很難處理。

24　But genes can be changed, they can be modified, and that's how you end up with a GMO, a genetically modified organism. (CNN)

但是，基因可以被改變，可以被修改，這就是最終的 GMO 基因改造生物。

要點解析

① modify 修改；更改。

② end up with... 以……而結束。

③ organism 有機體；生物體；微生物。常用片語有 marine organism 海洋生物。

25　Now a team in Oregon has used a skin sample and a woman's egg to produce some early cloned human embryo. (BBC)

奧勒岡州的一個小組使用皮膚樣本和女性卵細胞製造了早期的複製人類胚胎。

要點解析

① cloned 無性繁殖的。常用搭配語有 cloned sheep 複製羊。

② embryo 胚胎；初期。常用搭配有 embryo stage 胚胎期。

相關句子

Another US company, Geron, is also reported to be attempting to make human embryo clones for therapeutic purposes. (BBC)

根據報導，另一家美國公司傑龍也在嘗試製造用於醫療目的的人類複製胚胎。

26　When they get to the International Space Station, the Endeavour crew will be delivering and installing a module known as Tranquility, which will provide additional room for crew members. (VOA)

當他們到達國際太空站的時候，奮進號太空梭的機組人員將傳送並安裝叫做「寧靜」的機艙，它將提供航空工作人員額外的空間。

要點解析

① deliver 運輸；傳送。deliver goods 是「交貨」的意思。

② install 安裝。full install 意為「完整安裝」。

③ module 原指「模組，元件」。在航太學術語中，有「艙」的意思。

---

27   Scientists at the Smithsonian's Museum of Natural History say some-body tried to pry open her skull to remove the brain. (BBC)

史密森尼自然歷史博物館的科學家稱，有人曾試圖撬開她的頭顱以取出大腦。

要點解析

① pry 撬動；刺探；槓桿。常用片語有 pry about 窺探。
② skull 頭蓋骨，腦殼。常用片語有 skull fracture 顱骨骨折。

---

28   There is no way to overstate the importance of this case to the future of science and medicine. (NPR)

根本無法誇大這個案例對於未來科學和醫藥的重要性。

要點解析

① overstate 誇張，誇大的敘述。常見用法有 to overstate the facts 言過其實。
② case 情況；實例；包圍；把……裝於容器中。常用片語有 criminal case 刑事案件。

---

29   Day and night existed long before the first primitive cells came into being. (Scientific American)

在出現晝夜很久之後，第一批原始細胞才開始形成。

要點解析

① primitive 是「原始的；粗糙的；原始人」的意思，常用片語有 primitive culture 原始文化。
② come into being 可以表示「形成，產生」。

---

30   A pressure cooker is interesting because by pressurizing the vessel, you're able to cook much hotter than the boiling point of water, and still have water be present. (Scientific American)

壓力鍋非常有意思，因為透過給容器增壓，你能煮出比沸點溫度更高的開水，而水依然存在。

① pressurize 密封；增壓；使......加壓。如：air pressurize 空氣增壓法。

② boiling point 是「沸點」的意思，常見搭配有 boiling-point thermometer 沸點溫度計。

31　Since the system requires at least two phones to work, researchers say it would be ideal for a security force fanned out around a likely target. (NPR)

由於這個系統需要至少兩部電話來運作，研究人員認為，這對於安保部隊分散在潛在目標周圍是一個理想的方式。

要點解析

① security 安全，抵押品。security force 指「安保部隊」。其他常用片語有：security rules 安全規則，security van 保安車。

② target 作名詞表示「目標」；作動詞可以表示「把......作為目標」。常用片語有 target market 目標市場，meet the target 達成目標。

32　He is meant to ensure that the internet service providers can not block or slow down internet traffic like the ban with hogging video downloads. (BBC)

他的目的是確保網路服務供應商不能像禁止影片下載那樣封閉網路流量，或是降低網速。

要點解析

① be meant to do sth. 意圖做某事，企圖做某事。

② hog 指「豬」，也常用來形容「貪心和自私的人」。作動詞則有「霸占」的意思。

33　It doesn't matter who you are or where you live—if you have access to a computer, you are a potential target for cyber criminals. (VOA)

無論你是誰，無論你生活在哪個地方，只要你能夠使用電腦，你就會是網路犯罪分子的潛在目標。

要點解析

① have access to 使用；接近；可以利用。

② cyber 網路的，電腦的。如 cyber world 網路世界；cyber terrorism 網路恐怖主義。

③ potential target 潛在目標。

34　Not only was this pretty feasible, at least at the early look of it ... but it was the only way that humans would actually get out beyond the moon. (NPR)

不僅僅是因為這非常可行，至少在早期看上去是可行的……但這是人類探索月球之外的唯一途徑。

要點解析

① pretty 漂亮的；可愛的；相當地。其常用搭配有 pretty women 風月俏佳人。

② feasible 可行的；可能的。其常用片語有 feasible idea 可行的想法；feasible suggestion 可行的建議。

35　They will also convert several nuclear research facilities to use low enriched uranium. (BBC)

他們也會將幾個核研究設施進行改造，以便利用低濃縮鈾。

要點解析

① convert 改變……的形式或用途；使改變信仰。

② facilities 的複數形式表示「設施」，常用搭配有：sports facilities 運動設施；medical facilities 醫療設施；traffic facilities 交通設施。

36　Some of the biggest technology companies in the country—from Facebook and Google to Microsoft and Amazon—are trying to figure how to best monetize mobile advertizing. (NPR)

本國最大的幾個大型科技公司——從臉書和 Google 到微軟和亞馬遜都在努力想辦法如何從行動廣告業務中獲得最大的盈利。

① technology 技術，工藝。常用片語有 computer technology 電腦技術；science and technology 科學技術。

② monetize 使成為合法貨幣，鑄造成貨幣。在這句話裡引申為「盈利」。

③ advertizing 廣告,廣告業。常用片語有 commercial advertizing 商業廣告。

要點解析

37 Big Data is like gathering digital dust, says New Yorker tech blogger Gary Marcus. "It's a very valuable tool," he says, "but it's rarely the whole solution by itself." (NPR)

大資料就像搜集數位塵埃,《紐約客》的技術部落客蓋瑞‧馬庫斯說道。「這是一個非常有價值的工具,但它本身無法解決問題。」他說。

要點解析

① Big Data 即「大數據」,也稱為「巨量資料」,是一個熱門詞彙。指的是資料量規模巨大,無法透過目前主流軟體工具在合理時間內實現擷取、管理、處理,並整理成為幫助企業經營決策的資訊。

② digital 數字的;數位的。其常用片語有 digital signal 數位訊號;digital camera 數位相機;digital TV 數位電視。

③ dust 塵埃;灰塵。常用片語有 dust cover 防塵罩。

④ blogger 寫部落格的人。其常用片語有 enterprise blogger 企業部落客。

38 Without their research, modern communications technology including digital cameras and the internet might not exist. (BBC)

如果沒有他們的研究,包括數位相機和網路在內的現代通訊技術也許可能根本不存在。

要點解析

digital 數字的;手指的。相關的表達有:digital signal 數位訊號;digital camera 數字攝影機;digital technology 數位技術。

相關句子

The work by British scientist James Maxwell and German scientist Heinrich Hertz led to the development of modern communications technology. (VOA)

英國科學家詹姆斯‧馬克士威和德國科學家海因里希‧赫茲的非凡工作引領了現代通訊技術的突飛猛進。

39　For 18 months researchers rotated 17 trained detection dogs through three different diets: high protein, regular adult dog food, and regular adult dog food with corn oil. (Scientific American)

十八個月以來，實驗者讓 17 條訓練有素的偵查犬輪換三種不同的飲食：高脂肪狗糧、普通成年狗糧和拌有玉米油的普通成年狗糧。

要點解析

① rotate 旋轉；循環。
② detection 偵查；探測；察覺。

相關句子

The researchers say that dogs fed high fat diets are less fatigued after exercise, which reduces panting and sensitizes sniffing. (Scientific American)

研究人員稱，高脂肪食物餵養的偵緝犬在運動後不會感覺太過疲勞，這會減輕牠們的喘息，從而使嗅探更加敏感。

40　The research was funded by the Department of Justice and presented at the recent Companion Animal Nutrition Summit in Atlanta. (Scientific American)

這項研究由司法部門提供資金，並於近期在亞特蘭大舉行的寵物營養峰會上提出。

要點解析

① companion animal 的字面意思是「陪伴動物」，即我們常說的「寵物」。這個說法比 pet 更正式。
② summit 頂點，在這句話裡是「峰會」的意思。常用片語有 a summit talk 最高級會談。

41　What's unique is that we utilize a lot of data that's currently become available including traffic data, weather data. (VOA)

難得的是我們利用了很多目前可利用的資料，包括交通資料和天氣資料。

要點解析
① utilize 利用。常用搭配有 utilize solar power 利用太陽能。
② traffic data 交通資料。這個片語也可以指「流量資料」。

42　Beyond spilling drinks, severe clear-air turbulence can injure or kill passengers, and damage planes, too—it once ripped an engine off a DC-8. (Scientific American)

嚴重的晴空亂流除了會灑漏飲料，會使乘客受傷或死亡，也會損害飛機——這種氣流曾讓 DC-8 噴氣式客機的一個引擎脫落了下來。

要點解析
① clear-air 晴空的。
② turbulence 動盪；狂暴，亂流。其常用片語有 atmospheric turbulence 大氣湍流。

43　Nass says an app like Esquire's can only work well when it tightly limits what the conversation we are having is about. (NPR)

納斯表示，像 Esquire 這樣的應用程式只能在它密切限制我們談話內容的時候才能正常工作。

要點解析
① tightly 緊緊地，堅固地。常用片語有 grasp tightly 握緊。
② conversation 交談，會話。如：have a conversation with sb. 與某人談話。

44　When termites cluster together, feeding on and destroying vegetation, they leave a roughly circular bare patch that stores more water than the surrounding soil. (Scientific American)

白蟻聚集在一起時會啃食並破壞植被，牠們留下一個近乎圓形的空地用於儲存比周圍土壤更多的水。

要點解析
① vegetation 植被；植物，草木。
② circular 循環的；圓形的。常用片語有 circular tour 環線旅行。這個詞也

可以作名詞，表示「通知，傳單品」。

③ patch 在這句話裡是「一小塊地」的意思，還可以表示「斑點；補丁」。

---

45   The study also adds to the growing evidence that sensory-motor and language experiences are linked in the brain. (Scientific American)

該研究發現了進一步的證據，證明運動系統和語言感受在大腦中是有連鎖效應的。

要點解析

sensory-motor 運動系統上的，sensory 是「感覺上的；知覺的」意思。

要點解析

This is a rather sophisticated sensory-to-motor transformation and the search is on to find the place in the brain where this happens. (NPR)

從感知危險到採取行動是一個非常複雜的過程，而我們也在尋找這一過程發生在蒼蠅大腦的哪個部位。

---

46   The towers are staffed by contract air traffic controllers at smaller air-ports that's specialize in general aviation. (BBC)

控制塔上安排了專門在小型機場負責普通航空業的空中交通管制員。

要點解析

① staff 在這句話裡作動詞，意思是「為……配備職員」。

② aviation 航空，飛行，航空學。

---

47   Some reach for cigarettes, or at least the fluffy white fibers found in their filters. (Scientific American)

有人找到香菸，或者至少是篩檢過程中飄散出來的柔軟的白色煙霧。

要點解析

① reach for 有「伸手去拿」的意思。常見搭配有 reach out for 設法獲得。

② fluffy 蓬鬆的，毛茸茸的，柔軟的。常用搭配有 fluffy snow 鵝毛大雪。

48　A panel of experts appointed by the White House has warned that current plans to send astronauts back to the moon in preparation for manned missions to Mars are just not viable. (BBC)

白宮指定的專家組已經發出警告，讓太空人重返月球為人類登陸火星任務做準備的計畫目前是不可行的。

要點解析

① panel 常指「面板」，但在這句話裡是「研究小組」的意思。
② appoint 任命；指定；約定。常用片語有 appoint as 任命為。
③ in preparation for... 為……做準備。

49　He performed while floating weightless aboard the International Space Station, at times with a view of our planet out the window. (VOA)

他還表演了在失重狀態下飄浮在國際太空站裡，同時欣賞了窗外我們的地球。

要點解析

① float 飄浮。
② weightless 失重的，無重量。其常用片語有 weightless condition 失重狀態。

50　Some of the outrage was sparked by these shocking photos showing massive tumors that developed on these rats after they ate genetically modified corn over their lifetimes. (CNN)

這些令人震驚的照片顯示這些老鼠在長期食用基因改造玉米後長出了巨大的腫瘤，從而引發了眾怒。

要點解析

① outrage 作名詞可以表示「眾怒」；作動詞則有「引起眾怒」的含義。
② tumor 腫瘤。常用片語有 benign tumor 良性腫瘤；malignant tumor 惡性腫瘤。
③ lifetime 一生；壽命；終生。其常用片語有 during one's lifetime 在某人的一生中。

51   Debris fell across a sparsely populated part of Western Australia and
      the southeastern Indian Ocean. (VOA)
      殘骸墜落在人煙稀少的澳洲西部和印度洋東南部。

要點解析
   ① debris 碎片，殘骸。rock debris 岩屑；cell debris 細胞碎片。
   ② sparsely 稀疏地，貧乏地。sparsely populated 人口稀少的。

52   When they work well, they're fantastic; when they work poorly, they're
      really insulting and disturbing. (NPR)
      它們正常運行時會覺得它們很棒；但當它們運行不順利時，會覺
      得很無禮且讓人厭煩。

要點解析
   ① fantastic 在這句話裡表示「極好的；不可思議的」。這個詞還有「空想的」
      的意思，常用搭配有 fantastic idea 想入非非。
   ② disturb 打擾；妨礙；使惱怒。常用片語有 disturb sb. 打擾某人。

53   Avoiding the time and cost involved in commuting and presumably
      having a more flexible schedule and a better work-life balance are all
      potential pluses. (Scientific American)
      節省了時間和交通費用，有更靈活的工作計畫安排，以及一個更
      好的工作和生活的平衡點，這些都是潛在優勢。

要點解析
   ① involved in 涉及，包含。常用搭配有 be actively involved in 積極參與。
   ② commuting 意為「搭公車上下班，通勤」。
   ③ work-life balance 工作與生活的平衡。

54   If basic skills of math and reading are still a challenge in our primary
      schools, then it means, therefore, that the introduction of technology in
      schools through laptops may not be a viable component of our learn-
      ing circumstances now. (VOA)
      如果基本的數學和閱讀技能對我們的小學生來說仍是挑戰，那就

意味著在我們這樣的學習環境中利用筆記型電腦來引進科技是不可行的。

要點解析

① laptop 膝上型輕便電腦，筆記型電腦。「電腦包」則可以說成 laptop bag。

② component 成分；組件。如：television component 電視元件。

---

55 The imaginary spacecraft led to the name of the American space agency's first space shuttle. (VOA)

美國航太總署的第一架太空梭得名於人們對太空梭的想像。

要點解析

① spacecraft 太空船，太空飛行器。

② shuttle 太空梭；公共汽車。常用片語有：space shuttle 太空梭。而 shuttle bus 則表示「往返的班車」。

---

56 But the scientists predict advancing technology will lower prices and make their method cost-effective within a decade. (Scientific American)

不過，科學家們預測先進的科技會降低價格，他們的方法將會是未來十年內最具有成本效益的。

要點解析

① advancing technology 先進科技，其中 advancing 作形容詞，意思是「前進的；超前的」。

② cost-effective 節約成本的；划算的。

---

57 These stars are about a third the size of our sun, which is a plus for detecting planets, because an Earth-size body would block more of a smaller star's light, making it easier to spot. (Scientific American)

這些行星大小約是太陽的三分之一，這是探測行星的一個優勢；因為一個類似地球大小的行星會更多擋住小行星的光芒，使它們更容易被發現。

要點解析

① plus 正號，加號。常用搭配有 plus symbol 加號，但在這句話裡是「好處」的意思。

② block 阻止，擋住。

③ spot 作動詞有「發現」的意思。

58　The world is becoming a small village and you need to connect with the rest of the world, only if you're computer literate. (VOA)

世界變成了一個小村莊，你只需要精通電腦，就能與世界的其他地方聯繫起來。

要點解析

① connect with 連接；與......聯繫。

② the rest of 其餘的；剩下的。常用片語有 the rest of life 餘生。

③ literate 受過教育的；精通文學的。在這句話裡是「有文化的」的意思，指的是「懂得如何使用電腦的」。

59　It's based on Near Field Communication, or NFC—a way to send data wirelessly over short distances. Many Android phones already have NFC chips built in. (Scientific American)

它採用近距離無線通訊技術，即短距離內無線傳送資料的 NFC 技術。很多安卓手機已經內置了 NFC 晶片。

要點解析

① wirelessly 無線的；另外還特指「用電磁波傳導的」。常用片語有 wirelessly transferring 無線傳輸。

② Android phone 安卓手機。

相關句子

At present only a handful of phones support NFC, including Google's Android-based Nexus S, which is produced by Samsung. (Scientific American)

目前只有少數手機支援 NFC 技術，其中包括三星生產 Google 安卓系統的手機 Nexus S。

143

60   During their six-week voyage, researchers will employ a range of techniques to unlock some of the secrets of the giant marine mammals. (VOA)

在為期六個星期的航程中，研究人員將採用一系列技術來揭開一些巨型海洋哺乳動物的祕密。

要點解析

① voyage 航行；航海；航太。在口語中常用 bon voyage 表示「一路順風」。
② giant 巨大的，巨人。常用片語有 giant star 巨星。

61   The mission was needed to advance human knowledge and experience. (BBC)

這項任務將擴展人類知識和經驗。

要點解析

① mission 任務；使命。相關表達有：space mission 太空任務；rescue mission 營救任務；mission impossible 不可能的任務。
② advance 在這句話裡作動詞，表示「促進」的意思。

62   If you're tech savvy, you can even watch it on your TV. (NPR)
如果你是一個技術達人，你甚至可以在電視上觀看。

要點解析

savvy 表示「理解；悟性；理解能力」，也可以指「內行的人」，也就是我們常說的「達人」。

63   The project will depend on citizen scientists providing information about all of the world's power plants. (VOA)
該項目將依靠公民科學家來提供關於全世界所有發電廠的資訊。

要點解析

① citizen 公民。相關搭配有：senior citizen 老年人；corporate citizen 企業公民；fellow citizen 各位公民。
② plant 作名詞使用有「植物；設備；工廠」的意思。

64   An unmanned space cargo capsule carrying food, scientific equipment
      and spare parts has arrived at the international space station. (BBC)
      一艘載有食物、科研設備和零配件的無人太空運輸艙已抵達國
      際太空站。

要點解析

① space cargo capsule 太空運輸艙。其中 cargo 的意思是「貨物，負荷」；
capsule 的原意為「膠囊」，在這句話裡表示「航太艙」。
② space station 太空站。

65   In humans, when we're awake, our brain accounts for 20% of the ener-
      gy we use when just sitting around. (BBC)
      對於人類而言，當我們清醒時即便只是無所事事，大腦也會消耗
      20% 的能量。

要點解析

① account for... （資料、比例上）占......；對......負責。
② sit around 閒坐著。這個片語也有「無所事事」的意思。

66   Mission control said the incident was a mystery but still asked the as-
      tronauts to replace the 117-kilogram pump control box. (BBC)
      指揮中心稱這起事故非常神祕，但仍要求太空人換掉重達 117 公
      斤的泵控制箱。

要點解析

① incident 事件；事故；騷亂。
② astronaut 太空人。

相關句子

At 9 o'clock this morning, Mission Control in Houston lost contact with our
space shuttle Columbia. (CNN)
今天早上九點鐘，休士頓的航太地面指揮中心與我們的哥倫比亞號飛船
失去了聯絡。

67　Most people watch seven or eight channels, even though they have 500 channels, and a third of the households effectively just watched network television. (NPR)

即使有五百個電影頻道，大多數人也只會看其中的七八個，而且大約三分之一的家庭只看網路電視。

要點解析

household 家庭；全家人；家屬。

68　Last week, senators debated whether states could require food labeling for products with genetically engineered ingredients. (CNN)

上週，參議員就各州是否應該要求基因改造食品貼上標籤展開了辯論。

要點解析

① senator 參議員。相關搭配有：senior senator 資深參議員；life senator 終生參議員。

② genetically engineered 基因改造的。

69　French scientists believe they have come a step closer to understanding how the Vikings were able to navigate across the sea well before the invention of the magnetic compass. (BBC)

法國科學家確信他們進一步了解了維京人如何在磁羅盤發明之前順利橫渡大洋。

要點解析

① navigate 駕駛；航行；使通過。

② magnetic compass 磁羅盤。其中 magnetic 的意思是「有磁性的，有吸引力的」；compass 的意思是「羅盤；指南針」。

相關句子

The Vikings were skilled navigators and travelled thousand of kilometres between Northern Europe and North America. (BBC)

維京人是技藝高強的航海家，他們能在北歐和北美之間航行數千公里。

70   That requires solving difficult problems, like protecting astronauts from the radiation in deep space. (NPR)

這需要解決一些難題，比如讓太空人免受來自太空深處的輻射影響。

要點解析

protect... from... 防止……於。類似意思的表達還有 prevent sth. from 和 stop sth. from。

相關句子

Studies on biological effects of radiation can provide theoretical guide for astronaut health support. (CNN)

研究輻射生物學效應可以為保障太空人的生命健康提供理論指導。

---

71   Circadian rhythms may influence the timing of cell division, which could inform the timing of some therapies. (VOA)

畫夜節律可能會影響細胞分裂的時間，從而常推一些療法發揮的時機。

要點解析

① circadian rhythm 畫夜節律，生命活動以 24 小時左右為週期的變動。

② therapy 治療，療法。如：gene therapy 基因治療；radiation therapy 放射治療；drug therapy 藥物治療。

---

72   A spokesperson for the French company Areva said a team was going to assess the damage of the uranium sites of Arlit, but production has stopped for now. (BBC)

法國阿海琺公司的發言人表示，公司將派出一支隊伍對阿爾利特鈾礦的損失進行評估，但是目前已經停止生產。

要點解析

① spokesperson 發言人，代言人。

② uranium 鈾。uranium site 是指「鈾礦」，site 在這句話裡有「工地」的意思。

要點解析

According to government and local sources, the crushing and grinding units were particularly hit as a result of the accident. (BBC)
根據政府和當地人的說法，這些破碎的殘骸正是此次事故造成的後果。

73　The astronauts spent their workdays conducting experiments, including biomedical research, in microgravity. (VOA)
在微重力環境下太空人們把工作時間都投入在實驗上，包括生物醫學實驗。

要點解析

① biomedical 生物醫學的。其中詞根 bio 相當於 life，意思是「生命」。常見的單字還有 biochemistry 生物化學；biosphere 生物圈。
② microgravity 微重力。其中，micro 這個詞根表示「微，小」，如 microwave 微波；microworld 微觀世界；microscope 顯微鏡；microfilm 微縮膠片。

74　It turns out that early depictions of four-legged animals walking are more accurate in some ways than modern ones—even those crafted by the Renaissance master. (Scientific American)
實際上早期對四腳行走動物的描繪比現代更加準確，即便是文藝復興時期大師的精心創作也無法與之相比。

要點解析

① depiction 描寫；描繪。
② craft 手工製作；精心製作。
③ Renaissance 文藝復興。13 世紀末在義大利興起，後擴展到歐洲各國，於 16 世紀在歐洲盛行的一場思想文化運動。

75　NASA will use telescopes on Earth to track down a small asteroid passing by. (NPR)
美國國家航空暨太空總署將在地球上使用望遠鏡追蹤一顆與我們擦肩而過的小行星。

要點解析

① NASA 的全名為 National Aeronautics and Space Administration 美國國家航空暨太空總署，是美國負責太空計畫的政府機構。

② track down 追捕到；追查出；追尋。

相關句子

President Barack Obama wants astronauts headed to an asteroid and then Mars in the coming decades. (NPR)

歐巴馬總統希望太空人能夠在未來幾十年內前往小行星和火星進行控索。

76　The physicists think their research may also apply to other extreme situations, which could help us understand collective human movement in panics and riots. (VOA)

物理學家認為他們的研究也許還可以應用於其他極端情況，幫助我們理解在恐慌和騷亂中人類的集體行為。

要點解析

① collective 集體的，共同的。相關表達有：collective economy 集體經濟；collective ownership 集體所有制。

② panic 可以作名詞、動詞和形容詞使用，表示「恐慌」。

③ riot 騷亂，暴動。

77　The ClearPath app claims to do what other navigation systems cannot. (VOA)

這款「清路者」應用軟體宣稱具有其他導航系統沒有的功能。

要點解析

① app 即單字 application 的縮寫，在這句話裡的意思是「應用軟體，應用程式」。

② navigation 航行；導航。

相關句子

The navigation system leads the driver through unfamiliar territory in a natural, real and easy way. (NPR)

該導航系統將以一種自然、真實、簡便的方式引導司機在不熟悉的地段行駛。

---

78   It's been called a landmark moment in medical research. (NPR)
      這在醫療研究領域被稱為具有里程碑意義的時刻。

要點解析

landmark 里程碑；紀念碑；界標。

相關句子

The research was funded by the Stanley Medical Research Institute, nonprofit in Chevy Chase, Md. (BBC)
這項研究是由馬里蘭州切維蔡斯市的一個非營利研究所——史丹利醫研究所贊助的。

---

79   Command module pilot Michael Collins said the future of space exploration should be directed at getting to Mars. (BBC)
      指揮艙駕駛員麥可·柯林斯認為太空探索的未來趨勢應該是登陸火星。

要點解析

① exploration 是 explore 的名詞形式，意思是「探測，探索」。
② direct 在這句話裡作動詞，表示「指向」。片語 direct at... 就是「指向……；針對……」的意思。

---

80   That's according to a study published in the Personality and Social Psychology Bulletin. (NPR)
      這一說法是參照發表在《人格與社會心理學公報》上的一項研究得出的。

要點解析

① psychology 心理學；心理。
② bulletin 公告，公報。在新聞專業中還有「新聞快報；小報」的意思，如 news bulletin 新聞簡報。

相關句子

Research published in the Personality and Social Psychology Bulletin shows that eating with your non-dominant hand can help you to decrease the amount of food you consume, CNN reported. (CNN)

CNN 報導，發表在《人格與社會心理學公報》上的一項研究顯示，用不常用的那隻手進食有助於減少食物的攝取。

81　To summarize the tension around Big Data, New York Times reporter Steve Lohr quotes Albert Einstein:「Not everything that counts can be counted, and not everything that can be counted counts.」 (NPR)

為了總結海量資料所面臨的壓力，《紐約時報》的記者史蒂芬‧羅爾援引了愛因斯坦的名言：「不是所有有價值的都能被計算，也不是所有能計算的都有價值。」

要點解析

① tension 緊張不安；張力，拉力。

② 愛因斯坦的這句名言巧妙地運用了單字 count 的兩個不同的意思，一個是「計數，清點」，另一個是「有價值，有重要性」。如 count for much 關係重大，很有價值。此外，count 還有「依賴，指望」的意思，常用片語為 count on sb./ sth. 依賴某人／某事。

82　Canadian astronaut Chris Hadfield, who recently wrapped up nearly five months on the space station, has clearly adjusted to life away from Earth. (VOA)

剛剛順利結束在太空站裡近五個月生活的加拿大太空人克里斯‧哈德菲爾德表示，他已經完全適應了離開地球的生活。

要點解析

wrap up 有「包裹」的意思，但是在這句話裡表示「圓滿完成」。

83　Telecommuting for a portion of the workweek certain has its appeal. (Scientific American)

在一週的工作日裡進行部分時間的遠端辦公的確有一定的吸引力。

要點解析

① telecommuting 遠程辦公。將這個單字分解開來，commute 的意思是「通勤」，詞根 tele 表示「遠」。使用該詞根的單字有 telegraph 電報，telescope 望遠鏡，telemeter 測距儀。

② workweek 一週的工作。

相關句子

Most bosses who are hesitant to expand their telecommuting policies are afraid of giving employees too much room to mess up. (CNN)
大多數老闆不願擴大遠端辦公政策，他們擔心員工會浪費太多的自由時間。

84　Google's argument is that if you connect American homes to the Internet at these gigabit speeds, all kinds of Internet services and business that right now are basically impossible become possible. (BBC)
Google 的觀點是，如果美國家庭的連網速度提升至千兆級別，那麼目前基本無法實現的各種網路服務和商業行為都將變為可能。

要點解析

gigabit 千兆比特。Gb，千兆，用來形容網路速度。

相關句子

This is part of the "Gigabit Isles" programme that Jersey Telecom hope will bring "the world's fastest internet access to islanders". (BBC)
這是「千兆島」計畫的一部分，傑西通訊公司希望透過該專案為島民提供世界上速度最快的網路。

85　One research found that people like computers better if those computers flatter them. (NPR)
一項研究發現，如果電腦能迎合使用者的需求，他們會更加喜歡這部電腦。

要點解析

flatter 奉承，使滿意，使高興；flatter oneself 自鳴得意。

86　Scientists at the world's largest particle accelerator have successfully collided beams of protons at the highest energy levels ever seen. (BBC)

科學家已經用世界上最大的粒子加速器成功對撞出有史以來世界上能量等級最高的質子束。

要點解析

① particle 微粒，顆粒；質點；極小量。
② accelerate 是動詞，意思是「加快，增速，促進」。accelerator 是它的名詞，意思是「加速器」。
③ proton 質子，是物理專用名詞。

相關句子

Last week, the machine circulated two beams of protons for the first time and carried out its first low-energy beam collisions. (BBC)

上週，該機器首次傳輸了兩個質子束並且進行了第一次低能量束碰撞。

87　The researchers found that subjects increased their grip when listening to action words that involved hands or arms, such as scratch, throw or lift. (Scientific American)

研究人員發現，當受試者聽到與手或手臂相關的動詞如「劃」、「扔」、「舉」時，他們的握力會增加。

要點解析

① grip 在這句話裡作名詞，意思是「握力；緊握」。此外 grip 還有「掌握；勝任」的意思，如片語 take a grip of。
② scratch 刮，擦傷，抓破。scratch paper 有「便條紙」的意思。

88　What we learned was that simple exercise takes care of the problem, and there's no reason why a person can't stay in a weightless environment for a long, long time. (VOA)

我們發現，簡單的運動可以解決這個問題，但我們還不知道為什麼人們不能長時間待在失重環境。

要點解析

① take care of 在這句話裡的意思並非「照顧」，而是「解決」，相當於 solve。

② weightless 沒有重量的，失重的。

89　These are individual surveys in which people are contacted either by phone or in person. (VOA)

這些個人調查是透過電話或是面談約見的。

要點解析

① survey 調查；勘測。通常指「有資訊回饋的調查」，類似的詞有：questionaire 問卷調查。

② in person 親自；獨自；本人。

90　Contending that genes can be patented are the biotech and pharmaceutical industries, which see patents as the keys to new scientific exploration. (NPR)

生物科學機製藥行業主張可以為基因申請專利。他們將專利視作開啟新科技探索的鑰匙。

要點解析

① contend 爭奪；奮鬥；聲稱。contend...with... 與......鬥爭；對付。

② patent 獲得......專利，取得專利權。相關搭配：national patent 國家專利；patent law 專利法；patent office 專利局。

③ pharmaceutical 製藥的，配藥的。

91　I think we're still impressed with the amount of work that was accomplished and the foresight of the investigators in planning the experiments. (VOA)

我認為已經完成的工作量對規劃實驗的遠見性仍然讓我們感到印象深刻。

要點解析

foresight 名詞，意思是「先見；深謀遠慮」。

92   The world's biggest radio telescope has been inaugurated in Chile on a
      mountain high above the Atacama Desert. (BBC)
      世界上最大的電波望遠鏡已在智利阿他加馬沙漠的一座高山上
      投入使用。

要點解析

inaugurate 開創；創始；舉行開幕典禮或就職典禮。其名詞形式為 inau-
guration，如 the President's inauguration 總統就職典禮。

93   Finally almost half a million people have voted to name one of Pluto's
      newly discovered moons Vulcan in a tribute to the classic sci-fiseries
      Star Trek. (BBC)
      最後，將近五十萬人贊成將一個新發現的衛星命名為「火神」，
      以表達對經典科幻系列小說《星艦迷航記》的敬意。

要點解析

① name 在這句話裡作動詞，意思是「命名」。
② in a tribute to... 向……表示敬意。
③ Star Trek 星艦迷航記。科幻娛樂史上最受歡迎的作品，由金‧羅登貝瑞
   於 1960 年代初期到中期製作完成。

94   The California Science Center in LA, only a few miles from the side
      of the old rocket plant, where the shuttle was developed and from
      where its construction was managed, will be the new home of the shut-
      tle on the launch period preparing its final mission in Denver. (CNN)
      洛杉磯加利福尼亞科學中心距離舊火箭廠只有幾英里遠，該中
      心主要負責飛機研發和建設管理，它也將是太空梭在丹佛發射之
      前做最後準備工作的新基地。

要點解析

① shuttle 太空梭；短程穿梭運行的飛機或火車、汽車。相關表達有：space
   shuttle 太空梭；shuttle service 短程運輸。
② mission 代表團；使命。

95   It's a lot quieter than the standard demolition which keeps the neigh-
      bors happy, and no chance of explosion damaging other buildings.
      (CNN)
      它比普通拆遷的雜訊小，這使周圍的居民非常滿意，同時也不會
      產生爆炸對其他建築物造成損壞。

要點解析

demolition 是動詞 demolish 的名詞形式，意思是「毀壞；拆毀」。

相關句子

But some experts say the demolition of damaged heritage buildings has been
too aggressive. (BBC)
但是有一些專家認為對受損遺址建築的拆除行為有些太過激進。

96   Google Fiber is the tech giant's blazing fast Internet service, with
      current rates at 1 Gpbs, about 100 times faster than your typical cable
      broadband Internet service. (NPR)
      Google 光纖是科技龍頭 Google 公司推出的超高速寬頻服務
      專案，其目前的速度為 1Gpbs，比標準有線寬頻網路服務快
      上一百倍。

要點解析

① blazing 酷熱的；極其憤怒的；感情強烈的。在這句話裡 blazing 作副詞
   修飾 fast，意為「非常」，相當於 extremely。
② broadband 寬頻。

97   The theory goes that a giant asteroid crashed into the earth, wiping out
      half of all life on earth. (BBC)
      這一理論認為，有一顆巨型小行星撞上了地球，導致地球上一半
      的生物滅絕。

要點解析

① crash into 撞上，墜毀。當 crash 作名詞時，意為「撞擊」，如 car crash
   車禍，air crash 飛機墜毀。

② wipe out 擦淨，擦掉；澈底摧毀。

---

98   Some rights groups consider the scanners an invasion of privacy, be-
      cause they show private physical characteristics in detail. (BBC)
      一些人權組織認為掃描器侵犯了個人隱私，因為他們會將人們的
      身體特徵詳細地展示出來。

要點解析

① invasion 入侵，侵犯；它的動詞形式為 invade，入侵者是 invader。
② in detail 詳細地。

---

99   As they described in the Journal Science, astronauts in NASA's Aims
      research center found two planets, some one larger than earth orbiting
      a star called, Kepler 62, a star somewhat dimmer than our sun. (NPR)
      正如他們在《科學》雜誌上描述的那樣，美國國家航空暨太空總
      署艾姆斯研究中心的太空人們發現了兩顆行星，它們比地球體積
      稍大，圍繞著一顆行星運行，被命名為「克卜勒 62 號」，比太陽
      稍暗一點。

要點解析

① journal 日報；日誌；期刊。
② dim 黯淡的，昏暗的，看不清的，不顯著的。

相關句子

Astronomers estimate the newly-found planet is about 45 times more massive
than Earth, and has a year lasting 260 Earth days. (BBC)
天文學家推測最新發現的這顆行星質量比地球重 45 倍，並且它一年有
260 天。

---

100   Shuttle weather officer Kathy Winters said the skies should be clear
      for the evening launch, but storms could delay the delicate process of
      filling the shuttle's external fuel tanks. (VOA)
      航太飛船氣象官凱西·溫斯特表示，夜晚進行飛船發射能見度較
      高，但受風暴影響，向飛船的外側燃料箱注入燃料的精密程序

將被延後。

要點解析

① delicate 熟練的；易損的；微妙的。

② fuel tank 汽油箱。其中 tank 是「坦克」音譯的原詞，也有「油箱;蓄水池」的意思，還可以用於形容「酒量大的人」。

101　Microbes, plants, insects, mammals—we all experience circadian rhythms, due to molecular clocks in our cells. (Scientific American)
由於我們細胞中分子鐘的存在，無論是微生物、植物、昆蟲還是哺乳動物都會受晝夜節律的影響。

要點解析

① experience 原指「體驗」，在這句話裡表示「經歷......的影響」。

② circadian rhythm 晝夜節律。指生物體中由生理時鐘所控制的生理活動以 24 小時為單位循環。

③ due to 由於。也可以被 as a result of 或 owing to 替換。

相關句子

There's no exact formula for determining how much light is needed to reset a person's internal clock. (CNN)
沒有精確的準則能確定重設一個人的生理時鐘需要多少光線。

102　The camera-based ball-tracking system has been successfully deployed in other sports including tennis and cricket. (VOA)
這套基於攝影機的球類軌跡追蹤系統已被成功運用在包括網球和板球等其他運動中。

要點解析

① camera-based 基於攝影機的。其中 -based 這個尾碼表示「基於......的」，如：export-based 基於出口的。此外，它還可以表示「總部在......的」，如：a London-based company 總部在倫敦的公司。

② track 作名詞表示「軌跡」，作動詞則是「追蹤」的意思。

③ deploy in 部署在。這裡指「運用在......中」。

103   The long-awaited take-off of the Solar Impulse was greeted with delight by those who have spent the last seven years working on it. (BBC)

那些在過去七年中研製陽光動力號飛機的人們滿懷著喜悅，迎接期待已久的起飛。

要點解析

① long-awaited 期待已久的。
② greet with... 以……迎接。greet 有「問候，歡迎」的意思。

相關句子

The Solar Impulse doesn't use a single drop of aviation fuel, instead its giant wings are covered with solar cells. (BBC)

陽光動力號完全不消耗航空燃油，而是利用巨大機翼上覆蓋的太陽能電池提供動力。

104   The flies' intestinal stem cells got busy repairing the gut, most of them dividing in sync around dawn. (Scientific American)

蒼蠅的腸道幹細胞忙於修復內臟，大部分細胞在黎明時分同時進行分裂。

要點解析

① intestinal 腸的。
② stem cell 指「幹細胞」，在生物領域有關細胞分裂的話題中經常出現。
③ gut 內臟；腸子。其複數形式 guts 在口語中可以表示「膽量」，如：I have no guts to do that. 我沒勇氣這樣做。
④ in sync 同步地。sync 也可以作動詞表示「同步」，是 synchronize 的簡寫形式。

相關句子

But when researchers blocked the action of two clock genes in the intestine, the flies couldn't patch up the damage. (Scientific American)

但當研究人員干擾了腸內兩種生理時鐘基因的功能之後，蒼蠅便無法修復損傷。

105　A voice—even a synthetic one—is packed with information our brains are programmed to decode. (NPR)

聲音中包含大量的資訊，即使是人工合成的聲音也不例外，而我們的大腦被設定為能夠解碼這些資訊。

要點解析

① synthetic 綜合的；合成的。

② pack with 意為「擠滿」，在這句話裡指「大量含有」。

③ be programmed to do sth. 被設定去做某事。program 意為「設定……的程序」，在這句話裡是比喻的用法。

相關句子

When we talk to a computer and it answers back, most of us end up acting as if we're dealing with a real person. (NPR)

當我們與一台電腦進行交談時，多數人最終會覺得在與一個真人相處。

106　The scientists think the nucleus accumbens, which helps se expectations, draws on stored musical knowledge to predic how a new tune will play out. (Scientific American)

科學家認為，伏隔核有助於設定期望值，利用儲存的音樂知識預測如何演繹一支新曲。

要點解析

① draw on 利用；吸收。通常用於表示利用資訊或引用文獻，如：draw on the data from the experiment 從實驗中引用資料。

② predict 預測。

③ play out 演完。這個片語也有「將……進行到底」的意思，如：We have to play it out today. 我們今天必須要做完。

107　They say doctors might want to time surgeries or chemotherapy for when the body is primed to heal, helping patients clock a faster recovery. (Scientific American)

他們稱，醫生可能希望在身體做好治療準備時安排手術或化療，這樣能幫助患者快速康復。

要點解析

① time 為……安排時間。time 作動詞可以表示「為……安排時間；測量……的時間」。

② chemotherapy 化學療法。

③ be primed to 準備。prime 意為「使準備好」；作形容詞還可以表示「主要的，最好的」。

108　The human brain is built for speech, so anything that sounds like a voice, our brains just light up and we get an enormous range of social and other responses. (NPR)

人類大腦是為言語構建的，任何聽起來像聲音的事物都會讓大腦為之一振，使我們得到大量社交和其他方面的回應。

要點解析

① light up 照亮，點亮。這裡指呈現出興奮的情緒。

② social 在這句話裡指「社交的」。

Part 4

Culture & Arts

1   In the popular video, Hadfield plays David Bowie's rock classic Space
     Oddity on his acoustic guitar and sings the lyrics about a space travel-
     er. (VOA)
     在這個流行的影片中，哈德菲爾德用他的原聲吉他演奏了大衛‧
     鮑伊的經典搖滾歌曲《太空星塵》，並且演唱了關於一位太空遊
     客的歌詞。

要點解析

① rock classic 經典搖滾。
② acoustic 作形容詞，意思是「聲學的；聽覺的」。acoustic guitar 則是指「原
  聲吉他，木吉他」。
③ lyrics 歌詞。

2   The Potato Famine in Ireland killed a million people and led to mass
     emigration. (Scientific American)
     愛爾蘭馬鈴薯大飢荒造成 100 萬人死亡，並導致了大規模移民。

要點解析

① famine 指「飢荒；飢餓」。Potato Famine 指「愛爾蘭馬鈴薯大飢荒」，
  也叫 Great Famine。
② lead 表示「領導；導致」。如：lead an independent life 過著獨立的生活。
  lead 常與 to 搭配，lead to 表示「導致；通向」。
③ emigration 移民。如：Increase in population made emigration necessary.
  人口的增加使向外移民成為必要。在這句話裡的 mass 指「大規
  模的，集中的」，mass emigration 指「大規模的移民」。

3   Among them was American Jody Williams, who won the 1997 Nobel
     Peace Prize for her role in the campaign to ban landmines. (VOA)
     其中有美國的喬迪‧威廉斯，由於在禁雷運動中的傑出表現，她
     贏得了 1997 年度的諾貝爾和平獎。

要點解析

① campaign 運動；戰役；季節性競賽。campaign for... 為......助選；cam-
  paign against... 開展反對......的運動；election campaign 競選活動。

② landmine 地雷。

相關句子

He formulated the Theory of Relativity and won the Nobel Prize for Physics in 1921. (CNN)

他對相對論進行了闡釋，並且贏得了 1921 年的諾貝爾物理學獎。

4　Stars of the screen paraded up a rain-soaked red carpet as they arrived for the first event. (BBC)

影視明星紛紛走上被雨水打溼的紅地毯，參加他們到達後的第一場活動。

要點解析

① parade 遊行，列隊前進，展示，炫耀。

② rain-soaked 被雨水浸泡的。由名詞加動詞的過去分片語成的合成詞還有：man-made 人造的；poverty-stricken 貧困的；snow-covered 被雪覆蓋的。

相關句子

The 66th Cannes Film Festival has opened with the star-studded ceremony on the French Riviera. (BBC)

眾星雲集的第六十六屆坎城影展在法國里維埃拉開幕。

5　Local governments and businesses are still trying to figure out how the technology could transform sectors like education, health care and the arts. (NPR)

當地政府和企業仍在試圖弄清科技如何改變教育、衛生保健和藝術等領域。

要點解析

① figure out 是一個固定片語，意思是「解決，弄明白」。

② transform 改變。如：The event transformed the political landscape. 這一事件改變了政治形勢。

③ sector 表示「部門」，在這句話裡可理解為「領域」。

6　The first would be elementary schools, where all children could learn reading, writing, arithmetic and geography. (VOA)

首先是小學，在那裡孩子們可以學習閱讀、寫作、算數和地理。

要點解析

① elementary 表示「基本的，初級的」。elementary school 指美國的「小學」。而在英國，「小學」多用 primary school 來表示。

② arithmetic 算數，如：mental arithmetic 表示「心算」。

7　They hope to win permission for at least a temporary park when Burma hosts the Southeast Asian Games. (VOA)

當緬甸舉辦東亞運動會時，他們希望獲得至少建立一個臨時公園許可。

要點解析

① permission 是動詞 permit 的名詞形式，表示「允許，許可」。如：I pray your permission to speak. 我懇求您准許我發言。win permission 則表示「獲得許可」。

② temporary 臨時的，暫時的，如：a temporary chairman 臨時主席。

8　The painting fetch the most money ever paid for a work by a living artist at auction. (NPR)

這幅油畫取得了在世藝術家作品拍賣的最高收益。

要點解析

① fetch 是動詞，表示「取物；賣得」，這裡是「賣得」的意思。

② auction 是一個名詞，意思是「拍賣」。at auction 指「在拍賣會上」。

③ living artist 是指「在世藝術家」。

9　One of Britain's most popular reality TV programs has returned to our screens for a fifth series.(BBC)

英國最受歡迎的電視真人秀節目第五季已在本台回歸。

要點解析

① reality TV 指「電視真人秀」。

② screen 螢幕。如：They want to make a screen version of the novel. 他們想把那部小說改編成劇本。

③ series 指「系列，連續」。如：TV series 表示「電視連續劇」。

④ return 表示「回歸」。國外許多電視節目都是按季播出的，如果收視情況不好就會被停播，只有情況好的節目才能再度播出。

---

10 Wherever you can find a plug, because that's where your computer and entertainment system goes. (CNN)

無論在哪裡都要找到一個電源插頭，因為電腦和娛樂設備需要充電。

要點解析

① plug 作名詞，表示「插頭」。如：He put the electric plug into the socket. 他把電插頭插入插座。此外，plug 作動詞表示「塞住；插入」。

② entertainment 娛樂。如：It's not just mindless entertainment. 這並不是毋須動腦的娛樂。此外，還有「消遣；款待」的意思。

---

11 Some of the world's biggest hit records from the 1960s onward came from a recording studio in a little town in northern Alabama called Muscle Shoals. (VOA)

自 1960 年代以來，世界上最熱賣的一些唱片都出自阿拉巴馬北部一個叫做馬斯爾肖爾斯小鎮上的一個錄音工作室。

要點解析

① hit 作名詞，表示「成功」。如：hit the big time 表示「獲得成功，轟動一時」。

② onward 向前的，往前的。如：the period from 1969 onward 就是「1969 年以後的那段時間」。

---

12 So we must have the courage to knock them down and return the building to the simplicity and linearity of its origins. (VOA)

所以我們必須鼓起勇氣將它們全部拆除，還原建築物本來的簡潔和線條。

要點解析

① knock down 擊倒，撞到。與 knock 有關的片語還有：knock at 敲（門）；knock on 中斷。

② simplicity 樸素，簡單；如：for simplicity 簡單起見。

③ linearity 線性，直線性。

④ origin 表示「起源；原點」，如：country of origin「原產地，原產國」。

13　The Speed Ring Skate Club, comprise of 20 young Burmese with a passion for skateboarding in a country where skateboards are rare. (VOA)

速度環滑俱樂部是由 20 名對滑板充滿熱情的緬甸年輕人組成的，而滑板在那個國家很少見。

要點解析

① Burmese 緬甸的，緬甸人的；「緬甸」是 Burma。

② comprise of... 是一個片語，表示「由……構成」，相當於 include。

③ a passion for... 表示「對……的酷愛」。

14　A local archeologist called the pyramid's destruction an incredible display of ignorance. (CNN)

一位當地的考古學家稱破壞金字塔是一種令人難以置信的無知行為。

要點解析

① archeologist 考古學家。

② pyramid 金字塔。常用片語有 pyramid selling 金字塔式銷售。

③ destruction 破壞。

15　The tradition goes back to nearly 150 years started out with a way to pay tribute to troops who died during the Civil War. (CNN)

這個傳統可以追溯到近 150 年前，這是一種悼念內戰期間犧牲士兵的方法。

要點解析

① start out 出發；著手進行。

② pay tribute to 稱讚，歌頌。常用搭配有 pay warm tribute to 熱烈讚揚。

16　Not far away, Martin Luther King is remembered in a memorial whose centerpiece is a nine-meter white statue. (VOA)

不遠處是馬丁路德金的紀念雕像，它的主體是一個高達九公尺的白色雕像。

要點解析

① memorial 紀念碑；紀念儀式。相關表達有：memorial hall 紀念堂；memorial day 紀念日。

② centerpiece 核心部分。這個詞也可以表示「餐桌中心放的裝飾品」。

17　The care and affection he putting to them inspires us to one of these leave a legacy to our community, our children and our craft. (CNN)

他對它們的呵護和情感激勵，我們把其中一個作為遺產留給我們的社區、我們的孩子和我們的工藝。

要點解析

① affection 喜愛，感情。常用搭配有：business affection 商情；environment affection 環境影響。

② legacy 遺產，遺贈。

18　The company says Austin, famous for its South by Southwest festival, is a "Mecca for creativity and entrepreneurialism, with thriving artistic and tech communities". (NPR)

該公司稱，因南部西南藝術節而聞名的奧斯汀市，其蓬勃發展的藝術和科技社區被譽為創造力和企業家精神的「朝聖之地」。

要點解析

① festival 節日，慶祝，紀念活動。在這句話裡指音樂節這類的活動，類似的活動還有 gourmet festival 美食節。

② Mecca 麥加。沙烏地阿拉伯的一個城市，是一個朝聖聖地，可以引申為

「眾人都渴望去的地方」的意思。

③ entrepreneurialism 企業家精神，常用片語有 urban entrepreneurialism 都市企業主義。

④ artistic 藝術的，風雅的。常用片語有 artistic conception 意境。

19　The church is like certain old buildings that over the centuries adapt to current needs and become filled with partitions, staircases, rooms and closets. (VOA)

這座教堂就像幾個世紀前的那種老建築，有許多迎合當代需求的分區、樓梯、房間和衣櫃。

要點解析

① adapt to... 使自己適應於……。

② fill with 裝滿，充滿。常用片語有 fill sb. with desire 使某人充滿渴望。

20　The city pays for stamps and paper—promoting its identity as the hometown of Romeo and Juliet is not a bad thing for tourism. (NPR)

這個城市負擔了郵票和紙張的費用——將其宣傳為羅密歐和茱麗葉之鄉對旅遊業來說並非壞事。

要點解析

① pay for 賠償；為……付出代價。常用片語有 pay compensation for 支付賠償金。

② promote 促進；提升；推銷；發揚。常用片語有 promote sales 推銷商品。

21　Documentaries often get funding from non-profit groups and investors who care about the topic. (VOA)

紀錄片通常從非盈利組織和熱衷於該主題的投資人那裡獲得資金。

要點解析

① documentary 紀錄片；記錄的；記實的。documentary fiction 紀實小說；documentary movie 紀錄片。

② funding 提供資金。

相關句子

In the modern era, "Sports International" has focused on mini-series, one off documentaries and in-depth interviews. (BBC)

在現代社會,「國際體育」將重點放在短篇、 一次性播出的紀錄片和深度訪談上。

---

22 The route was crammed with spectators, hollering as their friends and family raced past. (VOA)

這條道路上擠滿了觀眾,他們在朋友或家人賽跑經過這裡時歡呼雀躍。

要點解析

① be crammed with 塞滿,填滿,「考試前突擊」 就可以說 cram for an exam。

② holler 發牢騷;叫喊;抱怨。

---

23 From the walkway that overlooks the head spring, the water is still blue and crystal clear, with fish, turtles and alligators clearly visible. (NPR)

從噴泉的上方的走道俯瞰,噴泉裡的水仍舊湛藍、清澈,魚兒、烏龜和鱷魚清晰可見。

要點解析

① crystal clear 明澈的,清楚易懂的。其中,crystal 作名詞表示「水晶」,作形容詞可以表示「水晶的,透明的」。

② turtle 甲魚;海龜。

③ alligator 鱷魚般的;鱷魚皮革的;短吻鱷。常用片語有 alligator sinensis 揚子鱷,中華短吻鱷。

---

24 Listening to her ethereal sound, you might not guess that Rachel Zeffira was classically trained as an opera singer. (NPR)

聽著她空靈的聲音,你可能不會想到蕾切爾·澤夫拉是一個科班出身的歌劇演唱者。

要點解析

① ethereal 輕巧的；超凡的；蒼天的。在形容歌聲時，有「空靈的」的含義。
② be trained as... 被訓練為......。

25　When the music fulfills or even exceeds these expectations, the listener feels rewarded. (Scientific American)
當音樂達到甚至超出聽眾的期望時，他們會覺得自己得到了回報。

要點解析

fulfill 滿足期望，願望。此外，fulfill 還有「履行；執行」的意思，常與 task, plan, purpose, promise 搭配使用。

相關句子

And I always had as much pleasure writing as playing because the thrill of hearing your music played back to you is almost indescribable. (NPR)
作曲對我來說與演奏一樣有趣，因為當你聽到你所創作的音樂被演奏出來時的那種激動的心情是難以形容的。

26　From classic novels to modern films, we'll talk about the unique delights of people who can't really be trusted to tell their own stories. (NPR)
從古典小說到現代電影，我們將談論那些在講述自己故事時不被相信的人們的獨特樂趣。

要點解析

① modern 近代的；時髦的；現代人。常用搭配有 modern art 現代藝術。
② delight 高興。常用片語有 delight in... 因......感到快樂。

27　How would you want to spend it, more academic, the focus on music and drama programs, getting internship or apprenticeship credit? (CNN)
你會如何分配時間？是從事更多的學術研究，專注音樂和戲劇節目，實習還是累積學徒學分？

要點解析
① internship 實習期。常用片語有 internship program 實習項目。
② apprenticeship 學徒期；學徒身分。
③ credit 可以表示「學分」。

---

28 They actually have a very holistic approach to teaching—ethics, morals, very, very important, music and the arts. (CNN)
他們實際上有一種全面的教學方法——倫理、道德，以及非常非
常重要的，音樂和藝術。

要點解析
① holistic 整體的；全面的。常用片語有 holistic marketing 全面行銷。
② approach to 接近；約等於；通往......的方法。

---

29 We've having a sushi and like matsuri sort of lunch type thing for the
Cherry Blossom Festival, which is another reason why we're here.
(VOA)
我們正在食用壽司，以及專門為櫻花節準備的鄉宴午餐，這也是
我們來到這裡的原因之一。

要點解析
① matsuri 鄉宴；祭。
② sort of 有幾分地；到某種程度。在這個句子中，表示「那一類」。

---

30 He also became known for his simple lifestyle, personal humility and
commitment to social justice. (VOA)
他還因其生活儉樸、為人謙遜以及承諾社會公正而著稱。

要點解析
① simple lifestyle 直譯為「簡單的生活方式」，在這句話裡是「生活儉樸」
的意思。
② social justice 社會正義，社會公正。

31　The first is when the light pink flowers swell their buds as they wait for warmth and sunshine to fully open. (VOA)

這朵淡粉色的花朵在等待溫暖和陽光的時候，花蕾首次完全綻放了。

要點解析

① light pink 淡粉紅色，light 在這句話裡是形容詞，表示「淡的」。
② bud 發芽；萌芽；蓓蕾。

32　The 5-hour event included the bands from 7 countries, it was organized by the Miami based Colombian rock star Wallace. (BBC)

在這五個小時的盛會上，有來自七個國家的樂隊表演，這一盛會是由主要在邁阿密活動的哥倫比亞搖滾明星華萊士組織的。

要點解析

① be organized by... 表示「由……主辦」。
② rock star 搖滾歌星，其中 rock 指「搖滾樂」。

33　People started by leaving notes on a local landmark said to be Juliet's tomb. (NPR)

人們開始在一個據說是茱麗葉墓碑的當地地標上留言。

要點解析

① landmark 地標，里程碑。常用片語有 landmark building 標誌性建築。
② tomb 墳墓。常用片語有 tomb stone 墓碑。

34　And it's made a lot of sense to make a spire-shaped building which has a light presence going to the top, and disappearing in the sky. (CNN)

而建造尖塔形的建築被賦予了很多意義，這樣的建築頂觀輕盈，直衝雲霄，消失在空中。

要點解析

① presence 存在；出席；風度。在這句話裡指「外觀」。
② disappear 消失。常用片語有 disappearing act 隱身術。

35   Revere Silver Shop made at least 90 different kinds of products, every-
      thing from spoons to parts for sword to a chain for a pet squirrel. (CNN)
      里維爾銀店製作了至少 90 種不同的產品，從湯匙，一把劍的一
      個零件，到一隻寵物松鼠的鏈子，應有盡有。

   要點解析

   ① parts 在這句話裡是「零件」的意思，在表達這一含義時常用複數。
   ② squirrel 松鼠。

36   Hereditary authority of itself did not give substance to a contemporary
      monarchy; rather, this was earned through willing service to the coun-
      try. (BBC)
      世襲王權本身並不能為當代王室提供資產，而是透過為國家效力
      而獲得的。

   要點解析

   ① contemporary 當代的，同時代的。常用片語有 contemporary design 現代
   風格設計。
   ② monarchy 君主政體，君主政治。常用片語有 constitutional monarchy 君主
   立憲制。

37   Using old films and photos, the documentary shows how Hall devel-
      oped a unique sound based on skilled studio ngineering and the sup-
      port of local talent, regardless of ace. (VOA)
      紀錄片透過老膠片和老照片展示了哈爾如何在當地各族眾多人才
      的幫助下，憑藉熟練的技藝成長為一個具有獨特聲音的人。

   要點解析

   ① documentary 記錄的；文件的；紀錄片。常用片語有 documentary film 紀
   錄片。
   ② regardless of 不顧，不管。常用片語有 regardless of the manner 不管用什
   麼樣方式。

38　Clarinetist Benny Goodman was known as the "King of Swing", and he kept Americans dancing in the 1930s and throughout World War II. (VOA)

單簧管手班尼‧古德曼以「搖擺樂之王」之名為人熟知，他讓美國人在 1930 年代和第二次世界大戰期間一直保持了跳舞。

要點解析

① clarinetist 吹木簫者；單簧管手。
② swing 搖擺；搖動。

39　When you can get people to build that confidence in themselves, it is something that they can then apply in other facets of life as well. (VOA)
當你幫助人們建立起自信心的時候，那麼在生活的其他方面他們也會如此。

要點解析

① confidence in... 對……信任。常用片語有 have confidence in each other 信任對方。
② facet 方面，小平面。常用片語有 triangular facet 三角面。

40　A television presenter in Nepal has set a new world record or hosting the longest TV talk show. (BBC)
一位尼泊爾的電視節目主持人錄製了史上最長的電視訪談秀，創造了一項新的世界紀錄。

要點解析

① presenter 提出者；主持人。常用片語有 television presenter 電視節目主持人。
② set a new world record 創造了新的世界紀錄。

41　The course spans 21km around the city of Bethlehem, and organisers could not find an uninterrupted 42km stretch of land for the race, so some 100 runners are attempting the fulmarathon ran the course twice.

(BBC)

跑道長達 21 公里，因為組織者無法為比賽找到 42 公里的直線
跑道，所以 100 多名馬拉松參賽選手將繞此跑道跑兩圈才能
完成全程。

要點解析

① uninterrupted 不間斷的，連續的
② stretch 這裡的意思是「直線跑道」。

---

42 The English football authorities have banned Liverpool's Uruguayan
striker Luis Suarez for 10 matches for biting an opponent in a game.
(BBC)

英國足球當局對利物浦烏拉圭前鋒路易斯‧蘇亞雷斯禁賽十場，
因為他在一場球賽中咬了對手。

要點解析

① authority 權威，權力，當局。在這句話裡指「官方」。常用片語有 legislative authority 立法權。
② opponent 對立的，對手，反對者。常用片語有 political opponent 政敵。

---

43 And one of the most intriguing things about it to me is when I first
heard the demo, which was, I think, really just an acoustic guitar
demo; I really had this feel of what I wanted to do. (VOA)

對我來說最有趣的事情之一是當我第一次聽到這個樣本的時候，
我真的以為這只是一個吉他原聲帶。我確實有種知道我想要做什
麼的感覺。

要點解析

① intriguing 有趣的，迷人的。這個詞來自動詞 intrigue「激起……的興趣」。
② acoustic 聽覺的；原聲的；音響的。

---

44 Unfortunately, the inside of the Washington Monument is closed for
repairs because of damage from a 5.8-strength earthquake in August

2011. (VOA)

不幸的是，由於 2011 年 8 月發生的一次強度為 5.8 級的地震使華盛頓紀念碑受到了損傷，紀念碑內部不得不關閉以進行維修。（編按：各國震度算法不同）

要點解析

① monument 紀念碑，豐碑，遺跡。相關表達有：historic monument 歷史碑石。

② strength 力量，優點，力度。相關表達有：economic strength 經濟實力。

相關句子

Must-sees like the Washington Monument and Lincoln Memorial are also just minutes away. (BBC)

像華盛頓紀念碑和林肯紀念堂這樣必看的景點也只有短短幾分鐘的路程。

45　Winner is the chair of psychology at Boston College and coauthor of the book Studio Thinking: The Real Benefits of Visual Arts Education. (NPR)

獲勝者是波士頓大學心理學院院長，他同時也是《工作室思考：視覺藝術教育的真正好處》的合著者。

要點解析

① psychology 心理學；心理狀態。

② co-author 合著者，通常指共同撰寫一本書的作者之一。

46　This period is called a gap year and is a time when British students can broaden their horizons by visiting foreign countries. (BBC)

這個階段被稱為間隔年，英國學生可以在這段時間裡出國旅行來開闊眼界。

要點解析

① gap year 間隔年。指的是在大學畢業或工作幾年之後，透過外出旅行一年來了解世界、成長見聞的一種行動。

② broaden 變寬；變廣。常用片語有 broaden business 擴大業務；broaden

horizon 則表示「開拓眼界」。

---

47 We have a particularly energetic segment regarding what's making us happy, beginning with Stephen's praise for a terribly underappreciated band and two songs that really need to work their way into your brain. (NPR)

我們有一個關於如何讓自己開心的特殊能量區,從史蒂芬讚美一個沒有得到充分欣賞的樂隊和兩首真正需要花費心思來印入我們腦海的歌曲開始。

要點解析

① energetic 精力充沛的;積極的;有力的。

② praise for... 因為……而讚美。常用用法有 praise sb. for sth. 因某事表揚某人。

---

48 Savoy Elementary isn't trying to turn these students into great artists; ultimately, they're trying to get them to improvethem. (NPR)

薩沃伊小學並沒有試圖把這些學生變成偉大的藝術家;他們努力讓這些學生最終實現自我提升。

要點解析

① ultimately 最終。

② improve 改善,提高。常用片語有 improve on 改進;勝過。

---

49 In a nation of immigrants, with a "melting pot" culture, it should not be surprising that American music is also an international blend. (VOA)

在一個有著「大熔爐」文化之稱的移民國度,美國音樂是國際化的融合不足為奇。

要點解析

① immigrant 移民的;遷入的;移民。常用片語有 immigrant inspection 移民檢查。

② melting pot 大熔爐。這個詞經常用來描述美國文化,因為美國是一個很大的移民國家,其文化正是由多種文化融合而來的。

③ blend 混合；協調；摻合物。

50　It's seen as one of the country's greatest sporting triumphs, but now a Dutch naval architect has come forward claiming that he designed the famous winged keel that helped propel Australial to victory. (BBC)
這被視為這個國家在體育方面獲得的最大成功，但是現在有一位荷蘭的造船工程師站了出來，聲稱幫助澳洲成功的帶翼龍骨是他設計的。

要點解析

① triumph 凱旋；歡欣；成功。常用片語有 triumph over 獲勝。
② architect 建築師。相關搭配有 software architect 軟體架構師。

51　He hopes his project will catch on in schools and beyond and bring more color to the world. (VOA)
他希望他的專案能夠在學校以及其他區域流行起來，並給世界帶來更多色彩。

要點解析

① catch on 變得流行，理解，明白。
② in... and beyond 可以表達「在......內外」的含義。

52　Miss Montana surrounded by more than 50 other beauty queens on stage, all hoping to become Ms. America. (CNN)
蒙大拿小姐被台上其他五十多名渴望成為美國小姐的佳麗們包圍著。

要點解析

① surround by... 被......環繞。相關詞 surroundings 則指「環境，周圍的事務」。
② on stage 在舞台上。

53 A record's been set in the world of art with the seller of huge painting last night at Sotheby's in New York. (NPR)

昨晚在紐約蘇富比拍賣公司，一幅巨型油畫的賣主在藝術界創造了歷史新高。

要點解析

① record 作名詞，意思是「紀錄，記載」。set a record 表示「創造紀錄」，break the record 表示「打破記錄」。

② the world of art 即「藝術界」，也可以用 art circle 表示。

---

54 In the United States, Los Angeles and San Francisco tie for second place for having the worst traffic problems. (VOA)

在美國，洛杉磯和舊金山並列第二，都有著嚴重的交通問題。

要點解析

① tie 作動詞，意思是「繫，栓，綁」。這個句子中的 tie for 表示「並列獲得」，如：tie for second place 並列第二。此外，tie 還可以作名詞，意思是「聯繫，連結」，如：a tie vote 表示「得票相等的選舉」。

② traffic problem 指的是「交通問題」，形容交通很糟糕經常用 bad，這裡用 bad 的最高級 worst 來形容交通問題非常糟糕。

相關句子

The road is narrow and the traffic is often slow as it travels through each of the small towns of the keys. (VOA)

這些小鎮的每條交通要道都很狹窄，車輛通過時需要緩慢行駛。

---

55 The television show Sea Hunt was filmed here, as were countless movies, including Tarzan and Creature from the Black Lagoon. (NPR)

電視劇《海獵》和不計其數的電影都是在這裡拍攝的，包括《泰山》和《黑狐妖潭》。

要點解析

① film 作動詞，意思是「拍攝電影」。film 最常用的是作為名詞，表示「電影」，如：The film was shooting. 那部電影正在拍攝中。

② countless 表示「無數的，多得數不清的」。如：I've told you countless

times. 我已經告訴過你無數遍了。

56　Facebook has announced plans to better deal with hit hateful pages and posts on the site. (BBC)

臉書已經宣布了能夠更好地處理網站中惡意網頁和文章的計畫。

要點解析

① page 本指「頁」。在這句話裡網路中表示「網頁」。
② post 本指「郵件」。用在網路上指「文章」。
③ site 指「地點；位置」。在這句話裡 on the site 表示「在網站上」。

相關句子

Facebook said it had over two hundred fifty million active users of July. (VOA)

七月，臉書宣布已經擁有超過 250 萬的活躍用戶。

57　There have been a lot of claims about the benefits of the arts on the mind: Listening to Mozart makes you smarter; playing an instrument makes you better at math. (NPR)

有許多關於藝術有益於大腦的說法：聽莫札特的音樂能讓你更加聰明；演奏樂器使你更擅長數學。

要點解析

① claim 在這句話裡作名詞，意思是「聲稱；斷言」。
② be good at sth. / doing sth. 擅長某件事情；擅長做某事。

相關句子

The report assesses the economic and social benefits of arts investment. (BBC)

這份報告評估了藝術投資產生的經濟和社會效益。

58　Even prestige magazines known for their lengthy pieces, such as The Atlantic and The New Yorker, are thinner than they used to be, and many articles are shorter than they once would have been. (NPR)

即便是《大西洋》和《紐約客》這些以長文著稱的知名雜誌也比以前薄了許多，許多文章的篇幅也有所縮短。

要點解析

① prestige 威信；聲譽。

② lengthy 冗長的；囉嗦的。常用搭配：lengthy process 很長的過程。

相關句子

He worked as editorial cartoonist for The Sunday Times and illustrator for The New Yorker. (BBC)

他曾在《星期日泰晤士報》擔任社論漫畫家，為《紐約客》提供插畫。

59　It touches people's hearts because they see something that they heard about, that all the church is about. (VOA)

它觸動了人們的心靈，因為他們看到了他們聽說過的關於教堂的事情。

要點解析

① touch 作動詞，有「接觸；觸動」的意思。這裡的意思是「觸動」。

② heard about 聽到或得知關於某人或某事的消息，與 hear of 同義，但比 hear of 知道的更詳細更具體。

60　The British artist Storm Thorgerson famous for designing album covers for the rock band Pink Floyd has died. (BBC)

為搖滾樂隊平克‧佛洛依德創作專輯封面而聞名的英國藝術家西德‧巴勒特已經逝世。

要點解析

① album 有「相簿；唱片集」的意思，這裡的意思是「唱片」。如：The album is a smorgasbord of different musical styles. 這個唱片集各種風格的音樂於一體。

② cover 是「封面」。

相關句子

The band's music is considered so influential that some critics say punk rock would not exist without the Stooges. (VOA)

傀儡樂隊的音樂影響如此之大，以至於一些評論稱如果沒有了這支樂隊，龐克搖滾也就不復存在了。

61   London is not known for its skyscrapers. It's not a city, even though
      as a world-class city, it's known n ot like New York, or Hong Kong,
      or even, some would say now Dubai with its high skyscrapers, as it is.
      (CNN)

      倫敦並不是以摩天大樓而聞名的。倫敦不像一座城市，儘管作為
      一個世界級城市，它也不像紐約或者香港那麼知名，甚至有人會
      說，事實上現在杜拜也有很高的摩天大樓。

要點解析

① skyscraper 摩天大樓。
② world-class 這裡作形容詞，表示「世界級」的。
③ as it is 表示「事實上」，相當於 in fact。

相關句子

An American stuck in London, already one of the world's highest priced cities,
found that her hotel had doubled its prices. (VOA)
倫敦是世界上物價最高的城市之一，一個在倫敦停留的美國人發現她住的
飯店價格翻倍了。

62   Royal watchers describe the 82 year old Queen as a silver surfer—
      someone who's enthusiastic about the Internet and who keeps in touch
      with younger members of her family by e-mail. (BBC)

      皇室觀察者將 82 歲高齡的女王形容為「老年線民」——她對網路
      充滿熱情，並且用郵件與家族裡的年輕成員保持聯絡。

要點解析

① surfer 衝浪運動員，在這句話裡的意思是「上網的人」。上網衝浪也可以
   表達為 surf on the Internet。而 sliver 在這句話裡是指「銀髮的」，引申為
   「老年人的」之意。
② ethusiastic 熱心的；熱烈的；狂熱的。

相關句子

The issue of Internet moral is in nature the surfer's moral problem in Internet.
(BBC)
網路道德問題的本質是在網路中上網者本身的道德問題。

63   Most states rely on gas taxes to raise the money for repairs and new construction, but that funding source is not the stream it used to be, says James Corless of Transportation for America. (NPR)

「美國很多州政府依靠收取天然氣稅獲得資金，用於維修和新建項目。但是這種資金來源將不再像過去那樣是主流了。」美國交通運輸系統詹姆斯．克萊斯說道。

要點解析

① raise 提高；上升；引起。在這句話裡則表示「募集」，相當於 collect。

② stream 河流，趨勢，流出，一連串。相關表達有：main stream 主要河流；a stream of 一連串。

64   The terminal here is packed with people wherever you can find space. (CNN)

在這個航廈，任何你能找到的地方都總是擠滿了人。

要點解析

① terminal 作名詞，意思是「終端，終點站，航廈」。做形容詞，則表示「末期的，晚期的，定期的，末端的」。

② be packed with... 擠滿……，塞滿……。其中 pack 作動詞，意思是「包裝；擠壓」。

相關句子

The terminal features shops and offshoots of local restaurants on both sides of the security checkpoint. (NPR)

這個航廈的特點是安檢口的兩側設有商店和當地餐館的分店。

65   The Scottish singer Emeli Sande has beaten a record set by the Beatles of the album with the most consecutive weeks in the British top 10. (BBC)

蘇格蘭歌手艾蜜莉．珊黛打破了披頭四創下的紀錄，其專輯連續數週名列英國前十名。

① beat 意為「打敗」，beat a record 表示「打破紀錄」。
② consecutive 連貫的，連續的。

66　The course is 26.2 miles long (42 km), and goes pa st many of London's landmarks, such as the Tower of London, the famous 19th century ship Cutty Sark, the Houses of Parliament and Buckingham Palace. (BBC)
這段路程共 26.2 英里（42 公里），途經很多倫敦標誌性建築，比如倫敦塔、19 世紀著名的「卡蒂薩克」號帆船、國會大廈和白金漢宮。

要點解析
① course 在這句話裡是「路程」的意思。
② goes past 經過，相當於 to pass by。
③ landmark 地標。如：The tower was once a landmark for ships. 這座塔曾經是船隻的陸標。

67　Archaeologists are digging up relics from the empire to this day and what they find can give a glimpse at what life was like back then. (BBC)
考古學家正在挖掘從帝國時代到如今的遺跡，他們的發現能夠讓我們對當時的生活有一點了解。

要點解析
① archaeologist 考古學家。
② glimpse 一瞥，隱約的閃現，瞥見。catch a glimpse of 瞥見。

相關句子
Chinese archaeologists have unearthed what they believe is a 2,400-year-old pot of soup, state media report. (BBC)
中國媒體報導稱考古學家發掘出了一個湯鍋，他們認為大約已經有兩千四百年的歷史了。

186

68   And band member Ezra Koenig sings about Zion, Babylon and a saint, or holy person, in the first verse. (VOA)
樂隊成員伊茲拉‧克恩寧在第一節中演唱了關於錫安人、巴比倫人和聖人的故事。

要點解析

① saint 聖人般的人，善良，有耐性的人。常用搭配有：patron saint 守護神。
② verse 詩，聖經中的節。常用搭配有：free verse 自由詩體；vice verse 反之亦然。

69   Roger Ebert was also known for his television reviews in which his thumbs-up or down influence to American filmgoers. (BBC)
羅傑‧伊伯特還是一位著名的電視評論員，他的喜好一直影響著美國影迷。

要點解析

① thumbs-up or down 的意思是「向上或向下豎起大拇指」，即「表示認可或否定」。
② filmgoer 愛看電影的人。

相關句子

In French cinemas, around 70% of filmgoers watch Hollywood movies.(BBC)
在法國的電影院裡，約有 70% 的電影愛好者看好萊塢電影。

70   And with yet another movie being planned, the series will continue to inspire people to think about space, the final frontier. (VOA)
隨著另外一部電影的計畫拍攝，該系列將繼續鼓勵人們對太空這一終極探索領域展開想像。

要點解析

① series 系列，連續，（廣播或電視的）系列節目。相關表達有：series of 一系列；in series with... 與......相連。
② frontier 邊疆，邊緣，尚待開發的領域。

71   The company says it's going to update its guidelines for identifying
      hate speech, and hold users more accountable for content considered
      cruel or insensitive. (CNN)
      該公司表示將更新識別仇恨言論的準則，並希望用戶對殘酷或麻
      木不仁的內容更加負責。

要點解析

① accountable 負有責任的，可解釋的，可說明的。
② insensitive 意思是「感覺遲鈍的；不敏感的」。在該句中引申翻譯為「麻
  木不仁的」，反義詞是 sensitive。

72   Tiger Woods regained golf's No.1 spot after winning the Arnold Palm-
      er Invitational in the US state of Florida. (BBC)
      在贏得了美國佛羅里達州阿諾‧龐馬邀請賽之後，老虎伍茲重新
      坐上了高爾夫世界第一的寶座。

要點解析

① spot 作名詞使用，意思是「地點，場所，汙點，職位」。在這句話裡則
  表示「地位，位置」。
② Arnold Palmer 阿諾‧龐馬，美國著名職業高爾夫球手，曾獲得數十個
  PGA 巡迴賽及冠軍巡迴賽的冠軍。龐馬還是美國第一位廣為人知的體育
  明星，是「高爾夫三巨擘」之一。

相關句子

At the age of 21, Tiger Woods blazed his way around the rhodedendron-lined
course. (BBC)
老虎‧伍茲在 21 歲的時候開啟了他在高爾夫球場上的傳奇征程。

73   People typically sort lo ng-form journalism into two categories—
      there's investigative or watchdog reporting. (NPR)
      人們通常把長篇新聞歸為兩類：一類是調查新聞，另一類是
      監督新聞。

要點解析

① sort 將……分類；category 種類，類別。

② investigative 調查性質的。如：investigative journalism 調查新聞業。
③ watchdog 監察人。如：a watchdog of public morals 公共道德的監督者。

相關句子

No history of journalism is complete without discussing the work of two young reporters from the Washington Post. (VOA)
如果不討論《華盛頓郵報》的兩名年輕記者的工作，新聞業的歷史是不完整的。

---

74 Unless you're at a Chaucer convention, speaking Middle English is not going to impress a potential romantic partner. (Scientific American)
除非你是在喬叟閱讀大會，否則說中世紀英語並不會讓潛在的戀愛對象留下深刻印象。

要點解析

① Chaucer 喬叟，英國作家，英國第一位詩人。
② convention 指「大會，慣例」，在這句話裡指「大會」。如：The southern delegates had the convention in a chokehold. 南方代表使會議陷入僵局。
③ potential 潛在的，有可能的。

---

75 James Bond—agent 007—has been saving the world from evil forces on movie screens since his first film. (VOA)
詹姆斯‧龐德——特務 007，從第一部電影上映後就一直在銀幕上與惡勢力鬥爭，拯救世界。

要點解析

① agent 最常見的意思是「代理人，代理商」。另外還可以表示「特務」。
② evil forces 惡勢力。其中，force 在這句話裡作名詞，意思是「勢力;力量;武力」。

---

76 Two Lanes of Freedom is Tim McGraw's debut album for the Nashville independent label Big Mac hine Records. (VOA)
《雙車道的自由》是提姆‧麥克羅的首張專輯，出自納什維爾獨立廠牌 Big Machine 唱片公司。

① debut 是一個法語詞，意思是「演員首次演出」，在這句話裡指「發行首張專輯」。

② independent label 是指獨立製作唱片的公司，譯為「獨立廠牌」。

77　She has directed three documentaries and two features also known as narrative films, all independently produced. (VOA)

她已經執導了三部紀錄片和兩部被認為是敘事電影的故事片，這些全部是由她獨立製作的。

要點解析

① direct 在這句話裡作動詞，意思是「指導，導演」。此外，direct 常被作為形容詞，表示「直接的」。

② documentary 紀錄片；feature 則指「專題節目」。

③ narrative 指「敘事的」。

78　Archaeologists in Mexico say they've uncovered three ancient playing fields at a pre-Hispanic site in the eastern state of Veracruz. (BBC)

墨西哥考古學家稱他們在維拉克魯茲東部的前西班牙地區發現了三個古代競技場。

要點解析

① archaeologist 考古學家。

② uncover 發現，揭開。

③ pre-Hispanic 前西班牙。pre- 首碼，表示「……之前」。

相關句子

The remains were identified as belonging to a man following forensi c archaeologist and anthropologist tests. (BBC)

經過法醫考古學家和人類學家檢測，該遺骸已被確認屬於一名男性。

79　Those civilizations included pyramids that looked like this one, some of them are still standing, like one that was the center of a settlement around 250 B.C. (CNN)

這些文明包括金字塔，看起來就像這一座，其中一些如今仍然矗

立，就像西元前 250 年矗立在定居地中央的這座一樣。

要點解析

① civilization 文明，文化。如：ancient civilization 古代文明。

② settlement 移居地，新住宅區。這個詞也有「移民」的意思。

---

80 A YouTube video of her audition has been watched by more than 26 million people, making it one of the most watched videos on the internet. (BBC)

超過兩千六百萬人在 YouTube 網站上觀看了她參加海選的一段影片，使其成為網路點擊率最高的一段影片。

要點解析

audition 作名詞使用，意思是「聽力，試聽，試音」；作動詞則有「對……進行面試；讓……試唱」的意思。

相關句子

The 17-year-old Canadian pop star's videos are among the most watched on YouTube. (BBC)

這個 17 歲加拿大流行歌手的影片是 YouTube 網站上點擊率最高的影片之一。

---

81 A recent study on women in American independent films reveals that there are more female content creators in independent films than in big Hollywood movies. (VOA)

最近針對美國獨立電影中女性的研究顯示，與好萊塢大片相比，獨立電影內容的女性作者更多。

要點解析

① reveal 意思是「顯示，透露」，通常指顯露某一事實。

② big Hollywood movie 就是「好萊塢大片」，也可以用 Hollywood blockbuster 表示。

---

82 But because of the tight economy, many colleges are eliminating full-time language-teaching positions or filling them with cheaper lecturers

who are not faculty members at all. (NPR)

但是由於經濟緊縮，許多大學都在減少全職語言教學職位，或者僱用薪酬較低的非教職員講師來滿足學校的需求。

要點解析

① eliminate 排除，消除；淘汰。相關搭配有：eliminate poverty 消除貧困；eliminate illiteracy 掃盲。

② faculty 全體教職員。

83　He brought in flamenco dancer and choreographer Melissa Cruz, and other musicians to create La Ruya's unique ound. (VOA)

他介紹了佛朗明哥舞者及編舞梅麗莎・克魯茲，以及其他一起創了 La Ruya 獨特聲效的音樂人。

要點解析

① bring in，意思是「介紹，引入」。如：He brought in two new members. 他介紹了兩名新成員。

② choreographer 舞蹈指導。

③ unique 唯一的，獨特的。

84　If there is a downside to that, it was tricky to find music teachers, so I had to travel to the States quite frequently to do violin lessons, and there wasn't an oboe teacher in the town, funny e nough. (NPR)

如果有負面的因素，那就是很難找到音樂教師，所以我不得不頻繁到美國去上小提琴課，而有趣的是，那裡的小鎮裡也沒有雙簧管老師。

要點解析

① downside 負面因素。

② tricky 的本意是「機警的，狡猾的」。在這個句子中引申為「困難的」意思，相當於 difficult。

③ oboe 雙簧管。

85 One of his favorite characters is a man who lives in a shack on the beach and rents lounge chairs to weekend visitors. (NPR)

他最喜歡的角色是一個住在沙灘棚屋裡，週末向遊客租賃躺椅的男人。

要點解析

① shack 窩棚，簡陋的小屋。

② lounge chair 躺椅。其中，lounge 作名詞的意思是「休息廳，客廳，等候室」；作動詞則表示「閒逛；懶洋洋地躺」。

86 Harvard University was founded in 1636, making it the oldest institution of higher learning in the U.S. (CNN)

哈佛大學成立於 1636 年，是美國最古老的高等學府。

要點解析

① found 是動詞 find 的過去分詞，同時也可以作動詞，意為「創辦，成立，建成」。

② institution 機構，慣例，制度。

相關句子

Harvard University has had its website hacked in what appears to be a 「sophisticated」 Syrian-related attack. (BBC)

哈佛大學網站遭到了駭客攻擊，且似乎是一個「複雜的」與敘利亞相關的攻擊行為。

87 The scandal began after a news magazine revealed that Gilles Bernheim had passed off another writer's work as his own. (VOA)

一家新聞雜誌曝光格列斯·伯海姆將另一作者的文章盜為己用後，這個醜聞開始流傳。

要點解析

① scandal 醜聞，丟臉的事情，恥辱。

② pass off 冒充。這個片語還有「逐漸消失；轉移注意」的意思。

88　Republicans don't often make high-profile speeches at Howard University, one of the country's most prominent historically black schools. (NPR)

霍華德大學是美國歷史上最著名的黑人學校，共和黨人通常不會在那裡進行高調演講。

要點解析

① high-profile 高調的，態度明確的；反義詞為 low-profile，意為「低調的」。其中 profile 作名詞使用，表示「側面，外形，輪廓」。
② prominent 突出的，傑出的，著名的。

相關句子

Hundreds of college students from historically black schools such as Howard University in Washington traveled to Jena, along with civil rights activists such as Al Sharpton and the Rev. (CNN)

來自華盛頓霍華大學等歷史悠久的黑人學校的數百名大學生正同阿爾·夏普頓及牧師等民權積極分子向耶拿前進。

89　Many ideas for the university buildings came from the architecture of ancient Greece and Rome. (VOA)

許多大學建築物的設計理念來源於古希臘和古羅馬的建築風格。

要點解析

① idea 意為「想法，概念」。在這句話裡表示「（設計）理念」。
② architecture 建築學，建築風格，建築式樣。

90　Perhaps those cave painters paid such close attention to detail because they wanted to avoid being starving artists. (Scientific American)

也許那些洞穴畫家如此關注細節，是因為他們不想成為受餓的藝術家。

要點解析

① pay attention to 是一個常用片語搭配，意思是「注意」；而 pay close attention to 則是「密切注意」的意思。
② avoid 作動詞，意思是「避免」。常用搭配是 avoid doing sth. 避免做某事。

相關句子

Ironically, the painter would probably have been forgotten but for the success of Chieko's Sky. (CNN)

諷刺地說,如果沒有《千惠的天空》的成功,這位畫家也許早就被遺忘了。

---

91 A crystal found in the wreckage of a British ship in the English Channel is believed to be what was referred as a "sunstone" in ancient Norse literature. (BBC)

在英吉利海峽一艘英國船隻的殘骸中找到的一顆水晶被認為是古挪威文學中提到的「太陽石」。

要點解析

wreckage 殘片,殘骸,折斷,失事。

---

92 The obelisk—the tall, slender column of marble—honors the United States' first president. (VOA)

那座方尖碑——細而高的大理石柱,是為了紀念美國第一任總統而建造的。

要點解析

① column 不但可以表示「列,專欄」,還可以表示「柱子」。

② honor 在這句話裡作動詞,表示「紀念」。相當於 commemorate。

---

93 The 11th century minaret of the Great Mosque in the city of Aleppo is part of a Unesco world heritage site. (BBC)

阿勒頗市大清真寺一個 11 世紀的尖塔是聯合國教科文組織世界遺產之一。

要點解析

① minaret(清真寺旁祈禱的人使用的)尖塔。

② Unesco 的全稱是 United Nations Educational, Scientific and Cultural Organization,表示聯合國教育、科學及文化組織,簡稱「聯合國教科文組織」,是聯合國的專門機構之一。

The Unesco World Heritage Site listing for numerous earth buildings highlights a growing sense of urgency regarding their preservation. (CNN)

聯合國教科文組織世界遺產清單中有許多土樓，這說明保護這些建築的緊迫性正在不斷增加。

94　　Nigerian writer Chinua Achebe was most famous for his first novel Things Fall Apart. (BBC)

奈及利亞作家奇努阿·阿切貝因為他的第一部小說《瓦解》而聞名。

要點解析

① be famous for 是「以⋯⋯而著名」的意思。

② fall apart 是「崩潰」的意思，在這句話裡翻譯成「瓦解」。其中 apart 是「分離的」的意思。

相關句子

Critics say this graphic novel artfully expresses the survivors' bravery and shows what it was like to live through this disaster. (VOA)

評論家稱這本繪本小說極富藝術性地表達了倖存者的勇氣，並向我們展示了這場災難經歷。

95　　Now, they are FA Cup winners and it is a story to breathe new life into the reputation of the old competition and on the day at Wembley, it was entirely deserved. (BBC)

目前，他們是足總杯冠軍，這為這個歷史悠久的比賽賦予了新的生機，溫布利的那一天絕對實至名歸。

要點解析

① breathe new life into 的意思是「給予生命，賦予生機」。

② reputation 名氣，名聲。如：reputation for... 以⋯⋯聞名。

③ deserve 表示「應得的」，在這句話裡是「名符其實」的意思。這個詞也可以表示「活該」。

相關句子

The FA had said its rules were clear and its requirements had not changed. (BBC)

足球協會稱它們的規則很明確，並且它們的要求也沒有改變。

---

96   There are reports that an artwork by the renowned graffiti artist Banksy due to be auctioned in Miami has been withdrawn from sale after an opening bid. (BBC)

有報導稱，原定在邁阿密拍賣的著名塗鴉藝術家班克斯的作品在開標後停止銷售。

要點解析

① renowned 有名的，有聲望的。
② graffiti 塗鴉。
③ auction 競拍，拍賣。相關表達有：auction house 拍賣行；at auction 拍賣；auction sale 拍賣。
④ withdraw 撤退，拿走，（從銀行）取（錢）。

相關句子

This helps auction houses such as Christie's to decide not just whether an artwork is by a master or his pupil, but also whether or not it is a forgery. (BBC)

這不僅有助於佳士得這樣的拍賣行判斷一個藝術品是由大師還是他的學生創作的，還能判斷該藝術品的真偽。

---

97   The leader of that movement has been honored with a commemorative statue in the capital building in Washington. (BBC)

那場運動的領袖被授予在首都華盛頓建立紀念雕像的榮譽。

要點解析

① be honored with... 被授予......的榮譽。
② commemorative 紀念性的；紀念品。

---

98   The artists visit the students in person, mentor them, teach master classes and give encouragement. (NPR)

藝術家與學生們面對面交談，成為他們的良師益友，教授他們重點課程並給予他們鼓勵。

要點解析
① mentor 有經驗可信賴的顧問;做……的良師;指導。
② master 作名詞有「主人,大師」的意思。在這句話裡 master 作形容詞,表示「主要的」。

99　These eight schools are getting intense intervention: more staff, supplies, professional development, and partnerships with local museums, dance companies and theaters. (NPR)
這八所學校受到越來越多的干擾:更多的員工、供給專業發展,以及更多的和當地博物館、舞蹈公司以及電影院的合作。

要點解析
① intervention 介入,調解;相關搭配有 market intervention 市場干預;surgical intervention 手術治療。
② partnership 夥伴關係,合作關係。ship 也是一個常見的詞綴,表示一種關係或者特性,如 friendship 朋友關係、membership 會員資格、leadership 領導才能。

要點解析
Intervention of foreigners will only make the problem that much bigger, and will never solve it. (CNN)
外國人的介入只會使問題變得更加嚴重,永遠也解決不了問題。

100　The famous Maracana football stadium in Rio de Janeiro reopened shortly after nearly three years of renovations. (BBC)
在完成近三年的改造後,里約熱內盧著名的馬拉卡納體育場很快就重新開放了。

要點解析
① stadium 體育場,運動場。
② reopen 是 open 加上表示「重複,再次」的首碼 re- 構成的,意為「重新開放」。
③ renovation 翻新;恢復活力。

相關句子

They've started work on a 44, 000-seat world-class football stadium and have many other plans. (CNN)

他們已經開始建造一個擁有四萬四千個座位的世界級足球場，並且還有很多其他的計畫。

101　Hungarian scientists recently analyzed a thousand statues, paintings and other art created in prehistory. (Scientific American)

匈牙利科學家們最近對一千件史前創作的雕像、繪畫和其他藝術品進行了分析。

要點解析

prehistory 史前(某件事)以前的發展背景。其中 pre 作為首碼，意為「在……前」，如 premature 不成熟的。

102　A funeral with full military honors traditionally includes a caisson to transport the body. (VOA)

一個最高榮譽的軍事化葬禮通常包含用彈藥箱運送遺體的環節。

要點解析

① funeral 葬禮；不愉快的事情。
② caisson 彈藥箱；(水下作業用的) 沉箱。

相關句子

The spokesman would not reveal any details about the location or time of the funeral. (BBC)

發言人不會透露關於葬禮時間、地點的任何細節。

103　The British Horse Racing Authority has disqualified a trainer of the leading Godolphin's stable in Newmarket for eight years for doping horses. (NPR)

由於給賽馬服用興奮劑，英國紐馬克特戈多爾芬馬場一名馴馬師被英國賽馬局禁賽八年。

要點解析

① disqualify 是 qualify 的反義詞，意思是「取消......的資格；使不合格」。

② stable 作形容詞表示「穩定的，沉穩的」；作名詞還有「馬廄，馬棚」的意思，在這個句子中翻譯為「馬場」。

③ dope 讓......用興奮劑；吸毒。作名詞則有「興奮劑；笨蛋」的意思。

相關句子

The doping of 11 horses was detected during sport checks by the authority at the Godophin's stables at Newmarket. The trainer himself admitted doping four others. (BBC)

當局在紐馬克特戈多爾芬馬場進行運動檢查時發現有 11 匹馬服用過興奮劑，而馴馬師承認另外 4 匹馬也服過藥。

104　The town of Verona, Italy—home of Shakespeare's Romeo and Juliet—receives thousands of letters of heartache and unrequited love addressed to the play's star-crossed heroine. (NPR)

義大利維洛納小鎮是莎士比亞小說《羅密歐與茱麗葉》的發生地，這個小鎮收到了上千封向劇中女主角表達心痛或者暗戀之情的信件。

要點解析

① heartache 心痛，悲傷。其中，詞綴 ache 表示「疼痛，病痛」。如 headache 頭痛；stomach 胃痛；toothache 牙痛。

② unrequited 得不到回應的。unrequited love 即我們常說的「暗戀」。

相關句子

Shakespeare's Romeo and Juliet, like many of his plays, originates from a much earlier Italian source, but many elements remain constant. (BBC)

莎士比亞的《羅密歐與茱麗葉》如同他的許多劇作一樣都來源於義大利早期的素材，並且將許多元素都保留了下來。

105　English is the dominant language of the Internet, which skews the language distribution in bilingual cities like Montreal. (Scientific American)

英語是網路主要語言，這導致像在蒙特婁這種雙語城市的語言分

布呈異常。

要點解析

① dominant 占優勢的，統治的。如：dominant role 主要角色；dominant effect 顯性效應。

② skew 偏離；歪曲；斜視。

相關句子

Observers say the company has struggled to establish its mostly Englishlanguage content in the region's TV and Internet markets. (CNN)

觀察人士稱，該公司一直試圖在該地區的電視和網路市場上推出以英語為主要語言的服務內容。

106　You're probably not familiar with armed forces day, as you're with Memorial Day or veteran day. (CNN)

與陣亡將士紀念日和老兵日相比，你也許並不怎麼熟悉軍人節。

要點解析

① be familiar with... 對……熟悉。

② armed forces 三軍，軍隊，武裝。其中 armed 作形容詞，表示「武裝的」。

③ veteran 老兵，退伍軍人。

相關句子

That year before the declaration of independent was signed, the navy was also established that year on Oct.13th. (CNN)

美國海軍是在獨立宣言簽署前一年的 10 月 13 日建立的。

107　The new study analyzed the residues on these unglazed pottery shards and found the remains of milk fat. (Scientific American)

新的研究分析了無釉陶器的殘留碎片，並且發現了乳脂殘留物。

要點解析

① residue 殘渣，殘餘物。相關搭配有：pesticide residue 農藥殘留物；oil residue 油渣。

② unglazed pottery shard 無釉陶器碎片。其中，unglazed 表示「無釉的」，這個詞源自 glaze「上釉」。

③ remain 在這句話裡作名詞，表示「剩餘物，殘骸」。

相關句子

In the meanwhile, oil residue continues to spread along the U.S. coastline, threatening livelihoods and sensitive wildlife in the areas. (VOA)
與此同時，石油殘渣繼續沿著美國海岸線蔓延，對區域內的人類和脆弱的野生動物造成威脅。

108　He suggests that the best advice might be to join a book group that walks and drinks red wine while talking about the book. (NPR)
他說，最好的建議也許就是加入圖書小組，在探討圖書的時候散步，並且喝點紅酒。

要點解析

① suggest 作動詞，意思是「建議，提議」。後面常跟動名詞形式。
② advice 作名詞，表示「建議，勸告」；是不可數名詞。「一項建議」應該用 a piece of advice 來表示。

Part 5

Medicine & Health

1   People should always be concerned whenever there is an emerging infectious disease, because we don't really know, we don't have ways in which we can predict and project, and appropriately prepare for some of these. (CNN)

無論何時出現新型傳染病，人們都應該保持重視，因為我們真的不知道，我們沒有辦法預測和計畫，也無法進行適當的準備。

要點解析

① emerging 新興的，出現的；來自表示「出現」的動詞 emerge。
② project 通常作名詞，表示「工程，計畫」；這裡作動詞，意思是「計畫」。

2   New York's mayor wants to make it illegal for restaurants to erve sugary drinks that are larger than 16 ounces. (CNN)

紐約市長希望對於餐廳提供超過 16 盎司含糖飲料的行為視為非法。

要點解析

① illegal 非法的，違法的。「違法行為」可以用 illegal activity 來表示。
② sugary 含糖的，甜的。sugary drink 無酒精飲料。
③ ounce 盎司，英國的計量單位。

相關句子

Drinking warm, non-alcoholic liquids and eating something sugary can stop the shivering. (VOA)

飲用熱的非酒精類飲料以及吃含糖食品可以停止顫抖。

3   Researchers in the United States have succeeded in making a working kidney and transplanting it into rats. (BBC)

美國研究者成功研製出一顆可運作的腎臟，並將它移植到了田鼠體內。

要點解析

① succeeded in... 在……方面成功。
② transplant 移植。organ transplant 器官移植；heart transplant 心臟移植。

相關句子

There's a chance that your body may reject the transplant, leading to life threatening complications. (CNN)

你的身體可能會對移植器官產生排斥，從而引發危及生命的併發症。

4　Most research on memory loss in the elderly focuses on dementia, Alzheimer's disease or other brain diseases. (NPR)

大部分針對老年人記憶減退的研究重點關注老年痴呆症、阿茲海默症或者其他大腦疾病。

要點解析

① memory loss 失憶，健忘。與 loss 相關的片語還有：weight loss 失重；energy loss 能量損耗。
② elderly 是形容詞，表示「上了年紀的，稍老的」。the elderly 表示「老年人」。
③ dementia 痴呆。

相關句子

A new study says the leading cause of disability in older people in low and middle income countries is dementia. (VOA)

一項新研究稱中低收入國家中，老年人能力喪失的直接原因是痴呆。

5　As far as we know, all the cases are individually infected in a sporadic and not connected way. (BBC)

據我們所知，所有病例都是單獨感染的，互相之間沒有關聯。

要點解析

① infect 感染，傳染。相關片語有 be infected with... 染上……。
② sporadic 零星的，分散的。

6　It says people are at great risk of getting diarrhea, cholera and other water borne diseases because of the bad sanitary conditions and contaminated water. (VOA)

據說，人們患上痢疾、霍亂和其他水生疾病的風險較高是因為惡的衛生條件和水汙染。

205

① at risk of... 有……的危險。

② sanitary 衛生的，清潔的。sanitary condition 表示「衛生條件」。

③ contaminated 受汙染的。如：contaminated area 受汙染區。

7　Once we got the virus, we took it immediately to the appropriate level of biocontainment. (NPR)

一旦我們感染了病毒，就必須立即採取適當程度的生物控制。

要點解析

① virus 病毒。相關片語有：influenza virus 流感病毒；virus infection 病毒感染。

② biocontainment 生物控制。這個詞由表示「生物的」的 bio- 和名詞 containment 「控制」合成而來。

③ take to 開始從事，喜歡，專心做。其中，to 是介詞。

8　He suffered from rheumatism and diabetes, and was so weak he could walk only short distances. (VOA)

他患了風溼和糖尿病，虛弱得只能走一小段路。

要點解析

① suffer from 忍受，遭受。在這句話裡指「患……病」。

② rheumatism 風溼病；diabetes 糖尿病。

相關句子

They may have a weak or damaged heart, high blood pressure or other problems of the blood system. (VOA)

他們的心臟可能很脆弱或易受損，並且患有高血壓和其他血液系統疾病。

9　They then injected a bit of saltwater into the subjects muscles and told them they'd be getting a little something to relieve the resulting pain. (Scientific American)

接著，他們向受試者的肌肉裡注射了一些鹽水，並告訴他們這會在某種程度上緩解之後的疼痛。

要點解析

① subject 受試者，被動作的對象。此外，它還有「主題，科目，主旨」的意思。

② resulting 作為結果的。在這句話裡可以理解為「隨之而來的」。

③ relieve 解除，減輕，救濟。relieve stress 緩解壓力；relieve oneself 方便一下。

10　Aspirin, for example, was derived in the 19th century from salicylic acid, a long-time remedy for pains and fever found in plants like willow and meadowsweet. (VOA)

比如，阿斯匹靈是 19 世紀時從水楊酸中提取的，長期以來它被用作止痛藥和退燒藥，發現於柳樹和繡線菊屬植物中。

要點解析

① derive 源於，得自。derive from... 表示「源於……」。

② salicylic acid 水楊酸。

③ remedy 藥品，治療法。

11　And from the answers to these questions, we can estimate the severity of food insecurity that has affected them and their families. (VOA)

從這些問題的答案，我們可以估計不安全的食品已經嚴重影響了他們和他們的家人。

要點解析

① estimate 估計，評價。相關片語有 estimate for... 對……估價；cost estimate 成本估算；rough estimate 粗算。

② severity 嚴重。disease severity 發病度。

12　Thousands of genetic tests carried out across the European Union have found that almost 5% of processed beef products on sale have been contaminated with horsemeat. (BBC)

歐盟進行的數千次基因測試顯示，幾乎 5% 正在出售的加工牛肉產品都被馬肉汙染了。

要點解析

① carry out 執行，實行。

② contaminated 是動詞 contaminate 的過去分詞形式。在這句話裡用作被動語態，意思是「汙染」。

③ processed 加工過的，處理的。如：processed food 加工過的食品。

13　We don't have well-equipped intensive care units to treat patients, so that is the gap that is missing. (VOA)

我們不具備治療患者的設備完善的加護病房，這是一片缺失的空白。

要點解析

① well-equipped 設備精良的。equip 作動詞，表示「裝備」。

② intensive 加強的，集中的。intensive care unit 指「加護病房」，即常說的 ICU。

③ gap 有「間隙，缺口，空白」的意思，在這句話裡表示「空白」。

14　Among other questions, the kids were asked to rate the importance of having "lots of money" and the stuff money can buy, like a house, a new car, or a "motor-powered recreational vehicle". (NPR)

在其他問題中，孩子們被要求評價「有很多錢」的重要性和錢能購買的東西，比如房子、新車或者「電動休閒類交通工具」。

要點解析

① rate 通常作名詞，表示「比率，速度」。在這句話裡作動詞，表示「估價」。

② recreational 娛樂的。消遣的；recreational activities 娛樂活動；recreational shopping 娛樂購物。

③ vehicle 車輛，交通工具。如：commercial vehicle 商用車輛；industrial vehicle 工業車輛。

15　Most deaths are in the developing world driven by high rate of infectious disease and of maternal mortality. (BBC)

在開發中國家，大多數的死亡都是由高感染率和產婦的高死亡

率導致的。

① developing world 在這句話裡泛指「開發中國家」，相當於 developing country。而 developed country 則指「已開發國家」。
② be driven by... 被……所驅使。在這句話裡是「由……導致」的意思。
③ maternal mortality 產婦死亡率。相關片語有：maternal instinct 母性本能。

16   We think antiviral medicines for them can be lifesaving, and that's a very important message. (BBC)
我們認為，抗病毒藥物對於他們來說是可以救命的，這是一個重要資訊。

要點解析

① antiviral 抗病毒的。antiviral medicine 指「抗病毒藥物」。
② lifesaving 救命的。由 save life 變形而來。

17   We have, of course, the sagebrush, which makes a very powerful pain-relieving liniment that I think we should all learn how to use, because it is much safer than the nonsteroidal anti-inflammatory agents. (VOA)
蒿屬植物可以起到很好的外用止痛劑的作用，我想我們每個人都應該學會使用，因為這比非類固醇消炎藥要安全得多。

要點解析

① sagebrush 灌木叢。
② liniment 擦藥，塗抹油。
③ anti-inflammatory 抗發炎的。其中 anti- 作為首碼，表示「防……、抗……」。
④ agent 有「代理人」的意思，但在這句話裡的意思是「藥劑」。

18   Researchers examined airway tissue to learn why bitterness makes the muscles relax. (Scientific American)
研究者檢查了呼吸道組織，了解了為什麼苦味能使肌肉放鬆。

209

要點解析

① airway 有「導氣管，呼吸道」的意思。在這句話裡可理解為「呼吸道」。

② tissue 組織，體素。相關片語有：soft tissue 軟組織；muscle tissue 肌肉組織；fat tissue 脂肪組織。

19　Not taking the elevator is a good way to sneak in a little extra exercise every day. (Scientific American)

不搭乘電梯是每天忙裡偷閒進行額外鍛鍊的一個好方法。

要點解析

sneak in 在這句話裡表示「忙裡偷閒」。 其中 sneak 是「偷偷摸摸做事」的意思。

20　And a handful of studies have actually shown that infecting human patients with worms can reduce symptoms of the disease. (Scientific American)

事實上，一些研究顯示，感染寄生蟲的患者的疾病症狀可以減輕。

要點解析

① a handful of 少量的，少數的。在這句話裡有「一小部分」的意思。

② worm 表示「蠕蟲」。在這句話裡是「寄生蟲」的意思。

21　You may have some of the classic symptoms including sore throat, but also specifically muscle aches, or something that distinguish flu from a regular cold. (CNN)

你可能會有一些典型症狀，包括喉嚨痛尤其是肌肉疼痛，或是不同於普通感冒的一些其他流感症狀。

要點解析

① sore throat 咽喉痛。其中，sore 表示「疼痛的」。

② distinguish 是「辨別，區別」的意思。distinguish... from 表示「把……和……區別開來」。

22 And one potential source of sickness when you dine out is the dinner-
    ware. (Scientific American)

    當你外出就餐時，餐具是潛在的疾病來源。

要點解析

① dine out 外出就餐，dine in 則表示「在家吃飯」。
② dinnerware 整套的餐具。

相關句子

The spokesperson said they were also reviewing occupational health
arrangements and sickness absence policy. (BBC)

發言人稱他們也在修訂職業保健安排和病假政策。

23 When scientists share genomic data, they first strip away identifying
    information, like the individual's name and date of birth. (Scientific
    American)

    當科學家們分享基因組資料時，他們首先會篩除識別資訊，比如
    個人姓名和出生日期。

要點解析

① strip away 除去，揭掉。還可以用 wipe off 和 get rid of 來表示這個意思。
② identifying 識別，表示。動詞形式為 identify。

24 A new study shows that sugar pills are less effective for people who
    are quick to anger. (Scientific American)

    一項新研究顯示，糖衣藥片對易怒患者的效果不太明顯。

要點解析

① pill 是「藥片」的意思，sugar 在這句話裡指「糖衣」，因此 sugar pill 就
是「糖衣藥片」。
② effective 有效的。相關片語有 effective management 有效管理；effective
measure 有效措施；cost effective 有成本效益的。

25 One of the world's best restaurants based in Copenhagen has apolo-
    gised after dozens of people who dined there suffering from vomiting

and diarrhea. (BBC)

哥本哈根的一家世界一流餐廳向幾十名用餐後嘔吐和腹瀉的顧客致歉。

要點解析

① based 表示「基於……」。在這句話裡有「在……的」的意思。常用搭配有 be based on 基於；computer based 基於電腦的。
② dozens of 幾十，許多。其中 dozen 表示「十二個」。
③ vomit 嘔吐，diarrhea 腹瀉。

26　The commission calls for better management of medical device alarms and recommends hospitals take inventory of all alarms, know where there are located and determine whether they are really necessary for patient care. (NPR)

委員會呼籲更好地管理醫療報警設備，建議醫院列出所有警報目錄進行定位，並決定患者是否真的需要護理。

要點解析

① commission 委員會。常用搭配有 arbitration commission 仲裁委員會；on commission 抽取傭金。
② call for 要求，提倡，邀請。call in for refills 為患者配藥。
③ inventory 詳細目錄。常用搭配有 merchandise inventory 商品存貨。
④ be necessary for... 對……有必要。

27　British and Canadian scientists say they have identified a potential treatment for sleeping sickness. (BBC)

英國和加拿大的科學家稱，他們確定了治療昏睡症的可能方法。

要點解析

① identify 表示「確定」。
② potential 表示「潛在的」。在這句話是「有希望的」的意思。

相關句子

Until now the drug melarsoprol was used to treat patients in the advanced stage of sleeping sickness. (VOA)

目前為止，硫肿密胺藥物被用於治療晚期昏睡症的患者。

28　The brain loves novelty, so if you do crossword puzzles, try shifting to a different type of puzzle. (NPR)

大腦喜歡新奇的事物，所以如果你玩縱橫字謎，可以嘗試不同的類型。

要點解析

① novelty 新奇，新奇的事物。
② crossword puzzle 即「填字遊戲」。
③ shift 移動，變化。在這句話是「改變」的意思，相當於 change。

相關句子

Only cells in your brain make the enzymes that produce certain neuron transmitters that are responsible for brain function. (VOA)

只有腦細胞才能產生促進神經傳導的酶，並以此維持大腦功能。

29　A study finds that elderly people who played a video game or at least 10 hours gained three years of protection from ognitive decline. (Scientific American)

一項研究顯示，每天至少玩十個小時電子遊戲的老人可以使認知能力減退延緩三年。

要點解析

① video game 需要依賴影片設備來玩，即我們常說的「電子遊戲」。
② cognitive 認知的。相關片語有 cognitive psychology 認知心理學；cognitive ability 認知能力。
③ decline 在這句話裡作名詞，表示「下降」。cognitive decline 表示「認知能力減退」。

相關句子

The finding suggests that even a half-hour walk at a quick speed every day could lower the risk of cognitive impairment. (VOA)

這一發現說明，即使是每天半個小時的快速行走，也可以降低認知損傷的危險。

30   Poor nutrition can cause some hair follicles to stop growing or cause
      the hairs that grow to become weak or thin. (VOA)
      缺乏營養毛囊會停止生長，頭髮變得脆弱或稀疏。

要點解析

① nutrition 營養。poor 原指「貧窮的」。在這句話裡是「缺乏的」的意思。
② follicle 淋巴結。hair follicle 是「毛囊」。
③ thin 原指「薄的，瘦的」。描述頭髮時，有「稀疏的」的意思。

相關句子

Your doctor may want to perform some tests to check for nutrition problems
or an illness. (CNN)
你的醫生也許想透過測試來檢查營養或疾病問題。

31   The researchers say that dogs fed high fat diets are less fatigued after
      exercise, which reduces panting and sensitizes sniffing. (Scientific
      American)
      研究者稱食用高脂肪食物的狗運動後不會很疲勞，喘氣也有所減
      輕，且嗅覺更加靈敏。

要點解析

① fatigued 疲勞的。如：fatigued test 疲勞試驗。
② panting 在這句話作名詞，表示「喘氣」。
③ sensitize 使某事物或某人敏感。
④ sniff 聞，嗅。如：sniff out 發現；sniff at 嗤之以鼻。

32   By straining out the lactose-rich whey and transforming the milk
      solids into cheese, dairy farmers gained nutrition from cows without
      slaughtering their food source. (Scientific American)
      透過過濾富含乳糖的乳清把固體牛奶變成乳酪，奶農不需要屠殺
      食品源，就可以從母牛身上獲取營養物質。

要點解析

① strain out 過濾，濾去。
② lactose 乳糖。lactose-rich 則可理解為「富含乳糖的」。

③ transform 改變，使……變形。transform into 表示「轉變成」。

④ slaughter 殺戮，屠殺。

---

33   People with asthma, chronic obstructive pulmonary disease and oth-
      er breathing disorders need fast relief when their airways tighten up.
      (Scientific American)
      患有哮喘、慢性阻塞性肺病和其他呼吸性疾病的患者在呼吸道收
      縮時需要立刻緩解。

要點解析

① asthma 哮喘。

② disorder 混亂，騷亂。如：in disorder 慌亂地；mental disorder 精神病；
anxiety disorder 焦慮症。

③ tighten up 拉緊，加強。在這句話裡是「收縮」的意思。

---

34   The findings support earlier animal research in which rodents that were
      exercised had a number of favorable physiological changes. (NPR)
      早期動物研究發現，經過鍛鍊的齧齒類動物的確發生了有利的生
      理變化，而這些研究得到了證實。

要點解析

① rodent 齧齒目動物。

② favorable 有利的。如：favorable to 贊成，對……有利。這個詞還可以表
示「討人喜歡的」。

③ physiological 生理的。如：The doctor had a test on the physiological reaction of human being. 醫生做了一項有關人類生理反應的測試。

---

35   And now archaeologists have turned up some of those ancien medi-
      cines, which were preserved in a shipwreck for closet two millennia.
      (Scientific American)
      現在，考古學家在失事船隻中發現了部分古老的藥品，這些藥品
      已經保存了將近 2,000 年了。

要點解析

① turn up 是一個固定片語搭配，意思是「找到，出現」。

② preserve 用作動詞，表示「保存，保護」。如：preserve from... 保護……免遭傷害。

③ shipwreck 海難，失事船隻。如：The shipwreck was a harrowing experience. 那次海難是一次慘痛的經歷。

36　The science of pharmacology originally was the science of going out, talking to traditional healers, finding out which plants they used in their healing. (VOA)

藥理學最初是一門走出去的科學，需要和傳統的醫治者交流，找到他們用來治病的植物。

要點解析

① pharmacology 藥理學，藥物學。比如：clinical pharmacology 臨床藥理學，herbal pharmacology 中草藥理學。

② healer 來自 heal，意思是「醫治者」。heal 表示「治癒，痊癒」，如：heal over 癒合。

37　The oth er residents remember him jumping on the chest of a patient in just the sort of most dramatic fashion. (NPR)

其他住院醫師記得他以極具戲劇性的方式在患者的胸口跳躍。

要點解析

① jump on... 在……跳躍，注意介詞要用 on。

② the sort of 那種，那一類的。

③ resident 常用的含義是「居民」。在這句話裡是「醫師」的意思。chief resident 就是「總住院醫師」。

38　A United Nations report has highlighted the important role that dible insects could play in the fight against global hunger. (BBC)

聯合國的一份報告強調了可食用昆蟲在應對全球飢餓問題上發揮的重要作用。

要點解析

① highlight 用作動詞，意思是「強調，突出」，相當於 emphasize。

② edible 可食用的。如：edible fungus 食用菌，edible oil 食用油。

③ hunger 作名詞時表示「飢餓，渴望」。global hunger 意為「全球飢餓問題」。

39　If a patient reaches an advanced medical center quickly enough, doctors can open the blocked artery before the damage is done. (VOA)

如果患者能足夠快地到達先進的醫療中心，那麼醫生就能在損傷之前將堵塞的動脈疏通。

要點解析

① medical center 醫療中心。

② blocked 堵塞的，這個詞來自動詞 block「阻塞」。

③ artery 動脈。如：brachial artery 臂動脈，carotid artery 頸動脈等。

40　Schools are well-known reservoirs of contagion where students share all sorts of communicable conditions: coughs, colds, flu, you name it. (Scientific American)

學校是眾所周知的傳染病集中地，學生們在這裡共同接觸如咳嗽、感冒、流感等各種你能想得到的傳染病。

要點解析

① reservoir 儲藏，彙集；contagion 傳染。其形容詞形式是 contagious。

② communicable 意為「可傳達的，會傳染的」；表示這個含義還可以用 infective。

③ You name it 的字面意思是「凡是你叫得出名字的」，也就是「你能想得到的」，還能表示「應有盡有」。

41　The cortex is comprised of dense layers of nerve cells, and its thickness indicates the health of the brain. (NPR)

大腦皮層由神經細胞的緻密層組成，其厚度可以顯示出大腦的健康程度。

要點解析

① cortex（腦或者其它器官的）皮層。

② dense layer 緻密層。其中，dense 表示「稠密的，濃厚的」；layer 是「層」的意思。

③ indicate 指示，指出。

42　Underst anding these preferences could help treat skin diseases, leaving our hides footloose and infection-free. (Scientific American)
了解這些偏好有助於治療皮膚病，使我們的皮膚不受束縛，免受感染。

要點解析

① preference 喜好，偏好。

② treat 治療。如：treat by fomentation 用熱敷處理。

③ footloose 自由自在，無拘無束。infection-free 是用名詞＋形容詞構成一個新的形容詞。

④ hides 用複數形式有「獸皮」的意思。在這句話裡指代人的皮膚。

43　Alda Gross is neither terminally nor chronically ill, but she is 82 and apparently wants to end her life before she becomes incapacitated. (BBC)
阿爾達‧格羅斯沒有絕症也沒有慢性病，但是她已經 82 歲高齡，希望在行動不便之前結束自己的生命。

要點解析

① terminally 表示「處於末期症狀上」。如：a terminally ill patient 晚期疾病患者。

② chronically 慢性地。

③ incapacitate 使無能力。如：He was incapacitated by a heart attack. 他因心臟病發作而喪失活動能力。在這句話裡這個詞可以指「行動不便」。

44　Doctors performed an emergency cesarean section without anesthetic after her heart stopped. (BBC)
醫生在她心跳停止後，沒有進行麻醉就實施了緊急剖腹產手術。

要點解析

① cesarean 既可以作名詞也可以作形容詞，意為「剖腹產（的）」。cesarean section 指的是「剖腹產手術」。在這這句話裡的 section 表示「手術」。

② anesthetic 麻醉的。如：The patient remained fully conscious after the local anesthetic was administered. 患者在被施以局部麻醉之後仍能保持完全清醒。

45　There's a new procedure instead of the traditional method of giving trauma patients large amounts of intravenous fluids such as saline. (VOA)

一種新方法代替了為患者進行大量靜脈注射的傳統方法，比如注射生理鹽水等。

要點解析

① trauma 外傷。如：trauma surgery 創傷外科。

② intravenous fluid 進入靜脈的液體。其中，intravenous 表示「靜脈內的」。

③ saline 鹽水。如：normal saline 生理鹽水。

46　Autism is often diagnosed in childhood. It is a lifelong disorder. There is no cure for it, and for adult with autism, finding a job can be a very difficult struggle. (CNN)

自閉症通常在童年確診，是一種伴隨終生的疾病，沒有治療方法。對於成年自閉症患者來說，找工作是一件非常困難的事情。

要點解析

① autism 自閉症。如：child hood autism 兒童自閉症。

② diagnose 診斷，斷定。如：The doctor diagnosed the illness as influenza. 醫生診斷此病為流行性感冒。

③ disorder 混亂，障礙。lifelong disorder 即「終生疾病」。

④ cure 在這句話裡指「治癒方法」。cure for... 就是「治癒……的方法」。

相關句子

Several previous studies have suggested that underweight or premature infants have a higher risk of autism. (CNN)

早期一些研究顯示，體重過輕或者早產嬰兒患自閉症的機率要高得多。

47　The subjects who responded to the faux treatment actually produced more of the body's own natural painkillers. (Scientific American)

這些對安慰療法有反應的受試者的身體本身確實產生了更多的自然止痛劑。

要點解析

① respond to... 表示「作為對……的回應」。在這句話裡引申為「對……有反應」的意思。

② faux 假的。在這句話裡指利用安慰劑欺騙患者，因此，faux treatment 的含義引申為「安慰療法」。

③ painkiller 止痛藥。

相關句子

Arsenic was their aspirin, their common painkiller. (VOA)

砒霜對他們來說相當於阿斯匹靈，是他們最常用的止疼藥。

48　Campaig ners hope the developed embryonic cells can repair damaged tissues and cure diseases. (BBC)

倡議者希望成熟的胚胎細胞能修復受損組織並治癒疾病。

要點解析

① campaigner 競選者，倡議者。

② developed 在這句話裡是指「成熟的」，來自動詞 develop，表示「發育」的意思。

③ embryonic 胚芽的，胎兒的，初期的。如：embryonic cell 胚胎細胞；embryonic development 胚胎發育。

49　For centuries, physicians have known that some patients improve when given fake me dicine, like pills that contain no real drugs. (Scientific American)

幾個世紀以來，內科醫生已經了解到服用仿製藥品，也就是不含真正藥物成分的藥品，也可以改善一些患者的身體狀況。

要點解析

① fake medicine 假藥。其中 fake 表示「偽造的」，但這裡指的是「安慰劑」，

即 placebo。

② 表示「改善健康狀況」，可以用 improve one's health。

50　The human brain is built for speech, so anything that sounds like a voice, our brains just light up and we get an enormous range o f social and other responses. (NPR)

人腦是為聲音構建的，所以任何類似聲音的刺激都可以讓我們的大腦興奮，從而進行各類社交活動並做出其他反應。

要點解析

① light up 有「點亮」的意思。但在這個句子中，是「使……呈現興奮狀態」的意思。

② a range of 一系列，一些；enormous 大量的。

相關句子

They showed that patients who received deep brain stimulation had better control of their symptoms than those who only took medicine. (VOA)

他們發現，比起只服用藥物的患者，大腦受過深層刺激的患者病情更好控制。

51　The World Health Organization says reducing salt or sodium use can reduce your risk of heart disease, kidney failure or stroke. (VOA)

世界衛生組織稱，減少鹽或鈉的攝取量可以降低心臟病、腎衰竭和中風的患病機率。

要點解析

① sodium 鈉。

② kidney 腎，kidney failure 即「腎衰竭」。在這句話裡的 failure 有「故障」的意思，如：power failure 停電。

③ stroke 中風，如：have a stroke 中風。另外，sun stroke 可以表示「中暑」。

相關句子

There is a risk that giving a patient a strong blood thinner during a stroke can cause bleeding inside the brain. (VOA)

為中風患者注射大量血液稀釋劑會導致腦內出血。

52　Patients needed hours of surgery, but Mackey said it was just the be-
　　ginning for many victims. (NPR)

　　患者需要接受幾個小時的手術，但是麥基表示對於很多受害者來
　　說，這只是一個開始。

要點解析

　① surgery 外科手術。
　② victim 受害者。如：fall a victim to... 成為……的受害者。A woman is re-
　　covering in hospital after being rescued from the rubble of the garment facto-
　　ry. (BBC)
　　一名從服裝工廠的廢墟中救出的女子，已經在醫院康復了。

要點解析

　① recover 康復。常用搭配為：recover from an illness / injury 從疾病／受傷
　　中恢復。
　② rescue 營救，援救。這個詞既可以作動詞，也可以作名詞。
　③ garment 服裝。這個詞主要用在服裝生產和銷售的領域。

───────────────────────────────

54　The restaurant says it's working with agency staff to try to solate the
　　source of the infection. (BBC)

　　餐廳稱目前正與地區政府工作人員協同隔離感染源。

要點解析

　① agency 可以表示「代理，仲介」，但這個詞還可以表示「地區政府」。
　② isolate 使隔離。
　③ source of infection 感染源。

相關句子

　　They would have been tested to see if they needed treatment to prevent an
　　infection like HIV or hepatitis. (VOA)
　　他們會接受檢測，確定他們是否需要接受治療以阻止愛滋病毒或者
　　肝炎感染。

───────────────────────────────

55　So far, there are no reported cases in the United States. (CNN)

　　到目前為止，沒有報導稱美國有病例出現。

要點解析

① so far 到目前為止。也可以用 by now 或 until now 表示相同的意思。
② case 實例。

56　Queen Elizabeth has been admitted to hospital in London suffering from gastroenteritis—stomach infection. (BBC)

伊利莎白女王因患腸胃炎在倫敦入院接受治療。

要點解析

① be admitted to hospital 表示「被醫院收治」，即「住院」。
② suffer from 遭受，因……而蒙受傷害。在表示「患有……疾病」時常用這個片語。
③ gastroenteritis 腸胃炎。

相關句子

Breast-fed infants also have a lower risk of gastroenteritis and respiratory and ear infections, research shows. (BBC)

研究顯示，母乳餵養的嬰兒出現腸胃炎、呼吸問題及耳部感染的機率也較低。

57　By scanning the brains of 300 people between the ages of 14 and 24, they hope to identify how the wiring that controls impulsive and emotional behavior changes as they get older. (BBC)

透過掃描 300 名 14 歲至 24 歲青少年的大腦，他們希望識別出隨著年齡的成長，控制衝動和情感行為的大腦線路的變化。

要點解析

① identify 認出，識別。如：identify with... 與……一致，identify by 透過……認出。
② wiring 線路。在這句話裡指的是「大腦線路」。
③ impulsive 衝動的。

相關句子

The disease can also diminish brain tissue and is associated with memory loss, depression, impulsive behavior and rage. (CNN)

這種疾病也能減少大腦組織，並且與記憶缺失、憂鬱、衝動和暴躁行為都緊密相關。

58　With the biggest emergency care facility in the city, Medina serves as a referral hospital for trauma and surgery cases. (CNN)

麥地那市擁有這座城市最大的急診醫療設備，這裡成為了外傷和手術的轉診醫院。

要點解析

① facility 設備，設施。不僅可以指某種設備，也可以指代某種服務。常用搭配還有：recreational facility 娛樂設施。

② referral hospital 轉診醫院。其中 referral 是名詞，可以表示「參照，提及，轉診患者」。

59　So even th ough they're burning fewer calorie s per minute than the bounders do, they work out enough longer to burn more total calories. (Scientific American)

所以即使他們每分鐘燃燒的熱量不如那些鍛鍊強度大的人多，但他們鍛鍊時間長，可以燃燒更多的總卡路里。

要點解析

① calorie 卡路里。

② bounder 原指「粗魯的人，暴發戶」。在這句話裡指「鍛鍊強度大的人」。

60　The scientists at the University of Dundee in Scotland were funded to research diseases neglected by major pharmaceutical Companies. (BBC)

蘇格蘭丹地大學的科學家得到了資助，致力於研究那些被大型製藥公司忽略的疾病。

要點解析

① be funded to do sth. 意為「得到資助以做某事」。在這句話裡 fund 是動詞，表示「資助」，這個詞也可以作名詞，指「資金」。

② neglect 忽視，疏忽。如：neglect of 忽略。

③ pharmaceutical 製藥的，配藥的。

61　And researchers said Cambridge University has begun the details study to understand the working of the teenage brain. (BBC)

研究人員表示，劍橋大學開始詳細研究了解青少年的大腦活動情況。

要點解析

① teenage 作形容詞時，表示「青少年的」。此外，還可以作為名詞，表示「青少年時期」。

② working 在這句話裡不表示「工作」，而是表示「活動」的意思，也就是「大腦的活動狀況」。

62　Officials have found some clusters of cases where the disease has been transmitted between family members or in a health care setting. (CNN)

官員們已經在一些集群的病例中發現，病毒是在家庭成員之間或衛生保健機構內傳播的。

要點解析

① cluster 串，簇，群，組。在醫藥方面，這個詞可以指「群集」。

② transmit 傳播，同義詞有 spread。

③ health care setting 是「醫療保健機構」。setting 原指「環境」。在這句話裡指代「醫療保健機構」。

相關句子

In the Senate, he was a leader in the fight for health care for children. (CNN)

在參議院，他是為兒童醫療保健而戰的領袖。

63　Some of the well known threats include wheat rust, African army worms, Cassava Bacterial Blight and the European Grapevine Moth. (VOA)

小麥銹病、非洲黏蟲、木薯白葉枯病和歐洲葡萄蛾蟲害等都是眾所周知的威脅。

要點解析
① well known 眾所周知的；出名的。
② threat 用作名詞，意思是「威脅」。

64　Kramer did a study in which he scanned the brains of 120 older adults, half of whom started a program of moderate aerobic exercise. (NPR)

克雷默的一項研究掃描了 120 名中老年人的大腦，這些人中有一半已經開始了適度的有氧訓練專案。

要點解析
① scan 是「瀏覽，掃描」的意思。在這句話裡指「掃描大腦」。
② moderate 中等的，適度的。
③ aerobic 有氧的，增氧健身法的。如：aerobic respiration 有氧呼吸，aerobic exercise 有氧訓練，aerobic treatment 有氧處理。

相關句子
They have a full program with weights, aerobic training and cricket training as well. (BBC)
他們參加了一個全方位專案，包括有氧訓練和板球訓練。

65　Some hair loss can result from a combination of genetics, aging and hormones. (VOA)

有些脫髮是由基因、老齡化和荷爾蒙的因素共同引起的。

要點解析
① hair loss 脫髮。其中 loss 是「減少，損失」的意思。
② result from 起因於，相當於 the result of... 的意思。
③ combination 結合，合作。
④ genetics 遺傳學。如：behavioral genetics 行為遺傳學；nature genetics 自然遺傳學。
⑤ hormone 荷爾蒙。如：This hormone interacts closely with other hormones in the body. 這種荷爾蒙與體內其他荷爾蒙有著密切的相互作用。

66　Most of the cases and illnesses have been associated with the elderly and those with preexisting or severe underlying medical conditions.

(CNN)

大多數的病例和疾病都與老年人以及之前患有嚴重的潛在疾病有關。

要點解析

① be associated with 和……聯繫在一起；和……有關。
② elderly 在這句話裡是形容詞，指「上了年紀的」。這個詞也可以作名詞，前面加定冠詞 the，the elderly 可以表示「老年人」。
③ preexisting 先前存在的。這個詞是動詞 preexist 「先前存在」的現在分詞作形容詞。似 underlying 潛在的，根本的。medical condition 在這句話裡是「健康狀況」的意思。

相關句子

But it turned out the elderly patients had fewer adverse effects from the drugs than younger patients. (VOA)
但結果顯示這種藥物對老年人的副作用比對年輕人的要小。

---

67 That would be a so-called biosafety level 3 labs, where researchers can keep this demonstrably dangerous virus undertight control. (NPR)
那裡將是一個所謂的三級生物安全實驗室，在那裡研究者可以嚴格控制這種被證實有危險的病毒。

要點解析

① biosafety 生物安全，這個詞由表示「生物的」的詞根 bio- 和 safety 合成。
② demonstrably 可證明地，可論證地。
③ under tight control 處於嚴格控制之中。其中 tight 作形容詞表示「緊的；嚴屬的」。

相關句子

Georgiana would live in a beautiful room he had prepared nearby, while he worked tirelessly in his lab. (VOA)
喬治安娜會住在他在附近準備的那所漂亮屋子裡，他卻在實驗室裡不知疲倦地工作。

---

68 A youthful cortex and thicker cingulate suggest to Rogalski that these two brain regions have been spared the typical age-related shrinkage.

(NPR)

年輕的皮層和較厚的扣帶皮層使羅加爾斯基認為這些都顯示這兩個大腦區域沒有出現典型的與年齡相關的萎縮。

要點解析

① cingulate 有色帶環繞的，在醫學用語中表示「扣帶」。如：cingulate cortex 扣帶皮層。
② brain region 指「大腦區域」。這句話裡 region 也可以用 section 表示。
③ be spared 的字面意思是「省去」。在這句話裡引申為「沒有出現某種症狀」的意思。
④ shrinkage 收縮，皺縮。

相關句子

For instance, the prefrontal cortex emerged late in evolution and is among the last to mature. (BBC)
例如，前額皮層在進化中出現較晚，也是最後成熟的。

69　In the view of Myriad and its supporters in the biotech and pharmaceutical industries, patents are the keys to making these medical discoveries possible. (NPR)

Myriad 公司及其生物技術和製藥業的支持者認為，專利授權是使這些醫學發現成為可能的關鍵。

要點解析

① in the view of... 根據……的觀點。
② pharmaceutical 製藥學的。此外，還可作為名詞，表示「藥物」。
③ patent 表示「專利，專利權」。

70　The commission says all the beeps and buzzing can distract caregivers and endanger patients. (NPR)

委員會稱，這些嗶嗶聲和嗡嗡聲會分散護理人員注意力，並且危及患者性命。

要點解析

① beep 嗶嗶聲，buzzing 嗡嗡聲。

② caregiver 是一個合成詞，care 表示「照顧」，giver 表示「給予者」。因此 caregiver 的字面意思是「提供照顧的人」，也就是「護理人員」的意思。

④ endanger 危及，使遭受危險。

---

71 The family of the Nobel Prize-winning Chilean poet Pablo Neruda has agreed that his remains should undergo toxicology tests in the United States. (BBC)

諾貝爾獎得主智利詩人巴勃羅·聶魯達的家人同意在美國對他的遺體進行毒理檢測。

要點解析

① remains 作名詞，意思是「遺骸」，通常要用複數形式。

② undergo 經歷，忍受。

③ toxicology 毒理學，毒物學。

相關句子

The human remains were moved from other places on the battlefield and put into graves in the new cemetery. (VOA)

人類遺體從其他地方的戰場轉移過來，安葬在新墓地的墳墓裡。

---

72 For practice, the patient is a remote-controlled mannequin who blinks and cries. (VOA)

在實驗中，患者是一個遠端控制的人體模型，可以眨眼和哭泣。

要點解析

① remote-control 指「遙控，遠程控制」。其中 remote 表示「遙遠的」。

② mannequin 人體模型。

③ blink 有「閃光」的意思，也可以指「眨眼」。

---

73 A study finds that a specific brain region gives the song a thumb up or down. (Scientific American)

研究發現，大腦的特定區域能夠判斷歌曲的好壞。

要點解析

thumb 的本意是「拇指」，give a thumb up 字面意思是「豎起拇指」，意為「讚揚」，與之相反的 give a thumb down 就是「貶低」。

74　The plant called chamise can be used in a balm that helps with skin problems, and the anesthetic qualities of California bay help with toothaches. (VOA)

一種叫做下田菊的植物可以用於製作鎮痛軟膏，幫助解決皮膚問題，而加州月桂的麻醉特性可以解決牙痛問題。

要點解析

① balm 鎮痛軟膏，有時候也指「軟膏」。比如：lip balm 潤唇膏。
② anesthetic 麻醉的，感覺缺失的。

相關句子

Its toxin is used as heart stimulant and as a diuretic as well a remedy for sinusitis and toothache. (VOA)

其毒素被用於製作心臟興奮劑和利尿劑，還可以治療鼻竇炎和牙痛。

75　There have be en a couple of family clusters that have been investigated, but the cases in general have been sporadically spread around the country, and the source of infections remains under active investigation. (BBC)

有幾個家族群體接受了調查，但全國還是有零星案例，人們仍在積極調查感染源。

要點解析

sporadically 偶發地，零星地。

相關句子

And what we see is a little bit late stage of the progression of the infection. (CNN)

我們看到的只是傳染過程中的一個較晚階段。

76　One of the most popular and famous musketeers Annette Funicello died and she suffered for more than decades with multiple sclerosis.

(NPR)

最受歡迎的著名火槍手之一安妮特‧弗奈斯洛逝世，她幾十年來一直受到多發性硬化症的困擾。

要點解析

① musketeer 火槍手。

② sclerosis 硬化症，multiple sclerosis 則指「多發性硬化症」。

相關句子

Disease such as multiple sclerosis and type-one diabetes are more common among whites. (VOA)

多發性硬化症和第一型糖尿病等疾病在白人中比較普遍。

77　Scientists believe they could use this genetic material or DNA from a skin cell of someone with Parkinson's disease to create a personalized treatment. (VOA)

科學家相信，他們可以用帕金森氏患者皮膚細胞的基因組織或者 DNA 來創造個性化治療。

要點解析

① genetic 基因的，遺傳的；genetic material 指「遺傳物質」。

② personalized 個人的，個性化的。

相關句子

This week, we will tell about what is said to be the largest study yet of a treatment for Parkinson's disease. (VOA)

這週，我們將談論的帕金森氏療法課題研究據說是規模空前的一次。

78　The Food and Agriculture Organization says two billion people already supplement their diets with insects such as grasshoppers and ants. (BBC)

糧農組織稱，有 20 億人已經將蚱蜢和螞蟻等昆蟲作為飲食補給。

要點解析

① supplement 作動詞，表示「增補」。在這句話裡是「作為飲食補給」的

意思。這個詞也可以作名詞,表示「補充,補充物」。

② grasshopper 蚱蜢。

相關句子

The American government also says a healthy diet is one that is high in fruits, vegetables and whole grains. (BBC)

美國政府還表示,健康飲食應該富含水果、蔬菜和全麥食品。

79　The researchers say extra-virgin olive oil contains aromatic compounds that block the absorption of glucose from the blood, delaying the recurrence of hunger. (Scientific American)

研究者稱,特級初榨橄欖油富含芳香烴化合物,該物質阻礙人體從血液中吸收葡萄糖,延緩飢餓感。

要點解析

① virgin 未經利用的,處於原始狀態的。extra-virgin olive oil 則表示「特級初榨橄欖油」。

② aromatic compound 芳香烴化合物。compound 在化學裡是「化合物;混合物」的意思。

③ absorption 是動詞 absorb 的名詞形式,意思是「吸收,同化」。

④ recurrence 反覆,重現。

80　Tufts University School of Medicine has a clinical skills and simulation center where medical students and hospital trauma teams get trained. (VOA)

塔夫茨大學醫學院擁有臨床技術和模擬中心,醫學院學生和醫院外傷救治團隊可以接受培訓。

要點解析

① clinical 臨床的,診所的。

② simulation 是 simulate 的名詞形式,表示「模仿,模擬」。

③ trauma 是「創傷,外傷」的意思。

81　The people who never left their home—even though they didn't seem to have any cognitive problems when we started following them—

were twice as likely to develop Alzheimer's disease over five years.
(NPR)

即使是當我們對那些從未離開過家的人們展開追蹤調查的時候，他們似乎也沒有認知能力問題，但在未來五年，他們患上阿茲海默症的機率卻是普通人的兩倍。

要點解析

cognitive 認知的，認識能力的。

相關句子

It's also helped inspire others to support people with the disease and
Alzheimer's research and awareness. (VOA)

這也鼓勵了其他人對阿茲海默症患者提供幫助，並且加強了這種疾病的研究和意識。

82　They say countries overburdened by diseases, such as HIV/ AIDS,
tuberculosis and malaria, will have great difficulty dealing with the
surge of pandemic flu cases. (VOA)

他們稱那些因愛滋病、肺結核和瘧疾等疾病的救治而負擔過重的國家會很難應付流感病例的激增。

要點解析

① overburden 在這句話裡用作被動語態，意思是「使負擔過重」。

② tuberculosis 肺結核；malaria 瘧疾。

③ surge 在這句話裡作名詞，表示「洶湧，激增」；也可以作為動詞，表示「激增」。

④ pandemic（疾病等）全國流行的，普遍的；如：pandemic influenza 大流行性流感。

83　These include rheumatoid arthritis, type I diabetes and celiac disease,
a condition that affects the digestive system. (VOA)

這些疾病包括風溼性關節炎，第一型糖尿病和一種會影響消化系統的乳糜瀉病症。

① rheumatoid arthritis 風溼性關節炎；diabetes 糖尿病。

② condition 在這句話裡表示「病症」。

③ digestive 是動詞 digest 的形容詞形式，意思是「消化的」。digestive system 即「消化系統」。

84　The researchers say that gum increases the flow of oxygen to regions of the brain responsible for attention. (Scientific American)

研究者稱口香糖可以增加負責注意力的大腦區域的氧氣輸送。

要點解析

① gum 口香糖。此外，這個詞還可以作為動詞，表示「使……有黏性」。

② flow 作名詞可以指「流動，流量」。在這句話裡是「氧氣流量」的意思，引申為「氧氣輸送」。

85　The country will launch an ambitious plan to provide free health care to lactating and pregnant women and children under five, in an attempt to reduce maternal and child mortality in the country. (VOA)

國家將發起一項宏偉的計畫，為哺乳期和孕婦及五歲以下的兒童提供免費醫療，試圖降低孕產婦和兒童死亡率。

要點解析

① launch 在這句話裡作動詞，表示「發起，發動」。如：launch strike 實施罷工。

② ambitious 有抱負的，雄心勃勃的。

③ lactating 哺乳的。動詞原形為 lactate，表示「授乳」。

④ mortality 死亡率。

86　Numerous studies indicate African-Americans and Hispanics receive a poorer quality of health care than non-Hispanic whites, even when they have the same levels of income and health insurance coverage. (VOA)

大量研究顯示非裔美國人和西班牙人獲得的醫療保健比非西班牙裔白人差一點，即使他們擁有相同的收入水準和醫療保險範圍。

要點解析

① numerous 許多的，很多的。

② indicate 顯示，預示。

③ coverage 指「覆蓋，覆蓋範圍」。但是在保險業，這個詞的含義是「承包範圍」。

87　Boston hospitals always staff up their emergency rooms on Marathon Day to care for runners with cramps, dehydration and the occasional heart attack. (NPR)

在馬拉松日，波士頓醫院總會增加急救室的工作人員來照顧那些抽筋、脫水和偶發心臟病的運動員。

要點解析

① staff up 為……增補人員。staff 在這句話裡作動詞，表示「為……配備職員」。staff 也經常作集體名詞表示「全體員工」。

② cramp 抽筋，痙攣。

③ dehydration 脫水。

④ heart attack 表示「心臟病」，其中 attack 有「發作」的意思。

88　Too much salt activates the cells that sense sourness and bitterness, sending unpleasant signals to the brain and transforming a tasty bite into a turn-off. (Scientific American)

過多的鹽分會啟動感知苦味和酸味的細胞，為大腦發送不愉快的訊號，並把一口美味的食物變得倒人胃口。

要點解析

① activate 啟動。

② sourness 酸味，其形容詞形式為：sour 酸的，bitterness 苦味。表示「味道」的詞還有：sweet 甜的，spicy 辣的。

③ a tasty bite 是「一口美味的食物」的意思，其中 bite 作名詞表示「一口」。

④ turn-off 來自片語 turn off，這個詞可以表示「倒人胃口的事物」，如：The movie is a turn-off. 這電影特別無聊。

89　Consuming too much sugar will eventually lead to diseases and cause immense medical expenses. (CNN)

攝取過多的糖最終會導致疾病，並造成龐大的醫療費用。

要點解析

① consume 消耗。在談論健康與飲食的關係時，通常用這個詞表示「食用」的意思。

② lead to 導致，通向。此外，lead up to 也可以表示「導致」，但偏向於「逐漸導致」。

③ immense 極大的，龐大的。

90　Lack of essential drugs to keep pregnant women and young children healthy is a major hurdle to providing comprehensive care. (VOA)

缺乏必需的藥物來保護孕婦和兒童的健康是提供綜合性醫療的一大障礙。

要點解析

① hurdle 在這句話裡作為名詞，表示「障礙」。此外，還可以作為動詞，表示「克服；跳過」。

② comprehensive 綜合的。常見的搭配有：comprehensive analysis 綜合分析；comprehensive control 綜合治理。

91　One of the measures sets a limit for driver similar to blood alcohol standard for drunk driving. (VOA)

其中一項措施是替司機設定一個限制，類似血液酒精濃度的酒駕測試。

要點解析

① limit 在這句話裡作為名詞，表示「限制，限度」。此外，還可以作為動詞，表示「限定」。

② alcohol 酒精。blood alcohol 就是「血液酒精含量」。

③ drunk driving 酒駕。

相關句子

So people with poor oral hygiene who drink alcohol may be placing themselves at higher risk. (BBC)

因此，口腔衛生不好的人喝酒是把自己置於更加危險的境地。

---

92   All mammals, us included, sense temperature and touch through nerve cells in the skin. (Scientific American)

包括我們在內的所有哺乳動物都透過皮膚神經細胞來感受溫度和觸摸。

要點解析

① mammal 哺乳動物。
② sense 通常作為名詞使用，表示「感覺，觀念」；但在這句話裡用作動詞，表示「感覺到」。

相關句子

Rescuers said the meter-long mammal had suffered a few scratches but was otherwise healthy. (VOA)

營救者稱這個身長一公尺的哺乳動物身上有幾處刮傷，但還是健康的。

---

93   Studies have shown that the fatter your friends, the more likely you're also overweight. (Scientific American)

研究顯示你的朋友越胖，你就越有可能超重。

要點解析

① show 經常用來表示某一研究「顯示」了某種結論，也可以用 reveal 替換。
② overweight 在這句話裡作為形容詞，表示「超重的，過重的」。

相關句子

About four out of five African-American are overweight or obese. (CNN)

約五分之四的非裔美國人都超重或者過胖。

---

94   He said the aim would be to find treatments and cures for a number of disorders including Alzheimer's and post-traumatic stress disorder known as PTSD. (BBC)

他表示目標是發現治療和治癒一些疾病的治療方法，包括老年痴呆症和創傷後壓力症候群，俗稱 PTSD。

要點解析

① Alzheimer's 在這句話裡相當於 Alzheimer's disease，表示「阿茲海默症」。

② PTSD 是 post-traumatic stress disorder 的縮寫，指的是「創傷後壓力症候群」。

相關句子

Several others were injured, including goalkeeper who was taken to South Africa for treatment. (BBC)

其他幾個人也受了傷，包括守門員，他已經被送往南非接受治療。

95　Olive oil is thought to be healthy because it's mostly monounsaturated fat. (Scientific American)

橄欖油被認為是健康的，因為它含有大量單元不飽和脂肪。

要點解析

monounsaturated fat 單元不飽和脂肪。fat 在這句話裡作為名詞，是「脂肪」的意思。

相關句子

A low-fat diet is one in which less than thirty percent of a person's daily calorie intake comes from fat. (VOA)

低脂肪飲食就是食用者每天從脂肪中攝取的卡路里低於 30%。

96　Figuring out this connection could lead to new therapies for speech and language disorders. (Scientific American)

弄清這種聯繫可以找到治療語言障礙的新方法。

要點解析

① therapy 治療，療法。

② speech and language disorder 指「語言障礙症」。

相關句子

But there was one therapy that made me sullen, resentful and depressed: speech therapy. (VOA)

但是有一種治療方法讓我感到沉悶、厭惡和沮喪，這就是言語治療。

97　But researchers also detected starch, pollen, charcoal, fats and linen fibers. (Scientific American)

但是研究者也檢測到澱粉、花粉、木炭、脂肪和亞麻纖維。

要點解析

① detect 察覺，發覺，探測。在這句話裡相當於 find。

② starch 澱粉，pollen 花粉，charcoal 木炭。

③ linen fiber 表示「亞麻纖維」，其中 fiber 表示「纖維」。

98　In theory this could be used to repair the damage after a heart attack or the brains of patients with Parkinson's disease. (BBC)

理論上，這可以修復心臟病的損傷或者帕金森氏患者的大腦。

要點解析

① in theory 理論上，從理論上來講。相當於 in the abstract。

② be used to do 被用於。類似的片語 be used to doing 則表示「習慣於做某事」；used to do 表示「過去常常做某事」。

相關句子

Doctors say that over time the damage interferes with the natural exchange of oxygen and carbon dioxide in the lungs. (VOA)

醫生稱久而久之這些損傷會妨礙肺部氧氣和二氧化碳的自動交換。

99　One of the advancements is a change from having paramedics stabilize the patient at the scene to what is called "scoop and run". (VOA)

其中一項進步是從護理人員在現場安頓患者轉變為採取所謂的「拉起就跑」原則。

要點解析

① paramedic 護理人員。

② stabilize 使穩定，使穩固。在這句話裡有「安置患者」的意思。

③ at the scene 在現場。scene 在這句話裡是「場面，現場」的意思。此外，scene 還有「風景」的意思。

④ scoop and run 拉起就跑。指的是對一些無法判斷、無法採取措施或即使採取措施也無濟於事的危重傷病，應該盡快將患者送到有條件治療的

醫院，而不要在現場進行無價值的搶救。

100　Check out this map, all those states in red, that's where officials are reporting widespread outbreaks of the flu. (CNN)

看看這張地圖，所有這些標記成紅色的州就是官方報告的流感廣泛爆發區域。

要點解析

① check out 在這句話裡是「檢查，查看」的意思。除此之外，還有「結帳離開，通過考核」的意思。

② widespread 廣泛的，普遍的。

③ outbreak 爆發，突然發生。通常指戰爭爆發或者疾病發作。

相關句子

But last week, two teams working independently reported a discovery that could help lead to a universal flu vaccine. (VOA)

但是上週，兩個獨立工作的小組報告了一項發現，透過這個發現可以製造一種通用的流感疫苗。

101　Her first step was to see if the brains of the super agers looked any different than those of other 80-year-olds. (NPR)

她第一步就是觀察這些正值盛年的人和 80 歲人的大腦的區別。

要點解析

① step 在這句話裡作為名詞，表示「步驟」；當作為動詞時，表示「踩，踏」的意思。

② ager 這個詞表示「處於某個年齡層的人」，如 super ager 表示「正值盛年」，也可以用 best ager 表示這個意思。

102　The pills primarily contained zinc compounds, probably the active medicinal ingredients. (Scientific American)

這些藥片主要成分是鋅化合物，而這可能就是活性藥物成分。

要點解析

① zinc 鋅。此外，身體需要的微量元素還有：calcium 鈣，iron 鐵，vitamin

維他命等。

② ingredient 組成部分，即「成分」。active 在這句話裡是「活性的」的意思。

相關句子

Teenagers were told the pill was good for them, helping with weight loss and productivity. (CNN)

青少年被告知這種藥片對他們有好處，能幫助他們減肥，促進成長。

103　It's a sedative used for surgery and you certainly were not the first doctor to give Michael Jackson propofol. (CNN)

異丙酚是一種用於手術的鎮靜劑，而你肯定不是第一位替麥可‧傑克森開異丙酚的醫生。

要點解析

① sedative 止痛藥，鎮靜劑。

② 表示給某人「開藥」也可以用 give 這個動詞。

相關句子

By measuring subsequent brain activity they found that alcohol no longer had the same sedative effect. (VOA)

透過對大腦活動的連續監測，他們發現酒精不再有相同的止痛作用。

104　In places without access to large sewage systems, bacterialaden human waste passes into septic tanks. (Scientific American)

在沒有大型汙水處理系統的地方，含有細菌的人類糞便將進入化糞池。

要點解析

① sewage 下水道。sewage system 就是指「下水道系統」。

② bacteria-laden 含有細菌的。bacteria 指「細菌」，laden 則指「裝滿的」。

③ septic tank 化糞池。

105　Health officials say that region seems to be the starting point for a dangerous new virus. (CNN)

衛生部官員表示那塊區域似乎是一種新型危險病毒的起源地。

① starting point 的字面意思是「開始的點」，也就是「發源地」的意思。

② virus 病毒。如：influenza virus 流感病毒；virus infection 病毒感染。

106　Flu shots can be very effective, you know there is a number of that varies every year, but it's in the 70% to 80% range, and not a 100%. (CNN)

注射流感疫苗非常有效，你知道疫苗種數每年都在變化，但是在 70% 到 80% 之間，而不是 100%。

要點解析

① shot 作為名詞時，是「發射」的意思。在這句話裡是「（疫苗等的）注射」的意思。

② effective 有效的，生效的。

③ vary 的意思是「變化，使多樣化」。

107　When you're on the high salt intake you always have some extra salt in you and a slightly greater volume of blood. (VOA)

當你攝取的鹽量偏高，你的身體裡就總會有些多餘的鹽分，血液中的含鹽量也稍微偏高。

要點解析

① intake 在這句話裡作為名詞，表示「攝取量」。

② slightly 輕微地，稍稍。其形容詞形式為 slight，表示「輕微的」。如：slight pain 輕微疼痛。

③ volume 含量。這個詞還可以表示「體積，容積」。

108　Our skins play host to a huge variety of microbes, but previous studies focused on bacteria. (Scientific American)

我們的皮膚寄居著多種微生物，但以前的研究主要集中在細菌上。

要點解析

① play host to 本指「招待」，在這句話裡可以理解為「是……的主人，

是……的宿主」。host 在生物學中，有「宿主」的意思。

② microbes 細菌，微生物。

相關句子

And in another one, scientists are studying microbes in search of a cure for cancer. (VOA)

另外，科學家們正在研究微生物，以尋找治療癌症的方法。

109　When bacteria, like some strains of E. coli, enter the water supply they can threaten public health. (Scientific American)

當細菌，像大腸桿菌的菌株進入到供水系統會威脅公共健康。

要點解析

① strain 可以指「微生物菌株」。

② E. coli 是 Escherichia coli 的縮寫，指的是「大腸桿菌」。

③ water supply 供水系統。

相關句子

E. coli can cause a range of symptoms from mild diarrhea to severe vomiting. (BBC)

大腸桿菌會引起輕微腹瀉和嚴重嘔吐等一系列症狀。

110　Scientists have cloned for the first time human embryos that can produce some cells, opening the door for treatments of various diseases. (NPR)

科學家首次複製出人類胚胎幹細胞，這為治療各種疾病打開了大門。

要點解析

① clone 通常作名詞，表示「複製」。在這句話裡作為動詞，表示「複製，複製」。

② embryo 胚胎。

相關句子

Dr. Antinori said he hoped to produce the first cloned human embryo within eighteen months. (BBC)

安蒂諾里博士稱他希望在 18 個月內培育出第一個人類複製胚胎。

111　But we also have the highest rates of inflammatory bowel disease.
(Scientific American)
然而，我們患上炎症性腸疾的機率是最高的。

要點解析

① inflammatory 炎症的，發炎的。
② bowel 腸。此外，還有「內臟」的意思。

112　A trial is being held in the California courtroom today on whether Ger-
ber Products, Del Monte Foods, Beech-Nut Nutrition and many other
baby food makers should put warning labels on products sold in California. (NPR)
審訊將於今天在加利福尼亞法庭進行，判定嘉寶公司、台爾蒙食
品公司、比納保健公司和許多其他嬰兒食品製造商是否應該在加
州出售的產品貼上警示標籤。

要點解析

① trial 審訊。如：on trial 在審訊中。
② courtroom 法庭，審判室。
③ put warning labels on... 是「在......上貼警示標籤」的意思。

113　By reducing the amount of dead space in the syringe design, researchers say they can reduce the amount of infectious blood trapped inside
by a factor of a thousand—and thus vastly reduce the numbers of viral
particles available to spread disease. (Scientific American)
透過減少注射器的無效區，研究者稱他們可以透過多種方式減少
注射器吸入被感染的血液，這樣就能大量減少可傳播疾病的濾過
性毒菌顆粒的數量。

要點解析

① dead space 在這句話裡並不是「死亡空間」的意思。在解剖學上，這個
片語可以理解為「死腔；無效區」。

② syringe 注射。

③ viral 濾過性毒菌的。

④ particle 顆粒。

114　It causes blurred vision, rapid breathing, heavy sweating, confusion, headaches, nausea and at the very worst cases, convulsions, paralysis and death. (CNN)

這會導致視力模糊、呼吸急促、大量出汗、精神錯亂、頭痛、噁心，最糟糕的情況還會抽搐、癱瘓甚至死亡。

要點解析

① blurred 模糊的，是用動詞 blur 的過去分詞作形容詞。blur 的意思是「玷汙，使……模糊不清」。

② confusion 混亂。如：in confusion 表示「亂七八糟」。

③ nausea 噁心，反胃，convulsion 抽搐，paralysis 癱瘓。

115　That's because today's vaccines train your immune system to recognize specific strains of flu. (Scientific American)

那是因為如今的疫苗會訓練你的免疫系統識別特定的流感菌株。

要點解析

① vaccines 疫苗。

② immune system 免疫系統。train 在這句話裡是「訓練」的意思。

相關句子

While research had progressed rapidly in recent years, vaccines currently being tested only offered 30% protection. (BBC)

然而，近年來研究取得了很大進步，經臨床試驗的疫苗僅提供了 30% 的保護。

116　The National Turkey Federation says it's supportive of the Food and Drug Administration's efforts to create strategy for judicious use of antibiotics that, they say, are needed to keep flocks of turkeys healthy. (NPR)

美國國家火雞協會稱，支持食品和藥物管理局為制定合理使用抗

生素策略方面所做的努力，他們稱抗生素對保證火雞群的健康是必要的。

要點解析

① judicious 明智的。
② antibiotic 抗生素。
③ flock 群。這個詞常指鳥群或獸群，如：flocks of 成群的。

117　The study of more than 60,000 people in the British Journal of Cancer suggests they have a lower risk of getting cancers of the stomach, bladder and blood. (BBC)

《英國癌症雜誌》一項針對 60,000 多人的研究顯示，他們患上胃癌、膀胱癌和白血病的機率較低。

要點解析

bladder 膀胱。此外，還有「空話連篇的人」的意思。

相關句子

Four out of 10 had a low understanding of various methods used to detect bowel cancer. (BBC)

40% 的人對於腸癌檢查的各種方法了解甚少。

118　Particularly with the penetrating trauma because if you got a vascular injury to the chest torso, there is nothing else than surgery that will stop the bleeding. (VOA)

如果有穿透性外傷，情況更加嚴重，因為如果你胸部軀幹的血管受傷，只有手術可以止血。

要點解析

① penetrating 敏銳的。
② trauma 創傷。通常指由心理上的創傷造成精神上的異常。
③ vascular 血管的。
④ stop the bleeding 的意思是「止血」。其中，bleeding 「出血」是動詞 bleed 的現在分詞作名詞。

119　We believe we're on the cusp of a revolution of how we treat our patients in this country, by translating personalized medicine into the clinic. (NPR)

在如何救治患者這個問題上，透過將個人化醫療轉化為臨床醫療，相信我們正處在改革的前端。

要點解析

① cusp 尖端，尖頭。在這句話裡比喻「前端」。

② revolution 革命。在這句話裡指「改革」。

相關句子

Two-thirds of the clinic's patients are under 20 and a third are between 20 and 35. (BBC)

三分之二的臨床患者年紀在 20 歲以下，另外三分之一則在 20 到 35 歲之間。

120　Researchers are looking at whether it was initially passed from animals to humans. (CNN)

研究人員正在探尋這種疾病最初是否是由動物傳染給人類的。

要點解析

① initially 開始，最初。

② pass from... to... 從……傳給……。這個片語可以用來指病毒的傳播。

Part 6

Environmental Protection

1   There's no sign though that world governments have the political will to make real their promises to reduce emissions of greenhouse gases. (BBC)

但是沒有跡象顯示各國政府做出減少溫室氣體排放承諾的政治意願。

要點解析

① there is no sign... 沒有……的預兆。其中 sign 作名詞，是「標誌；跡象」的意思。

② emission 排放，散發。相關片語有：exhaust emission 廢氣排放；carbon emission 碳排放；dust emission 粉塵排放。

③ greenhouse 溫室，而 greenhouse gases 則指「溫室氣體；溫室效應」。

相關句子

The reduction in emissions of sulphur dioxide, which causes acid rain, has increased the impact of greenhouse gases. (BBC)

引起酸雨的二氧化硫氣體排放的減少，增加了溫室氣體的影響。

2   The aircraft's wings and rear stabilizer are covered with some 12,000 solar cells which in daylight charge batteries that are hung below the wings. (BBC)

飛機的機翼和後方穩定裝置上覆蓋著大約 1,200 塊太陽能晶片，白天可以為懸掛在機翼下的電池充電。

要點解析

① rear 在後面。常用搭配有：rear wheel 後輪；rear end 後部；rear area 後方。

② be covered with... 被……覆蓋。

③ charge 這裡的意思是「使充電」。此外還有「飽和，承擔……責任」的意思。

3   But wild coffee forests have a much bigger gene pool than cultivated crops, meaning more resistance to disease, pests and drought. (Scientific American)

但是野生咖啡林比種植農作物擁有更大的基因庫，這意味著它能

更好地抵抗疾病、害蟲和乾旱。

（要點解析）

① gene pool 基因庫。pool 本身是「泳池」的意思，在醫學用語中，有「庫、血庫」的意思。

② drought 乾旱。drought resistance 耐旱性；drought relief 乾旱救災；drought control 抗旱

③ pest 害蟲。

---

4 Humans are impacting the global water systems by building dams, through land use changes, and it influences the global water cycle. (VOA)

人類正在透過建造大壩和改變土地的用途影響全球水系統和水循環。

（要點解析）

① impact 在這句話裡作為動詞，表示「影響」。常用搭配是 have impact on... 對......產生影響。

② dam 壩，堤。concrete dam 混凝土壩；earth dam 土壩；dam up 築壩攔水。

（相關句子）

Its prevalence has raised concerns about the potential impact on water quality and quantity. (NPR)

它的流行提高了對水質和水量潛在影響的關注。

---

5 The company also is pumping ethanol into the ground to start a chemical reaction designed to neutralize the chromium. (VOA)

這家公司也用幫浦為土地輸入乙醇來產生化學反應，中和土壤中的鉻。

（要點解析）

① pump 作名詞表示「幫浦」。相關搭配有：water pump 抽水機；作動詞表示「抽水，打氣」，如：pump in 用幫浦吸入。

② ethanol 乙醇，酒精。

③ design to 旨在；目的在於。

④ neutralize 抵消，中和，使無價值。如：be neutralized by... 被……銷毀。

---

6 After member states failed to agree on the issue, the European Union's executive body said it would impose a moratorium on the chemicals. (BBC)

成員國就這一問題未達成一致，歐盟行政機構稱他們將停止使用這些化學製品。

要點解析

① executive body 表示「執行機構」。其中 executive 是「行政的，執行的」的意思。

② impose on 利用，施加影響於。

③ moratorium 暫停，正式的延緩。相關片語有：transfer moratorium 延期償付。但在這句話裡，這個詞有「停產」的意思。

相關句子

And across bee species, mated females appear to express a csshemical that virgin females do not. (BBC)

在蜜蜂種群中，交配過的工蜂攜帶一種未交配工蜂沒有的化學物質。

---

7 There's particular environment that water was there for significant amount of time, that it was neutral, wasn't too salty. (BBC)

這是一個水資源已存在一段時間的特殊環境，且水質為中性，鹽度不大。

要點解析

① significant amount of 大量。其中 significant 除了常用意思「重大的；有意義的」之外，還有「顯著的，有效的」的意思。

② neutral 中性的。此外，「酸性的」可以用 acidic 表示；「鹼性的」可以用 alkaline 表示。

相關句子

This makes the freshwater salty, and means it can't be used for drinking water. (CNN)

這使淡水變鹹，也就是說這些淡水不能飲用。

8   It doesn't use a single drop of aviation fuel, instead its giant wings are
     covered with solar cells. (BBC)
     它一滴航空燃料也不需要，取而代之的是布滿太陽能電池的
     巨型機翼。

要點解析

① be covered with... 布滿著......。
② aviation fuel 航空燃料。
③ solar cell 太陽能電池。cell 在這句話裡是「電池」的意思。

9   Engineers added a concrete lining to the bottom of the waterway in the
     1930s after years of periodic flooding. (VOA)
     經過多年的定期洪水氾濫之後，工程師於 1930 年代在水道底部
     安裝了混凝土襯砌。

要點解析

① concrete lining 混凝土襯砌。其中 concrete 在這句話裡是「混凝土」的
   意思。
② periodic 週期的，定期的。
③ waterway 航道，水道，排水溝。

相關句子

Worries about flooding are now focused to the east and west of the city center.
(NPR)
對於水災的擔心主要集中於城市中心東西部地區。

10   But the signature attraction of the springs—its famous glassbottom
     boats—will remain. (NPR)
     然而泉水的標誌性景點——著名的玻璃底小船也將會保存下來。

要點解析

① spring 在這句話裡並不是「春天」的意思，而是表示「泉水」。
② signature attraction 標誌性景點。其中 signature 作為形容詞，表示「特點
   顯著的」的意思。

11 Pollution from agriculture and residential development has helped coat the spring with algae. (NPR)
農業到住宅等方面的發展造成的汙染使泉水上布滿一層藻類植物。

要點解析

① residential 住宅的，與住宅有關的。
② coat 在這句話裡作動詞，表示「覆蓋在......表面」的意思。
③ algae 藻類，海藻。

相關句子

Researchers at Bournemouth University found the structure has attracted species including algae, mollusks, crustaceans and fish. (BBC)
伯恩茅斯大學的研究者發現這種構造所吸引的物種包括海藻、軟體動物、甲殼動物和魚類。

12 This proposal will ban the use on a variety of crops of three specific pesticides for two years. (BBC)
這項提議規定兩年內禁止在多種農作物上使用三種特定的殺蟲劑。

要點解析

① proposal 在這句話裡作為名詞，表示「提議，建議」。
② ban 禁止，後面通常接動名詞形式。
③ pesticide 殺蟲劑。

相關句子

The committee also discovered traces of at least one pesticide in a range of food. (BBC)
委員會還在一系列食物中發現含有至少一種殺蟲劑的跡象。

13 If it is produced water and it just has oil in it, then there is going to be substantial value because you can simply put it back in the pipeline that goes to the refinery. (VOA)
如果生產水裡含有石油，那麼會很寶貴，因為你可以直接將其透

過輸油管送進煉油廠。

要點解析

① substantial 重大的，大量的，實質的。如：substantial factor 實際性因素；substantial presence 實質性存在。

② pipeline 管道，輸油管。

③ refinery 煉油廠。

14　A new study shows that animals evolved weight-bearing limbs long before they had the chompers to really take advantage of a terrestrial diet. (CNN)

一項新的研究顯示，動物在吃陸地食物時可以咀嚼了，因為牠們早已進化，長出可以負重的四肢了。

要點解析

① limb 肢，臂。

② chomper 咀嚼者，在這句話裡暗指「獲得咀嚼能力」。

③ take advantage of 利用。還可以用 advantage over 表示「占有......的優勢」的意思。

④ weight-bearing 負重的。這個詞由動詞片語 bear weight 變形而來。

15　Commercial jets pump out some 700 million tons of CO2 a year—about two percent of global emissions. (Scientific American)

商務噴氣式飛機每年噴射 700 萬噸二氧化碳，相當於全球排放量的 2%。

要點解析

① jet 噴氣式飛機。

② 與 pump in 相反，片語 pump out 表示「排出」。

相關句子

They ask how many of these projects really deliver the emission reductions they promise. (NPR)

他們問有多少項目真正實現了承諾的排放減少量。

16　　I hear there's 95% of the construction materials are as from recycled materials. (CNN)

　　我聽說有 95% 的建築材料都來自可再生材料。

要點解析

① material 材料。如：raw material 原料；building material 建築材料；composite material 複合材料。

② recycled 回收利用的，可循環再造的。

相關句子

He and a team of researchers there have built a house made out of straw bale and hemp material. (VOA)

他和一組研究者使用稻草和麻類材料在那裡建造了一棟房子。

17　　Thousands of volunteers turned out to remove the trash that has been deposited by winter rain storms. (VOA)

　　有上千名志願者出去清掃冬季暴風雨過後堆積的垃圾。

要點解析

① turn out 在這句話裡理解為「出動」。此外它還有「證明」的意思。

② trash 垃圾。

③ deposit 沉積，寄存；這個詞還有「存款，保證金」的意思。

相關句子

Brawn said miners often pull trash from rivers and leave areas cleaner than they found them. (CNN)

布朗稱礦工通常會收拾河水中的垃圾，使這些地方比他們剛找到時還要乾淨。

18　　A mild wind is combined of low spring precipitation levels to leave vegetation dry and prone to fire, especially its daytime high temperatures reached triple dangers. (NPR)

　　溫和的風伴隨著低降雨量會導致植物乾旱、發生火災，特別是白天的高溫會使危險增加三倍。

要點解析

① mild 溫和的，mild wind 指「和風」。

② precipitation 在這句話裡指某地區的「降水量」。如：annual precipitation 年降水量；acid precipitation 酸性降水。

③ vegetation 植物，草木。

④ prone to 有......傾向的。

19　The relationship between carbon dioxide uptake and canopy colour from two camera systems in a deciduous forest in southern England. (Scientific American)

英格蘭南部落葉森林裡的兩個拍攝系統記錄著二氧化碳攝取量與天空顏色的關係。

要點解析

① uptake 攝入，攝取。相關片語有：water uptake 水吸收；oxygen uptake 耗氧量。

② deciduous 每年落葉的。

③ carbon dioxide 二氧化碳。

20　So far the agency hasn't closed any recreation areas but has imposed severe restrictions on smoking and camp fires. (NPR)

目前為止，代理商還沒有關閉任何娛樂場所，但是已經對吸菸和篝火進行了嚴格限制。

要點解析

① recreation area 娛樂場所。

② severe 嚴厲的，苛刻的。如：severe restrictions 嚴厲的限制。

相關句子

Last year, a study found smoking to be an established risk factor in developing the disease. (VOA)

去年，一項研究發現吸菸是疾病傳播的一個極其危險的因素。

21　Three-and-a-half million liters of oil have already poured into the river and the environmental devastation is there for everyone to see. (VOA)

350 萬升石油被倒入河中，這對環境的破壞人人可見。

要點解析

① liter 升，per liter 即「每升」。

② devastation 毀壞，破壞。類似的詞語有 demolition； disruption。

22　Many organisms live in and around fairy circles, which range from one to 50 meters in diameter and persist for decades. (Scientific American)

許多生物生長在仙女環裡和周圍，仙女環直徑有 1 到 50 公尺長，能存活幾十年。

要點解析

① diameter 直徑，半徑的表達是 radius。

② persist 存留。persistent in 是「堅持，固執於」的意思。

23　When we start removing too many of these individual sharks we've seen huge crashes in their populations. (VOA)

當我們開始大量移走這些鯊魚個體時，我們會發現鯊魚群體會遭到重創。

要點解析

crash 作為名詞，表示「崩潰，墜落」。這裡可以理解為「減少，下降」。

相關句子

The California Shark Protection Act would make it illegal to possess, sell or trade shark fins. (CNN)

加利福尼亞鯊魚保護法將規定持有、 販賣或者交易魚翅是違法的。

24　Scientists hope that removing lionfish one by one may help preserve native fish populations in some reefs that are important for tourism, conservation or fishing. But it can't stop the lionfish's explosive foray into the Atlantic and the Gulf of Mexico. (NPR)

科學家希望將獅子魚一條一條地移走能保護暗礁中的本土魚類種群，這對旅遊業、自然保護和漁業都很重要，但這並不能阻止獅子魚大規模侵略大西洋和墨西哥灣。

要點解析

① native 本土的。常用片語有 native species 原生種；native fiber 天然纖維。
② explosive 爆發性的。如：explosive force 爆炸力；explosive mixture 爆炸混合物。
③ foray 侵略，攻擊。

---

25   Italian authorities say it is a race against time to stop a massive oil slick flowing down Italy's longest river. (VOA)

義大利官方稱，阻止大量石油傾瀉到義大利最長的河中是一場和時間競爭的賽跑。

要點解析

① massive 大量的，整塊的。如：massive coal 塊煤；massive earthquake 大地震。
② slick 在這句話裡作副詞，表示「靈活地」。引申為「傾瀉」。

---

26   According to an international team of climate researchers, this cooling has been significant enough over the past decade to slow human-induced global warming. (VOA)

根據國際氣候研究小組的研究顯示，這種冷卻在過去十年對延緩人類導致的全球變暖速度十分重要。

要點解析

① cooling 冷卻。
② human-induced 人類導致的。其中 induce 表示「誘導；引起」。

---

27   Most of the world's remaining 3,300 one-horned rhinos live in India's Kaziranga National Park which is a world heritage site. (BBC)

世界上僅存的 3,300 隻獨角犀牛，大多數生活在世界遺產地印度

加濟蘭加國家公園。

要點解析

① one-horned rhino 獨角犀牛。

② heritage site 遺址。其中 heritage 有「遺產，傳統」的意思。如：culture heritage 文化遺產；natural heritage 自然遺產。

相關句子

There is also a running battle between heritage and municipal authorities, often allied with business interests. (NPR)

在遺產和地方政府之間總是存在爭論，並且通常和商業利益有關。

These are things like the purification of water and air, the cycling of nutrients, which is very important for our agriculture, pollination, the provision of food and fuel for societies that depend on land, flood control and soil erosion, all of these are affected by ecosystems. (VOA)

這些就像水和空氣的淨化，以及營養物質的循環一樣，對一個依賴土地、防洪和土壤腐蝕的社會而言，這對我們的農業、授粉，以及食物和燃料供給非常重要，所有這一切都受到生態系統的影響。

要點解析

① purification 淨化。相關搭配有：water purification 水淨化；biological purification 生物淨化。

② nutrient 營養物。相關搭配有：soil nutrient 土壤養分；nutrient solution 營養液；nutrient element 營養元素。

③ provision 供給，條款。如：make provision for... 為……做好準備。

29　The idea is that you would put these tracers in a frank job and if there is contamination in the water from somewhere else, you could potentially trace the source of that contamination. (VOA)

這個想法就是你在壓裂作業時放入這些追蹤器，一旦水受到其他地方的汙染，你就可以追蹤汙染源。

要點解析

① tracer 追蹤者。這裡可以理解為「追蹤器」；這個詞來自動詞 trace，意為「追蹤」。

② contamination 汙染。

相關句子

Early tests don't show substantial chemical contamination, but monitoring might have to continue for decades. (VOA)

早期檢測沒有顯示嚴重的化學汙染，但是追蹤也許還會持續幾十年。

30　　The solar-powered plane has the wing-span of a jumbo jet, but weighs less than a family car. (BBC)

太陽能飛機擁有大型噴氣式客機的翼展，但總重量比一輛家用汽車還要輕。

要點解析

① solar-powered 太陽能的。
② jumbo jet 大型噴氣式客機。

31　　Unlike many animals that use sound to draw in potential mates, clown fish appear to use their calls only as labels of ocial status. (Scientific American)

不像許多動物用聲音來吸引潛在配偶，小丑魚僅用聲音作為社會地位的標籤。

要點解析

① draw in 引誘，吸入，吸收。
② status 身分，地位。如：social status 社會地位。
③ call 的意思是「電話，呼叫」等，但是這裡指代「聲音」。

32　　Russian officials said a nuclear-powered icebreaking ship was being brought in to move the station onto an island. (BBC)

俄羅斯官員稱將派遣一艘核能破冰船把考察站轉移到一座島嶼上。

要點解析

① icebreaking ship 相當於 icebreaker，指的是「破冰船」。
② bring in 引入，帶進。
③ station 在這句話裡是「駐地」的意思。

33 And we have evidence again, being from the U.S., of something like the Asian Longhorn Beetle, which has quite a voracious appetite for certain trees. (VOA)

我們又有來自美國的證據顯示，亞洲天牛這類生物對這種樹很有食慾。

要點解析

① voracious 貪婪的，貪得無厭的。
② appetite for... 對……的欲望，其中 appetite 表示「食慾，胃口」。

34 It's a vision that strives to meet the needs of a rapidly growing population. (CNN)

這是一種力求滿足迅速成長的人口需求的願景。

要點解析

① strive 努力，鬥爭。而 strives to 表示「努力做……」。
② meet the need 滿足需求。need 在這句話裡作動詞，是「需求」的意思。

相關句子

Within around thirty years the Census Bureau expects racial and ethnic minorities to form the majority of America's population. (VOA)

人口普查局預計大約 30 年內，美國大部分人口將會是少數民族。

35 For the first time in human history, daily measures of CO2, which is an important factor in global warming, have topped 400 parts per million. (BBC)

二氧化碳濃度日均值是衡量氣候變暖的一個重要因素，這個數值在人類歷史上首次達到了 400ppm。

要點解析

① factor 因素。factor in ……的因素；key factor 關鍵因素。
② top 在這句話裡作為動詞，表示「超越，超過」的意思。

相關句子

Climate change is not a debate among the sellers and buyers of CO2. (BBC)
氣候變化不是一場二氧化碳買賣雙方的爭論。

---

36   There are plants growing along the water and some of the birds, fish and other wildlife have returned. (VOA)
植物開始在水邊生長，一些鳥兒、魚兒和其他野生動物也遷徙回來了。

要點解析

① wildlife 在這句話裡作名詞，表示「野生動物」。
② return 返回，回來。這裡根據上下文，可理解為「遷徙回來」。

相關句子

Park officials said the revised plans still posed a threat to rare wildlife such as capercaillie. (BBC)
公園官員稱改革方案仍會對雷鳥這樣的野生動物造成威脅。

---

37   Synthetic biologists design and make biological devices and systems for useful purposes. Conservation biologists study biodiversity to protect species and habitat. (Scientific American)
人造生物學家設計並製作了生物裝置系統以供備用。保護生物學家則研究生物多樣性來保護物種和棲息地。

要點解析

① biodiversity 生物多樣性。其中 bio- 作首碼時，表示「生物的」意思。
② habitat 棲息地。相關片語有 habitat destruction 毀壞棲息地；habitat condition 居住條件。

相關句子

As a result of the study, eleven species of mangrove have been placed on the Red List of Threatened Species. (VOA)
研究結果顯示，紅樹林裡的 11 個物種都在瀕臨滅絕物種的紅色名單上。

38   Using a sediment core as a detailed history of climate change, scientists can see how the forested Arctic gradually became covered in ice and snow. (Scientific American)

沉積岩中心可作為氣候變化的詳細歷史記錄,科學家們可以看出北極森林是如何逐漸被冰雪覆蓋的。

要點解析

① sediment 沉澱物,沉積。近義詞有 precipitate,是「沉澱物」的意思。
② core 核心,要點。sediment core 可以理解為「沉積岩心」。

---

39   We can't grow any food without water. We can't live without water. We can't run our cities without managing our water properly. (VOA)

沒有水我們就不能種植糧食,也不能生存。不能合理地管理我們的水資源,我們的城市就無法維持運轉。

要點解析

① run 的本意是「跑」。這裡引申為「營運,使運轉」的意思,相當於 operate。
② properly 適當地。

---

40   American scientists said carbon dioxide in Earth's atmosphere had risen to its highest level in 2.5 million years. (VOA)

美國科學家稱,大氣中的二氧化碳已經上升到了 250 萬年來的最高程度。

要點解析

① atmosphere 大氣,大氣層。相關片語有 atmosphere pressure 大氣壓;standard atmosphere 標準氣壓。
② level 水準,程度;如:highest level 最高程度。

---

41   The International Energy Agency said global carbon emissions hadn't fallen because a boom in solar and wind power had been offset by increasing use of coal. (BBC)

國際能源處稱,因為太陽能和風能的發展被日益成長的碳消耗抵

消了，所以全球碳排放量並沒有降低。

要點解析

① boom 繁榮。這裡是「成長」的意思。
② offset 抵消，補償。

42　For a second day the national weather service has issued a tornado watch for a large portion of Oklahoma. (NPR)
美國國家氣象局連續第二天向奧克拉荷馬州大部分地區發布龍捲風預警。

要點解析

① issue 發布。如：new issue 新發行的證券；key issue 關鍵議題；in the issue 結果。
② watch 在這句話裡作為名詞，可理解為「預警」。
③ a portion of 一部分。

43　Many scientists say carbon emissions are a major reason for rising temperatures in Earth's atmosphere. (VOA)
許多科學家表示，碳排放是全球大氣氣溫升高的一個主要原因。

要點解析

① carbon 碳。carbon emission 即「碳排放」。
② major 主要的，重要的。如：major reason 主要原因；major in 主修。

相關句子

The avalanche threat increases with the temperature, which is rising in the search area. (CNN)
搜尋區域內雪崩和氣溫的威脅有所成長。

44　Private companies are now rushing into the relatively new market for recycling drill site water. (VOA)
現在，鑽井工地循環水這個相對新興的市場吸引了許多私營企業。

> 要點解析
>
> ① rush into 突然衝入，突然出現；這裡可理解為「湧入」。
> ② drill 鑽孔。drill site 則表示「鑽井工地」。

> 相關句子
>
> People living in Wiltshire can now recycle their waste vegetable oil following a three-month trial. (BBC)
> 經過三個月的試驗，居住在威爾特郡的人們現在可以將廢棄的植物油循環利用。

45　The governor of Puerto Rico has signed a law which will protect a swath of land on the island's north-east coast that is a major nesting site for the world's largest turtle species, the Leatherback turtle. (BBC)
波多黎各州長簽署了保護該島東北海岸一片土地的法律，這裡是世界上最大海龜──革龜的主要築巢區。

> 要點解析
>
> ① a swath of 一片，一帶；其中 swath 是「細長的列」的意思。
> ② nesting 築巢。

46　Countries involved in such trade have to prove that the sharks and rays were, one, legally caught and, two, sustainably caught. (VOA)
參與這項貿易的國家必須證明用射線捕捉鯊魚首先是合法的，其次是可持續的。

> 要點解析
>
> ① trade 在這句話裡的意思是「行業」。
> ② ray 射線。相關片語有：ultraviolet ray 紫外線；infrared ray 紅外線。

47　This machine, developed by a company called 「Origin Oil,」 is re-moving sludge from water that came from an oil drilling site—with a process originally developed for extracting algae. (VOA)
由 Origin Oil 公司開發的機器正在清理石油鑽取站的爛泥，而這

種方法最初被用來清理海藻。

要點解析

① sludge 爛泥。
② oil drilling site 石油鑽取站。
③ extract 提取，取出。同義詞有 draw。

48　Right now we have to watch about the levee getting saturated and water trying to seep underneath of it. (VOA)
現在我們必須注意堤壩已經開始飽和，水會從下面滲出來。

要點解析

① levee 堤壩，為……築堤。如：levee breach 堤壩裂口；levee opening 陸閘。
② saturated 極溼的，飽和的。如：saturated fat 飽和脂肪；saturated soil 飽和土壤。
③ seep 滲出。常用搭配為：seep into 滲入。

49　He and colleagues decided to convince industry executives that protecting the oceans would also protect their bottom line. (NPR)
他和同事決定說服產業高管，保護大洋就是保護他們的底線。

要點解析

① convince 說服。convince sb. of sth. 說服某人去做某事。
② executive 行政部門。
③ bottom line 底線。其引申義表示「最重要的」。

50　A tropical cyclone is an area of low pressure that forms in the tropical regions of the world. (CNN)
熱帶氣旋是在熱帶地區形成的一個低壓區。

要點解析

① tropical 熱帶的。
② cyclone 氣旋。tropical cyclone 表示「熱帶氣旋」。

51   An attempt to ban the international trade in polar-bear parts has been
      narrowly rejected by delegates at an intergovernmental meeting on the
      endangered species. (BBC)
      在關於瀕危物種的政府間會議上，代表團以微弱優勢否決了禁止
      北極熊交易的提議。

要點解析

① narrowly 勉強地。這個詞來自形容詞 narrow，原意是「狹窄的」，可引
  申為「勉強的」的意思。
② delegate 代表，代表團成員。
③ intergovernmental 政府間的。

52   The leftover grains in the scrap heap may have attracted animals that,
      over time, evolved ability to carbo-load. (Scientific American)
      垃圾堆裡的殘留食物吸引著那些隨著時間已經進化到依靠碳水化
      合物生活的動物。

要點解析

① leftover 殘留物，吃剩的飯菜。
② scrap heap 垃圾堆。
③ carbo-load 吸收碳水化合物的。carbo- 指「碳水化合物」，load 指「負載，
  負荷」。因此，carbo-load 可理解為「吸收碳水化合物的」。

53   If those pests get an opportunity through an open container door to just
      wander out into a new environment, it can be pretty bad for the envi-
      ronment. (VOA)
      如果那些害蟲乘機透過打開的集裝箱門進入一個新環境，會對環
      境造成很糟糕的影響。

要點解析

① pest 害蟲。
② wander out into... 遊蕩到……。

相關句子

Professional pest control and agricultural workers would still be allowed to use them, the agency said. (CNN)
代理機構稱，專業的害蟲控制和農業工作者仍被允許使用它們。

54　The state is seeking hundreds of millions of dollars to detect and remediate ground water contaminated with that chemical. (NPR)
該州正在籌集數億美元來檢測和清潔含有化學成分的受汙染地下水。

要點解析

① detect 察覺，探測。這裡的意思是「查明」。
② remediate 補救。
③ ground water 地下水。

55　Starting with the pre-industrial revolution, of course, the anthropogenic emissions increased so much that the oceans suddenly started to take up huge amounts of carbon. (VOA)
從工業革命開始之前，人為碳排放開始大量成長，導致海洋突然開始吸收大量的碳。

要點解析

① anthropogenic 人類起源論的，人為的。
② take up 吸收。同義詞還有 intake, absorb。

56　So researchers got to wondering whether there might be an easier way to keep an eye on photosynthesis. (Scientific American)
所以研究者需要思考是否有更容易的方法來觀察光合作用。

要點解析

① get to 不得不，必須。相當於 have to。
② keep an eye on 留意，密切注視。這個片語也經常用來提醒人們注意自己的物品，比如：Keep an eye on your belongings 注意你的物品。
③ photosynthesis 光合作用。

57   Ecotourism may be good for a given species, as humans become engaged in its survival. (Scientific American)

生態旅遊對於某些特定物種是有益的，因為人類也在此生存。

要點解析

① given 作形容詞表示「贈予的」的意思，但這裡可以理解為「特定的」。

② become engaged in 在這句話裡相當於 be engaged in，表示「參與⋯⋯」的意思。

④ survival 生存，倖存。如：survival of the fittest 適者生存。

---

58   It has the same wingspan as that of an Airbus A-340 passenger jet, but thanks to its carbon fiber construction, weighs only as much as an average car. (BBC)

它的翼展和空巴 A-340 噴氣式客機相同，然而由於其碳纖維結構，它的重量和一輛普通小汽車差不多。

要點解析

① wingspan 是「翼展」的意思，是航空學裡的名詞。

② average car 普通小汽車。average 原指「平均的」。這裡有「普通的」的意思。

---

59   Now we know that to reinforce this social structure, the fish communicate with aggressive and submissive audio signals. (Scientific American)

現在我們了解，要加強這種社會結構，魚類要靠挑釁或順從的聲音訊號來交流。

要點解析

① reinforce 意為「增強，加強」。

② audio 聽覺的，聲音的。相關片語有：digital auto 數位音訊；audio signal 聲頻訊號。

③ submissive 是「順從的，唯命是從的」的意思。

60 The country's biggest maker of food is facing a lawsuit from environ-mental groups over the amount of lead in the food. (NPR)

這個國家最大的食品製造商因食物中鉛含量超標正面臨著環境組織的訴訟。

要點解析 lawsuit 是「訴訟」的意思，主要是指非刑事案件。如：Medical Lawsuit 醫療訴訟。

---

61 Samples of sediment layers beneath a frozen lake show this region used to be a lot warmer—and may thaw out again in the future. (Scientific American)

冰凍的湖面下的沉積層樣本說明該地區曾經氣溫很高，並可能在未來再次解凍。

要點解析

① sample 樣本。
② thaw out 解凍，融化，使暖和。其中 thaw 表示「解凍」。

---

62 Some ecotourism offers visitors close encounters with different species. (Scientific American)

一些生態旅遊提供遊客近距離接觸不同物種的機會。

要點解析 encounter 在這句話裡作為名詞，表示「偶然碰見，遭遇」。close encounter 即「親密接觸，近距離接觸」。此外，encounter 還可以作為動詞，表示「邂逅；遇到」。

---

63 A new study out this week highlights the role that coral reefs play in evolution, adding another reason to preserve these delicate, diverse, and often beautiful ecosystems. (NPR)

本週一項新研究強調珊瑚礁在進化中的作用，為保護這些微妙的、多樣的、美麗的生態系統又增加了一個原因。

要點解析

① highlight 強調，突出。也可以用 emphasize 表達這個含義。

② delicate 微妙的。

③ diverse 不同的，多種多樣的。

64　Maybe the trees are dead when being made into pallets and beetles will bore into that wood and then they'll emerge. (VOA)

也許大樹被製成貨盤時已經死亡，甲殼蟲會從木材中鑽出，然後爬出來。

要點解析

① pallet 有「踏板，簡陋的小床」等含義，但在貿易領域通常指「貨運托盤」。

② beetle 甲殼蟲。

③ emerge 浮現。這裡指「出現，露面」。

65　Currently, that water has to be trucked in—and the contaminated water then has to be trucked out—for disposal at great cost. (VOA)

現在，如果水被引進，那麼汙水必須被運走，處理水的成本很高。

要點解析

① truck 作動詞，意思是「交易」。因此，truck in 可理解為「買進」，而 truck out 則可理解為「賣出」。

② disposal 為名詞，表示「清理」。

③ at great cost 花了很大的代價，成本很高。

66　Drew Bartlett of Florida's Department of Environmental Protection acknowledges it's a massive undertaking that could take decades. (NPR)

佛羅里達環境保護部的德魯·巴特利特承認這是一個艱巨的任務，可能需要十年的時間。

要點解析

① Department of Environmental Protection 指「環境保護部」。

② acknowledge 是動詞，表示「承認」。如：It was officially acknowledged that the economy was in recession. 官方承認經濟處於衰退之中。

③ massive 巨大的；undertaking 表示「事業；任務」。

67   A wave of cold and snowy weather continues to grip Europe, grounding airplanes, trains and cars and causing dozens of deaths. (VOA)

一股冷空氣和降雪天氣襲捲歐洲，飛機、火車和汽車停運，導致幾十人死亡。

要點解析

① grip 指「緊握，抓緊」。在這句話裡可以理解為「襲捲」。
② ground 在這句話裡是動詞，表示「著陸」。引申為「使飛機停運」的意思。
③ dozens of 幾十個。

相關句子

These products are used for pain, high body temperature, colds and sleeplessness. (VOA)

這些產品可用於治療疼痛、發燒、感冒和失眠。

68   Bolortsetseg Minjin, one of Mongolia's chief paleontologists, said she'd been shocked to see the skeleton for sale. (BBC)

蒙古首席古生物學家布勒特特格·敏金稱在看到動物骨架出售時感到非常震驚。

要點解析

① chief 首席的，主要的；常用搭配有：chief executive 行政長官；in chief 主要地；chief editor 總編輯；chief engineer 總編輯。
② be shocked... 是「為……感到震驚」的意思，在這句話裡 shock 表示「使震驚」。
③ for sale 出售，待售。

69   But fisheries experts say plans by Cambodia, Laos and Thailand to build hydropower dams on the Mekong would block fish migration, threatening already endangered species. (VOA)

但是漁業專家表示，柬埔寨、寮國和泰國在湄公河上興建水電大壩的計畫將阻攔魚類洄游，對已經瀕臨滅絕的物種產生威脅。

要點解析

① hydropower 水力發電。如：hydropower station 水電站；hydropower engi-neering 水利水電工程。

② migration 移民，遷徙。如：bird migration 鳥類遷徙；data migration 資料移轉。

相關句子

Delegates from Laos, Cambodia, Thailand, and Vietnam postponed a decision Tuesday on Laos's plan to build a hydropower dam on the lower Mekong. (VOA)

本週二，來自寮國、柬埔寨、泰國和越南的代表團決定推遲在湄公河下游興建水電大壩的計畫。

70　It could mean a sharp decline in rainfall in some areas, flooding in others and extinction of about half of all the world's animal and plant species. (BBC)

這意味著某些區域的降雨量將急遽減少，其他地區會發生洪水，世界上近半的動植物物種都會滅絕。

要點解析

① decline 在這句話裡作名詞，意思是「下降，衰退」。另外，decline 還可以作動詞，表示「謝絕，婉拒」。如 She declined their invitation. 她婉拒了他們的邀請。

② extinction 滅絕，熄滅。

新聞英語必備指南——關鍵句

作　　　者：金利 主編

發　行　人：黃振庭

出　版　者：崧博出版事業有限公司

發　行　者：崧燁文化事業有限公司

E - m a i l：sonbookservice@gmail.com

粉　絲　頁：https://www.facebook.com/sonbookss/

網　　　址：https://sonbook.net/

地　　　址：台北市中正區重慶南路一段六十一號八樓
815 室

Rm. 815, 8F., No.61, Sec. 1, Chongqing S. Rd.,
Zhongzheng Dist., Taipei City 100, Taiwan (R.O.C)

電　　　話：(02)2370-3310

傳　　　真：(02) 2388-1990

總　經　銷：紅螞蟻圖書有限公司

地　　　址：台北市內湖區舊宗路二段 121 巷 19 號

電　　　話：02-2795-3656

傳　　　真：02-2795-4100

印　　　刷：京峯彩色印刷有限公司（京峰數位）

國家圖書館出版品預行編目資料

新聞英語必備指南：關鍵句 / 金利主編 .
-- 第一版 . -- 臺北市：崧博出版：崧燁
文化發行 , 2020.10
　　面；　公分
POD 版
ISBN 978-957-735-995-7(平裝)
1. 英語 2. 讀本
805.18　109015793

官網

臉書

定　　　價：380 元

發行日期：2020 年 10 月第一版

◎本書以 POD 印製